DEJA VU

LIZ LEIBY

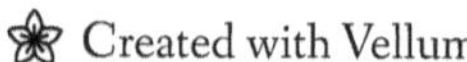 Created with Vellum

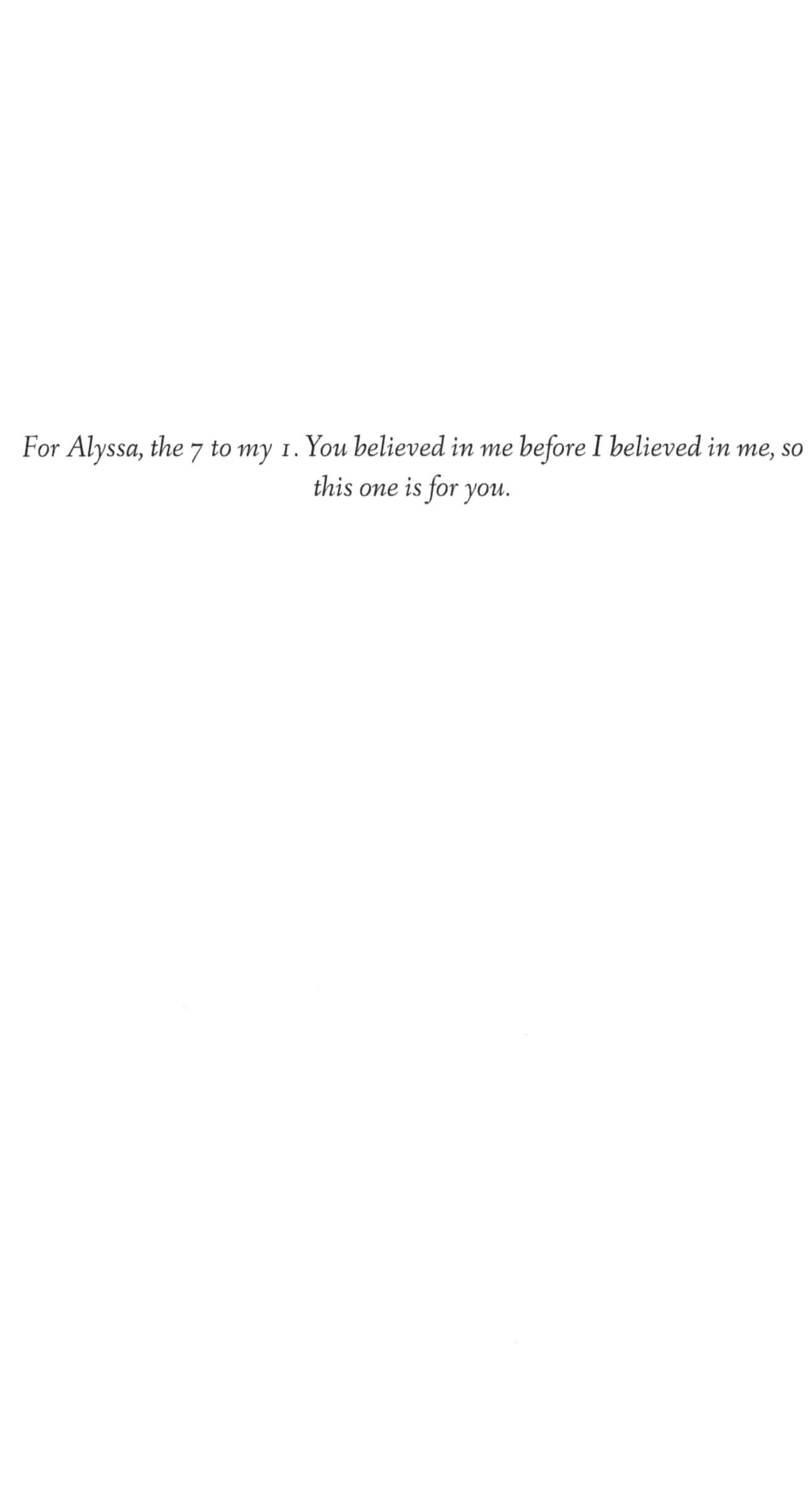

For Alyssa, the 7 to my 1. You believed in me before I believed in me, so this one is for you.

CHAPTER ONE

JESSIE

"I look ridiculous."

I'm wearing a cat-ear headband, a black leather corset top, and black leather pants so tight I think they might actually be a size too small. Oh, and there are eyeliner whiskers drawn on my cheeks.

"You look like a sexy cat," Jade says as she adjusts the neckline of my too-tight tank top, exposing more of my cleavage.

"Cats are not sexy."

"Tell that to Catwoman."

"They're aloof and mysterious." I tug my top back up as soon as she turns around.

"Then be aloof and mysterious as soon as we get to the party. But, Jessie Matthews, you *are* going to the party." She smacks her lips and fluffs her auburn hair.

I scowl at her, but Jade remains unfazed. She just adjusts her cleavage, pulling each breast up and out of her shirt a little more, then does a half-turn to check her butt in the mirror. It looks killer in her red leather pants, but she knows that. Jade is all curves, confidence, and sex appeal. Men literally whistle at her when we're out in public.

She's dressed as Wanda from the Marvel movies tonight. She tried to talk me into being a Marvel character too—Jade is very into the idea of matching costumes—but I don't watch the movies. I barely wanted to go to the party as it is, but if anyone knows how to talk me into getting out of the dorm, it's my best friend and roommate.

Behind Jade, I see myself in the mirror in my all-black getup, the corset giving my squarish body some shape. Jade insisted I use her curling iron, so my normally straight brown hair now cascades past my shoulders in voluminous waves. I don't look half bad, and something about that thrills me.

I tear my eyes away from myself in the mirror. Being all dressed up like this reminds me of Freshman Year Jessie, and the thought of being that Jessie again makes me feel a little sick.

"I should be studying," I say.

"And *Game of Thrones* season eight should have ended differently, but here we are."

"I can't afford to lose my scholarship, Jade." My words come out sharper than intended.

"You can't afford to spend one more Thursday night alone in your room or the library. Socially, you're almost a pariah. Plus, it's Halloween Weekend at Alpha Tau Zeta, and these parties are legendary, so we are not missing it," Jade says as she applies her lipstick. "I know you hate parties, but this one will be fun."

I roll my eyes. She says that every time. It's not that I hate parties; I just hate the person I become when I'm partying. It's not worth it to correct Jade, though. She already knows the whole story. She was there my freshman year when I started dating a guy who was a fraternity pledge. Every Thursday through Sunday I'd be at the frat house with him, drinking too much and not studying enough. It was so distracting that my grades suffered, which might not be a big deal for most students, but my scholarship depends on a certain GPA, and losing my scholarship means I lose my ability to be in school at all.

I almost lost my scholarship.

I quit partying after that.

Jade tucks her ID and phone into her already-too-full corset and strides into the living room. I follow, stuffing my things into my corset as well, though there's plenty of room in mine.

"Ready?" she asks without looking back at me. She snaps up the dorm key and tucks that next to a boob as well, then she walks out into the hall, but I'm still inside.

The door shuts heavily behind her.

Hand on the doorknob, I pause, debating whether I should cut my losses now. We're just six weeks away from finals, and if I don't start studying now, especially for statistics—I've got a B in that class—I'm at risk of dropping to a C. My brain starts to swirl the way it always does when I'm anxious. I wipe my sweaty palms on my leather pants, but to no avail: they're still wet. I look around for something to wipe my palms on. I can't leave when I'm this sweaty. Maybe I should change and then just go to the library. I don't sweat this much in the library. I don't want to sweat this much anywhere.

Why am I sweating so much?

Jade walks back in through the door to find me standing on the other side of it fanning my armpits. "Jessie?"

"Yeah, I should just not go. I have so much studying to do for finals."

"Finals are like two months—"

"Six weeks."

"—away. You have plenty of time, and I promised we'd study tomorrow." She slaps her hands onto my shoulders and takes a deep breath in, encouraging me with her eyes to do the same.

"It's okay," she says gently. "It's just one party. And this can be your party quota for the semester. Your grades are perfectly safe if you party once."

I nod. She's right. It's just one party. I breathe in and out slowly with her, and the swirling in my brain fades away.

"You're right. I'm sorry. That was stupid."

"Don't be so hard on yourself," Jade says, opening the door and gesturing for me to step through.

Easier said than done.

"Oh, wait!" Jade says, just as she's stepping through the door for a second time. She rushes back to her room and emerges seconds later holding two candy necklaces. She shoves one on my head, over my cat ears. I try to adjust it to make it more comfortable, but it pinches my neck and sits flush against my skin, feeling more like a choker.

"I haven't worn one of these in ages." I tug on the elastic and it pulls at my skin. The candy digs into my neck, determined to ruin my night. I start to remove it, but Jade slaps my hands away.

"Stop it! This is a prime man magnet."

"Man magnet?"

"Yes, a man magnet. You can thank me later." She totters away on her four-inch heels.

"Thank you later? For what?" I call after her, scurrying behind on my flats, probably a bit too much like a cat.

"If I told you, it wouldn't be as much fun as you figuring it out yourself," Jade says, practically power-walking out of our dorm building but turning to wink at me. She tugs on the elastic of her own candy necklace and licks her top lip. It's a sexy gesture, and I finally catch her meaning.

"Did you give me this so some guy could, like, eat this off my neck? Is that supposed to be sexy?"

"That's exactly what I mean, and trust me on this, it *is* sexy, and it usually leads to much more than just kissing." She winks over her shoulder at me again.

I should have expected something like this. When Jade and I first moved in together I remember being floored by how easily and openly she talked about sex. She was amused by how naïve I was. Until I started dating someone about a month into the semester, Jade was constantly offering to introduce me to "a nice young man" because she said I seemed "wound a little tight" and "could use a good screw" to loosen up a bit. I declined each time, but apparently now she's back to her old tricks.

I've obviously spent too much time with her because I wonder for a moment if she's right. Maybe I do need to loosen up a little. Just the idea of coming out tonight had me sweating like I was in a jungle.

No—I have to stay vigilant. What if I have so much fun I start partying again every week? Multiple nights a week? No. Just tonight. I'll take off the candy necklace when she's not looking and she'll never know.

"How thoughtful of you. Always looking out for me," I say, but Jade isn't fazed by my sarcasm.

"Jessie, if you don't get laid soon, I'm going to do it myself."

"I might be into that," I say as we make our way to fraternity row.

"You're not my type," Jade says.

"You always say that, and it hurts my feelings." I stick out my bottom lip, pouting, and Jade snaps my candy necklace. As the hard candy thuds against my vocal cords, something between a squeal and a groan comes out of my mouth. The sound sends us into a fit of giggles, and we walk the rest of the way to fraternity row bent over with laughter, trying to snap each other's candy necklaces.

The campus of Middle Penn College is small enough that everything is walkable. Our dorm is nestled at the top of a slope with the other on-campus dorms, farthest from fraternity row. The walk is only ten minutes, but it feels shorter, and by the time we hear the thumping bass and electronic beat I'm more relaxed and even a little grateful Jade convinced me to come out. I'll just stay until she finds someone else to hang out with and then sneak off.

As we crest the last hill, a row of six large houses comes into view. Red bricks and white columns make these houses look like they belong in the late 1800s, not the twenty-first century. From the outside one might assume the insides are spacious and bright with plush carpets, spiral staircases, and large chandeliers, but in reality they reek of beer, pot, cigarettes, and body odor, and their defining feature is crunchy carpet. Heavy wooden accents make them feel like a house someone's rich grandfather decorated and refused to let anyone change. They're crammed with thrift store furniture and somehow always littered with red Solo cups.

The legendary Halloween party Jade and I are attending is hosted by Alpha Tau Zeta, a house known for attracting science and math majors. I don't know any pledges or brothers at this house. Jade knows a few, but that doesn't matter for parties like this. Practically the whole campus is on fraternity row tonight because Halloween is a big deal around here. There's a yearly competition between the fraternities for "best decorated," and even though the only prize is bragging rights, these guys take it very seriously. This year on the ATZ lawn, twenty skeletons reenact a scene from *Pirates of the Caribbean*. It's impressive, with a massive cardboard ship, a slew of props—think empty rum bottles and treasure chests—and all the skeletons dressed in elaborate pirate costumes. I pause to take in the scene, but Jade pulls me along, dragging me into the house through the front door.

Jade likes to scope out who's upstairs before we head downstairs, where the real party is, and since I don't feel up to being super social tonight, while she makes her rounds I head to the kitchen for drinks.

I've always wondered if the guys who live in the frat house even use this kitchen. I've only ever seen it the way it looks now: the island in the middle a makeshift beer pong table, the counters absolutely packed with alcohol and various juice containers, the floor sticky with the cornucopia of drinks that have been spilled on it. There are always about four too many people in here, and I squeeze my way past a couple making out to pour a couple of drinks for me and Jade.

Two years ago I would have made two drinks for me and two for Jade and that would have just been the start. I didn't party in high school—I was too busy with school and extracurriculars and a weekend job—so when I got to college I got a little carried away with the freedom. I thought I'd be able to balance school and my social life, and I failed pretty hard. So I just make two drinks tonight—a vodka and cranberry juice for each of us.

"Hey, gorgeous," some drunk guy says, somehow appearing next to me without my noticing. He leans his elbow on the counter and stands way too close, his breath smelling like an ashtray took a bath in a tub of cheap beer.

"No, thank you," I say, clutching my drinks and walking away. I squeeze past the couple again, realizing they now have their hands in each other's pants. "Get a room," I mumble under my breath, rolling my eyes. I know this is a party, but there really should be a limit to how much touching people are allowed to indulge in publicly.

I find Jade flirting with a group of guys all dressed as pirates and hand off her drink. I stand with her for a bit, sipping my own, wishing I were back at the dorm. I'm out of place at parties like this, like a Cheerio box placed back on the wrong shelf at the grocery store because someone decided in the baking aisle to do muffins instead of cereal for breakfast. I give Jade my "Can we do something else, or I'm leaving" eyes, and she nods, makes her excuses, takes my hand, and leads me to the basement.

"Basement" feels like a generous word for the space, like maybe the place will be furnished and cozy, but it's just a spacious concrete room with a few measly places to sit and it happens to be under the house.

Colorful lights dot the room, but they do a poor job of lighting it—I can barely make out faces. As usual, the space is packed with people and reeks of cheap beer and sweat. A techno remix of the *Halloween* movie theme song blasts through large speakers that frame a wooden platform used as a stage when a live band or DJ plays for a party. Tonight it's being used as a makeshift bar with coolers holding drinks for people who don't want to schlep all the way back upstairs for a beer.

Jade and I hang at the edge of the crowd, judging costumes and waiting for our drinks to kick in. Or rather, I'm waiting for Jade's drink to kick in so she'll find a dance partner and I can sneak off. But Jade stays with me until we've finished our first drinks and then she gets us each a beer from the coolers. By the time I've reached the bottom of the second drink, I've started to succumb to the quirky Halloween techno beats and the mob of sweaty, dancing bodies, so the thought of leaving doesn't feel so urgent. We both sway and jerk to the music in a rhythmic fashion that could technically be called dancing until we really *are* dancing, joining in with the crowd.

There's a pleasant buzz in my brain and a looseness to my muscles that indicates I'm tipsy but not drunk. It feels good to move with the music. I let my arms swirl and move around my head. I keep telling myself I'll leave after the next song, but when the song ends I can't seem to remember why I want to go.

"This is fun!" I shout at Jade and give her a thumbs-up. She smiles at me, a big, bright smile, and I give her my biggest, brightest smile too. Why didn't I want to come out? This is great. I'm feeling myself. Why can't I always be this relaxed? Maybe I can party a little and study a lot. Finding that balance would...

Hands on my waist interrupt my thoughts; a chest against my back, hips against my own moving in sync with me. Before I can turn and see who the person is, Jade squeezes my hand and gives me the look that says "Hottie, not a creeper." She starts to dance away from me, and I try to grip her hand tighter, to make her stay, but she shimmies off, winking and snapping her candy necklace. I don't normally like to dance with strangers, but he's moving his hips with me and the music, not just smashing his junk against my ass and calling it dancing, so maybe one song won't be so bad.

I close my eyes and lose myself in our movement, in the way his broad chest feels against my back. His hands splay against my ribs and slide down to my hips, fingers digging into me, pinning me against him even as we sway to the music. The bass vibrates through me as if the speaker is inside my body, and when the beat drops I raise my arms, tossing my head from side to side, giving myself over to the music fully. My partner has no trouble keeping up, and when his hands graze my arms, goosebumps break out over my exposed skin. How long has it been since I've been touched like this?

When the song changes, he grips my hips and spins me to face him. My hands land on a broad, firm chest, and though we're still moving to the music I can finally get a good look at my mystery partner and see if Jade was right.

I don't know what I expected, but a half-masked man wearing a frilly blouse is not it. I suppress a burst of laughter. Most of the guys here are dressed like pirates or zombie-somethings. Zombie football players. Zombie doctors. Plain old zombies. This guy looks like Shakespeare. I do a quick once-over. A very sexy Shakespeare, but Shakespeare nonetheless. Pants tucked into knee-high boots, a Venetian mask —even his hair is giving Shakespeare, curled and kind of wild.

I fucking love it.

I can't see much else about the guy in the bright neon-green, purple, and blue light of the basement, but I can see a little stubble on the hard line of his jaw and the way his eyes drink me in. Even in this lighting, I can tell this guy is capital "H" *hot*. Guys this attractive haven't historically chosen me as their dance partner. It's gotta be the leather.

His lips quirk into a smile and the room gets warmer, but I don't think that's just the leather.

"I love your outfit!" I yell, but he doesn't hear me. He shakes his head and points to his ear. I grab the front of his frilly blouse and pull him closer, repeating myself, but with my lips pressed to his ear this time. When I pull back, the vaguest hint of that fresh laundry detergent scent bleeds through the smell of sweat and beer.

He mouths, "Thank you," and then smiles—a real smile, teeth and everything—and I thank all the Halloween gods I came to this party.

The music changes abruptly like someone picked a different song on a phone somewhere. Loud groans sound from various people around the room, but "I Put a Spell on You" by Annie Lennox blasts over their complaints. A noticeable number of people stop dancing, but for those who remain the vibe of the room totally shifts. People are pairing off, slowing down. I don't see Jade anywhere, but my dance partner presses a hand against my lower back and moves against me in a way that refocuses my attention fully on him. His tempo matches the music, hips swaying in a slow, sensual movement that implies these moves aren't just for the dance floor. Desire swirls around inside me like sand kicked up from a riverbed. It doesn't matter that a piece of paper couldn't fit between us right now; we aren't nearly close enough.

He leans in, his lips against my ear, sending a chill down my spine. "May I?" He loops a finger under my candy necklace, stretching it a little. The elastic pulls against the small hairs of my neck.

The bass of his voice, gravelly, deep, and accented, renders me speechless. I nod, moving my face against his. Is that the alcohol, or is this what happens when a man dressed like a literary character flirts with me?

I expect him to pull the necklace away from my neck and nibble off a piece of the colorful candy, but he releases it so it sits flush against my skin instead. I flinch as it snaps, but the pain disappears when he dips his head and presses his lips around the candy, right against my neck. I almost jerk back in surprise, but his tongue and teeth graze my skin, and it feels so good my knees buckle a little and I melt against him. He bites at a small, round candy piece, and I wait for the crunch, but he releases the necklace, not having taken a piece of candy at all. Instead he kisses my neck, tongue and lips soft against the sensitive skin. My pulse beats wildly at the sensation. I dig my fingers into his back, trying and failing to take a full breath. His mask scratches my face, but the sensation is overpowered by the ripples of desire radiating through my body. I forgot what it was like to be touched like this, to be wanted this way. I'm no longer sand kicked up in a riverbed; I'm a volcano once thought to be dormant. I'm not made of flesh and blood; I'm power and heat and—

He presses the softest trail of kisses up my neck, landing just behind my earlobe.

I am a goner.

Longing overtakes me, infuriating and luxurious. I grip the fabric of his shirt, desperate for more, desperate for him to be closer. He only barely grants my wish, moving his mouth along my jaw and cupping the back of my head, fingers entangled in my hair. Neither of us is moving with the music anymore.

His lips hover close to mine, prolonging my torture, but I am not a patient woman. I push up on my toes to meet them, relief flooding me. It is a chaste, sweet kiss. Nothing to write home about. And for a moment, I'm disappointed. What happened to our chemistry? He pulls back, his eyes searching mine for a split second and I don't know what he finds, but when he kisses me again, it's exactly the way I like to be kissed: as if oxygen is optional. He tastes like cinnamon schnapps and oranges.

Satisfaction creeps in at the edge of my longing, but when his tongue finds mine I can't even conjure the word "satisfaction." I'm insatiable, a caged animal set free, losing all sense of reality. The building could collapse around us, and I'd never know.

I have lost myself completely to this stranger.

That is until someone pours a drink down my back.

"Eugh!" I stumble out of my partner's embrace and try to find the guilty party. A very drunk zombie cheerleader is attempting to apologize, but she's having trouble with her words.

"I'm sssorr— It was not on purplesss..." she slurs, and a zombie football player puts his arm around her, issues an actual apology, and leads the girl away.

My back is soaked and already turning sticky. I make a beeline for the outside door, the spell of desire broken, cinnamon and oranges already a distant memory.

The cool air of the night refreshes me after the humidity of the basement. I gather my hair off my back and braid it to the side. It's half wet from the beer and half from sweat. I desperately need a shower. I don't even want to know what my eyeliner cat whiskers look like now given how much I'm sweating, and when I feel the top of my head for my cat-ear headband it seems to have disappeared. My ears feel full and everything sounds like it could be underwater. My buzz is wearing off.

I sigh heavily. Even out here, the basement music is too loud now. The people hanging out on the back patio above me scream and laugh, and I wish I had the balls to tell them to shut up.

I just need to go home, but Jade has the key.

"Drop something?" an accented voice asks from behind me.

I spin to find Sexy Shakespeare holding my cat-ear headband.

"Thank you," I say, suddenly feeling a little awkward. What do you say to someone you just made out with? "I'm Jessie, by the way."

He smirks, the corners of his mouth drawing up into a gorgeous smile. There's something familiar about him, but I can't quite put my finger on it. His smile manages to dissipate some of the awkwardness, like this situation is entirely comfortable for him. Amusing even.

Whatever it is, it rubs off on me.

"Will," he says and bows with a flourish.

My mouth tugs into a smile entirely of its own accord. Then my phone dings, jarring me from the moment, and I peel it out of my corset.

Jade.

> Won't be back tonight. Have fun 😌

> Need the room key. Don't go yet.

SHIT. I have to catch Jade before she leaves, but I don't want to lose this guy.

"Can I give you my number?" I ask, frantically searching the crowd for Jade. The beer on my back no longer feels wet, just sticky and swampy. I squirm in my too-tight corset, rolling my shoulders. An ache has started in my jaw, neck, and upper back.

I check my phone again to see if Jade has texted. The gray dots appear then disappear.

Sexy Shakespeare holds something out to me, and I give him my attention. In his hands are a mini scroll and a pen with a feather attached to it.

"Your commitment to this costume is impressive," I say as I scribble my number across the paper.

"Why, thank you, milady." He takes the scroll back and snatches one of my hands, pressing his lips to my knuckles, his eyes holding mine. It's singlehandedly the sexiest and most romantic thing I've ever experienced in my twenty-one years of life.

"Until next time," he says. He bows and disappears back into the frat house.

Fuck, that was something else. I touch my fingers to my lips, trying to conjure the taste of cinnamon schnapps and oranges. It comes back to me easily, and for a moment I let myself be free again.

DING.

I snap back to reality at a text from Jade asking me to meet her out front, and I do, retrieving the key and promising to unlock the door for her in the morning.

I walk back to the dorms in a trance. My lips are swollen and raw, my whole body buzzes with desire that was never fully satisfied, and my neck feels exposed after having the warmth of Will's face buried there. The pull to turn back and find Sexy Shakespeare is almost stronger than my desire to get out of my beer-soaked clothes.

By the time I've showered and crawled into bed, it's nearly midnight—much later than I intended on being out. I glance at the open textbook on the floor by my bed. Guilt settles on me, a knot in my stomach, and I turn off the light so as not to have to face the consequences of my actions.

I had fun tonight, but did I have too much fun?

I close my eyes, hoping I can sleep off my guilt, but all I can think of as I drift off is a masked stranger with a familiar smile...

CHAPTER TWO

"I put a spell on you and now you're mine."

His hand flexes and clenches my hip, and when he pulls me against him a thrill runs through me. I shiver. He's behind me, kissing that spot where my neck meets my shoulder. How do I get his lips back on mine? I reach up...

"Well done, Jessie. See me after class?" Professor Campbell drops a piece of paper on my desk, tapping her manicured nails against the fake wood.

I jolt as if pushed, my heart racing. *Am I in trouble? Did she notice me zoning out?*

I'm not much of a daydreamer, but I can't stop thinking about last night.

The room gets warmer. My cheeks must be so red. I redo my ponytail and push up the sleeves of my long-sleeve shirt.

Will has haunted me since I woke up today. While I was brushing my teeth, I got a flash of his hands skimming my ribs. On my walk to class this morning, my stomach flip-flopped when I remembered the way his fingertips dug into my hips, and just now at my desk, I zoned out thinking of the feel of his lips on my neck.

I'm getting all hot and bothered thinking about his touch. I don't remember ever feeling like this when my ex-boyfriends touched me. I thought it would come with time and maybe we just broke up before we got to the part where we had that kind of chemistry. I thought chemistry was something you built with someone, but maybe you either have it or you don't, and the rest is what you build.

Whatever it is, I'm on cloud nine today, and only this, the prospect of being in trouble with my professor, has knocked me clean off the cloud. Well, that and the fact he still hasn't texted me and it's nearly 9:30 a.m. It hasn't stopped me from checking my phone every ten minutes or so. But my only texts are from my mom and Jade.

And I have a lot of texts from Jade.

YOU LIL SLUT

I saw you hook up with that guy last night

Deets?????????

Coffee after class?????????

Jessie.

You cannot ignore me.

You cannot hoe it up and then go radio silent.

I know your class schedule.

I know where you sleep.

Ok fine, twist my arm, I'm bringing you coffee. I'll meet you outside your class.

I click my phone off and try to quell the rising disappointment. He might not even be up by now. It's still early. He could still text.

There's a jab on the back of my arm. I know exactly who it is without having to look. Sighing, I turn to face Mackenzie Baldwin.

"Why did you poke me?" I ask, not masking my annoyance.

"You did great," Mac says, pointing to my quiz, 99% in bright red at the top. There's a wide smile on his face, but in his eyes there's something mischievous.

He's always doing this, making snarky little comments disguised as compliments. I don't have the patience for it this morning. It's wearing thin as I wait for Sexy Shakespeare to text me.

"How did you do?" I ask, knowing that if I got a better grade than him it could buoy me for the rest of the day.

I've been in competition with Mac for two years. At first it was fun. We had nearly every class together freshman year by some weird scheduling fate, and every time there was a test he'd ask me how I did. For months we compared quiz scores and test results, egging each other on. Because I was partying a little too much, Mac did better than me a lot that first semester, but by second semester I had him beat at nearly everything.

I worked hard in high school. My grades were so good there the school created an award to give me at the end of the year. So when I got to college and found the classes to be surprisingly hard, having something to focus me—beating Mackenzie Baldwin—made me a better student. It was fun, actually. A little game.

Until The Incident. Then it stopped feeling like a game.

Mac flashes his paper at me. 98%.

Ha.

Smirk on my face, I turn back around to face the front of the classroom. I adjust in my seat, straightening my back and rolling my shoulders. When my phone buzzes I nearly drop it trying to check who the text is from.

> I'm bringing you a croissant so you're legally obligated to spill your stories. I don't make the rules.

Jade.

I click my phone off, slumping back down in my chair. 9:45 a.m. Maybe he just doesn't have a morning class.

Mac pokes me again, and I check the teacher's location. She's with a student, so I reluctantly turn back around.

Mac is easy on the eyes, with chestnut-colored hair that's shorter on the sides and just long enough on the top to be styled back or to swoop down into his rich brown eyes. He's smirking at me, and for a second I'm a little dazzled by how handsome he is.

"Did you have fun at the Halloween party last night?" he asks, leaning forward. His tone is playful, but his eyes hold an unfamiliar intensity.

Did he see me at the party last night?

"Yes...?" I narrow my eyes at him.

"ATZ has great parties, huh?"

I guess he did see me. What is this? We never socialize.

"Sure?" I say with a shrug.

He cocks his head to the side, a bit like a puppy. A confused puppy. A confused puppy who can smirk. "I was at the party too. Had a really great time." He pauses meaningfully, as if it's my turn to ask a question or share a story. But I don't have any stories to share with Mac.

Broad hands gripping my ass, pulling me against him, hard as his tongue slips across my neck...

Or, rather, I have stories, but I won't be sharing them with Mac.

"Cool?" I shrug again, shaking my head a little, and start to turn back around, but a hand on my arm stops my swivel. It's not an aggressive touch, but it surprises me.

My eyes dart between his hand on my arm and his face. *What is happening right now?*

"You okay?" he asks. He looks like he genuinely wants to know.

I give him my best "What the fuck?" face.

"You guys are dismissed," Professor Campbell announces from the back of the classroom.

"I'm fine," I whisper, yanking my arm away and sliding out of my seat to wait by Professor Campbell's desk. I relax only after Mac leaves without trying to talk to me again.

That was so fucking weird.

I pull my phone out of my pocket to text Jade back, but I've only composed half the text before Professor Campbell approaches. Butterflies go wild in my stomach and chest. I'm always worried I've done something wrong, especially with teachers.

"Jessie, thanks for staying back a few minutes."

"No problem."

Can she hear the way my voice just shook?

"Have you considered being a research assistant?" she asks.

My shoulders relax an inch away from my ears. "Um, not really. What does it entail?"

"You would assist with some experiments I'm working on, code the data. I can go over it in more detail if you think you're interested. It is an investment of your time, but I think you'd be well-suited for it. I'm not sure what path you'd like to take after you graduate, but it looks good on the résumé and gives you some experience if you're interested in research at all."

I'm not interested in research, but I also don't want to rule it out completely.

"Is it paid?" I ask, and instantly my cheeks heat. I hate even having to ask, but I don't know if I could take on being a research assistant without giving up my work-study job, and I need that job. My full-ride scholarship means I don't have to put any of my work-study money toward school, books, my meal plan, or housing. But I do need money for gas.

"It's not, and I understand if you couldn't take it for that reason, but I wanted to offer it to you anyway. If you're concerned about scheduling, we can work that out. I can always take on a second research assistant if you can't be around for some of the experiments. You're one of my top students, though, and it would be great to have you assisting me. Think about it and let me know."

I thank her and step out into the hallway. Jade isn't here yet, so I lean against a wall to wait for her.

Being a research assistant is a great opportunity, but is it the right one?

My first year of middle school was tough. I'd just hit a growth spurt and needed new clothes, but since my dad had just lost his job for taking too much sick time, money was tight. Mom hadn't picked up her second job yet, and we were just scraping by. I'd been getting teased on the bus for weeks, but one day I wore a shirt with a big hole in the armpit that stretched down the side that I didn't know was there until the girls pointed it out, laughing at me. When everyone else got off the bus, I stayed on and asked the driver, tears streaming down my face, to please take me back home. She didn't. Instead, she marched me right into the guidance counselor's office. Miss Julie, the guidance counselor, sat me down in a big comfy chair and let me cry until I didn't have any more tears. She let me hang out in her office all day and read and didn't make me go to class. She even brought me lunch from the school cafeteria and told me I could come back as often as I needed to. At the end of the day, she asked my mom to come get me instead of making me take the bus again.

I spent a lot of time on Miss Julie's big blue couch in middle school reading and telling her about my life. When it came time for me to go to high school, Miss Julie introduced me to the high school guidance counselor, Mr. Green, who was just as nice as Miss Julie and helped me through a lot of really hard times.

When I was thinking of what I wanted to do after graduation, I asked Mr. Green what he went to college for. He said both he and Miss Julie were psychology majors, that they'd known each other in college. They'd both gone to Middle Penn, and so that's where I applied too. I knew I didn't want to be a school counselor, but I would like to work with kids in a therapeutic setting, and I knew that the first day I left Miss Julie's office nearly a decade ago.

But to become a therapist I need to attend grad school, and in order to attend grad school I'll need an assistantship, for which my options are teaching or research. Since teaching holds no appeal to me, Professor Campbell's offer might just be what I didn't know I needed.

"WHAT'S that look on your face?" Jade asks as she approaches me, hands outstretched with coffee and a pastry.

I take them from her and stop myself before I can ask how much I owe her.

Jade's love language is gifts. That, and her college experience doesn't come from her pockets but her father's. According to Jade, his pockets are deep, and so is his guilt. He left her mom when she was young, and when Jade reconnected with him as a teenager he was nothing but apologies for leaving her life. They don't have a terrible relationship now, but it's hard to say how much Jade would talk to her dad without the money.

"My professor asked me to be a research assistant."

"Not interested?" Jade scrunches her face.

"Just not sure if I want to add one more thing to my schedule." I shrug and dig into my croissant before she even has a chance to respond, buttery, flaky bits spilling down the front of my top.

We walk toward the elevators, and I brush the flakes off my chest. I'm eager to tell Jade about Sexy Shakespeare. I need her reassurance he was actually into me despite his lack of contact today, and that it's totally fine and he will text and—

"It's a psychology thing, right?" Jade asks, interrupting my thoughts.

I nod, mouth full of croissant.

"Mac wasn't asked to be a research assistant, was he?"

"I hope not. He's already in two of my classes this semester."

"The woes of sharing a major at a small college. Hasn't he been in at least one of your classes every semester?"

I nod.

"You should consider breaking into the dean's office and fucking with the files so he's not in your classes anymore."

"I don't hate that idea."

We step in through the elevator doors as they open, then I press the ground floor button. A semester without competing with Mac sounds blissful.

"Shall we ring in the weekend by ruining Mac's life?"

"Cheers to that." I hold out my coffee cup.

She clinks her cup against mine and gives me her most devilish grin. This is why I love Jade. She's my ride-or-die. She's the most supportive presence in my life, and even if sometimes her support looks like tough love or aggressive and illegal suggestions, I wouldn't have it any other way.

"By the way, I'm mad at you," Jade says.

"What'd I do this time?" I take the first sip of my coffee, closing my eyes to savor the warm, bittersweet beverage. Jade knows I like my coffee tan-colored with two sugar packets. That's my love language: details.

"For not texting me a play-by-play of what happened with the yummy dude in the king costume," she says as the elevator door dings open.

"Okay, first of all, it wasn't a king costume. It was a Shakespeare costume. And it was sexy."

"Let's talk about that first. Who dresses like Sexy Shakespeare?" Jade asks.

"He was dressed LIKE Shakespeare, but he was sexy. It wasn't, like...a revealing costume."

"He might as well have tried to be an accountant, or Ben Franklin," Jade says.

"Sexy Ben Franklin?"

"Sexy Abe Lincoln."

"Sexy Teddy Roosevelt?"

"Are we just naming presidents now?" Jade asks.

"Look, that guy could have dressed as anything and I probably would have found him sexy."

"Jane Eyre?" she suggests.

"Yes, absolutely. I would be his Rochester. Oh! We could do a three-way costume—you could be the wife in the attic."

"The only part of that sentence I understood was 'three-way,'" Jade says.

"Why did you reference Jane Eyre then?"

"I don't know! It was the first book I thought of on your shelf."

I roll my eyes and chuckle. Jade is my favorite person to talk to about a lot of things, but books are not one of them.

"Well, anyway, there isn't anything to tell with Sexy Shakespeare.

We made out, and then I got beer dumped on me and I called it a night.”

“Why didn’t you just invite him back? Sexy shower?”

“Showers aren’t sexy, Jade. They’re practical.”

“You’re taking the wrong kind of showers.” She raises her eyebrows at me while taking a sip of her coffee. She starts walking down the path to the left that would take us to our dorm, but I’m taking the path in the opposite direction.

“Where are you going?” she asks, brow furrowed.

“I have that financial aid meeting,” I say, and my stomach does the tiniest flip. This meeting is the same check-in I always do with my financial aid advisor; it’s routine, but it still makes me nervous.

“Oh! I forgot. I’ll walk with you. But you have to explain why you skipped out on the opportunity for a sexy shower and if you have plans to see him again.”

“I just wanted to get out of my beer clothes, and I was sweaty and gross. I don’t know, it just didn’t feel right. But his name is Will, and I gave him my number! But he hasn’t texted.” I check my phone: no new messages. “Yet. He will text, right?”

Jade groans. “What!”

“What?” I ask.

“What have I always told you?”

“When it doubt, bang it out?”

“Well, yes. But—”

“Never trust a man with blond hair? He had brown hair. I mean, it was kind of a sandy brown—”

“No, not that. The—”

“Oh! Keep it tight unless the vibes are right?”

“Are you writing down everything I tell you?”

“I have a good memory.”

"Clearly, you don't. I told you to always get THEIR number. We don't give them all the power."

"Ohhh, I was going to say that one next. I swear."

She rolls her eyes at me, and I give her a smug grin. "We have to find him," she insists.

"That's a good idea. How hard could that be? This is a small campus—how many Wills are there? Oh! And he had an accent. He was definitely British. There are only so many exchange students, right?"

"Sure, assuming he's a student here."

I hadn't thought of that. He might have been visiting from another school. *Fuck.* I deflate, my shoulders slumping with the weight of that realization. Jade reads my body language and loops her hand through my arm.

"Look, let's just start here, and if he's not here, we'll deal with it then, okay?" Her voice is upbeat and positive, and her efforts to keep me focused on the present are working—for now.

"Thank you," I say.

We both take a sip of our coffees as we make our way to the financial aid office building. I crumple up my pastry bag, slipping it into my jacket pocket until I can find a trashcan.

Leaves crunch beneath our feet and the wind pinks our cheeks, whipping our hair around our faces. Middle Penn is beautiful in the fall, bright yellow and orange trees everywhere littering the sidewalks, making the whole campus feel like some kind of autumnal snow globe.

I can't decide if I should feel optimistic or hopeless. I didn't get his number, so my fate with this guy is in his hands. Unless I go searching for him, which would give me a little more control over the situation—but only if he's actually a student here. So much of it is up in the air and intangible and unknown, and I hate all those things. This might be an adventure for Jade, but I like predictable; I like knowing all the answers and outcomes. An uneasy discomfort settles in my bones like dust on a table. Except the table is covered in glue and one quick swipe won't clean it off.

It occurs to me as we're approaching the financial aid office building that I never asked Jade about her night.

"What did you end up doing last night? Who were you with?" I ask.

"Mmm, I may or may not have had a rendezvous with a very handsome young man."

"Say more." I take a sip of my drink. Jade always has the best stories.

"And a very beautiful young lady."

I nearly spit my drink out.

She throws her head back and cackles.

"A threesome! What!"

"Details later!" She spins on her toes and nearly jogs away, waggling her fingers at me, leaving me standing alone with my jaw dragging on the ground.

CHERI LAKEDON'S office is the epitome of 1980s fancy. Her desk is a dark wood monstrosity with cabinets and drawers that take up an entire wall, and a large L-shaped desk jutting out to hold her monitors and desk supplies. There isn't much by way of supplies besides a stapler, a tape dispenser, a cup of pens, and one stack of sticky notes. If it wasn't for the lady sitting behind it, the single picture frame, and the hum of a computer, I might think the desk was purely for display.

I knock on the open door, and Cheri pops her head out from behind her monitors.

"Hi, Jessie," she says with a smile so big her eyes disappear. She's all cheeks and teeth and it's so friendly I relax a little. But only a little. Coming to this office always makes me uncomfortable.

"Have a seat. How are you?" Cheri asks as she clacks away at the keyboard. Her nails are so long I'm genuinely surprised at how fast she's typing.

I stare a little too long and have to force myself to look away as my mother's voice hisses in my head. *"It's not appropriate to stare, Jessica."*

"I'm okay, thank you. How are you?"

"Good, good. I'm just finishing up this email, I'm so sorry."

"No problem."

I toe the floor, my old Converse looking particularly dingy against the plush white carpet. The tightness in my chest comes back the same way it always does when I'm in this office, and I trace a box on the floor with my toe, counting to four and breathing with each line the way Miss Julie taught me to a decade ago. *Inhale for 4, 3, 2, 1...hold the breath for 4, 3, 2, 1...*

Middle Penn College was my only choice for college. My junior and senior years were singularly focused on getting into this school and securing financial assistance. With my dad on disability and my mom working two jobs, there was no way I'd be able to attend without a scholarship or loans or some combination of both. My parents encouraged me to try for as many scholarships as possible before taking a loan, so I did, and I ended up with a full ride here. I knew being a Middle Penn student was my gateway into the future I dreamed of, so when Cheri sat me down at the end of my first semester of freshman year and told me I needed to get my grades up or I was in danger of losing my scholarship, I took her very seriously.

That entire meeting was a bucket of ice water over my head. I left her office and spent the next month in the library, my dorm, or my work-study job. I didn't go to a party again for five months. My boyfriend broke up with me a mere two weeks after that meeting.

So this office has come to feel a little bit like the dentist's office for me. And I'm not one of those weirdos who likes the dentist.

"Jessie, thank you for coming by to see me." Cheri wheels her chair over so she's no longer hiding behind her monitors. "I needed to talk with you about your scholarship for your senior year." She pauses.

I fiddle with the ends of my hair, needing something to do with my hands. My leg bounces of its own accord nearly as fast as my heart is racing.

"There's no easy way to say this, but the full scholarship program is being canceled next year. So you're all set for the rest of this year, but for your senior year, unfortunately, we won't be able to offer your full scholarship. I am really sorry about this. We can offer half of what you're getting now, but I know that won't fully cover all your needs."

One of my best friends in elementary school had a pool at her house, and I spent at least three days a week there in the summer swimming from dawn until dusk. Her mom would bring us Goldfish and watermelon and let us watch movies while our hair dried and we waited for my mom to come pick me up. We'd play this game where we'd dive under the water, purple goggles tight over our eyes, and one of us would sing while the other tried to guess the song. But it was hard because sound doesn't travel as well underwater, and we couldn't read each other's lips because the goggles made everything go kind of "funhouse mirror."

Right now I'm underwater watching Cheri open a drawer, riffle through some papers, and pull out a folder—it's all muffled, all funhouse mirrors and unintelligible gurgles. I can hear my own breathing. I can hear my own heartbeat. She slides the paper across the desk to me, but it's blurry, tears marring my vision like the goggles. I would reach for the paper, but I'm shaking so hard I don't know if I'll be able to hold it.

What the hell am I going to do?

I think Cheri starts talking again, but I haven't come up from underwater yet. I don't know if I ever will. I'm in an endless pool, drowning under the reality of my situation.

I'm not going to be able to come back next year. I'm not going to be able to graduate.

My chest is so tight it physically hurts. Something dark rises from my belly—anxiety or rage or the kind of sadness that will chain me to my bed for days—but I don't have time to fall apart. I have to fix this.

I press my lips together and furiously swipe at the tears coming down my cheeks. I force myself to break the surface, come back up for air, get out of the water.

"Oh, honey, I'm sorry. I know this is hard news." Cheri's voice isn't muffled anymore, but I'm still trembling. "But listen, in this folder is a list of scholarships and grants you can apply for to cover the cost. I'll help however I can—that's what I'm here for. I'm on your team. And if you need to take out a loan, I can help you fill out that paperwork too."

Just nod and smile so you can get the hell out of here.

I nod and stretch my lips into some vague smile-like shape.

"Do you have any questions?" she asks, her eyebrows pulled down in concern or sympathy—probably a mix of both.

I shake my head, stretching the sort-of smile as far as it will go.

"I'll send you an email to check in in a couple of weeks, okay?"

I give a tight nod, snatch up the folder, and bolt through the door before she can say another word.

The cool afternoon air hits my face, and for the first time since Cheri said the word "canceled," I'm able to take a deep breath. I pull the fresh air into my lungs, noticing the way my body temperature starts to drop. I hadn't realized I was so warm. *Am I sweating?* I touch the back of my neck to find that yes, in fact, I am sweating. I make my way to a bench across from the financial aid office and sit, dropping my face into my hands.

This is bad. This is, like, worst-nightmare bad. And there is no trust fund to rescue me; there is no backup plan; there is no plan B. This was it. Middle Penn College and then grad school and then join a practice and become a child psychologist with a steady paycheck and health insurance was the plan. Graduate from college, graduate from grad school, get a job, and help support my parents was the plan. Help pay for some of my dad's medical procedures. Help pay their mortgage so Mom wouldn't have to work two jobs. So Mom could—

Nausea hits me like a wave, and I sit back against the bench, allowing the cool air on my face again. I'm still trembling a little, and I try some deep breaths.

I can't afford to spiral like this. It's useless. What I need is a plan.

I flip open the folder and scan the list of scholarships available. There are five pages of them. It makes my head swim. I don't really have the time in my schedule to deal with the time it will take to figure out if I'm eligible for these, much less the time it will take to apply for them.

But I have to. I have to stay in school because I am not going to spend my future just surviving. I want to thrive. And if that means I sacrifice a little sleep now to get the future I know I deserve, so be it.

CHAPTER THREE

MAC

Girls are weird.

Guys get a bad rap for sending mixed signals, playing hot-and-cold, and acting differently from one day to the next, but Jessie Matthews put all that behavior to shame this morning. Girls play games too, apparently, and damn, if it doesn't feel like getting the breath knocked out of you.

It seems it's possible to have the greatest make-out session of your life one night, with chemistry off the charts, and then act like it meant nothing at all less than twelve hours later.

I wasn't expecting her to go all doe-eyed around me today, batting her lashes or throwing herself into my arms, but I also wasn't expecting her to act as if last night didn't happen at all. It's a little harsh, even for Jessie.

We've always had a playful dynamic in the way competitors do. Freshman year, when we basically shared a schedule, I noticed how hard she worked. The way she turned in assignments before anyone else, the praising comments professors gave her for her work. One day I nearly aced a test. It was the best I'd done since starting school, and I was proud. I'd been having trouble balancing soccer and school, so this felt like a victory. I asked Jessie how she did, thinking maybe I'd beat the teacher's pet. She'd outdone me by two points. It knocked my confidence down a few pegs and fueled the competitive spirit in me. I studied harder and longer for the next test than I ever had. I missed practice and asked to be benched for a game just so I could study, and when I got a better grade than Jessie I almost did the same dance I do after scoring a goal.

Sparring with Jessie has always felt as heated as any match I've ever played, and I compete with her as often as I can.

Eventually, with all our classes, I got to know her. How witty and sharp she is, dishing out sarcastic comments as often as I do. So is it really a surprise I've developed a crush on someone as sharp and brilliant as her? I knew a year ago that I'd shoot my shot as soon as I could. And last night I got my chance, so I took it.

And, *goddamn*, it was...everything.

Except she just spent our entire Friday morning class acting like it was nothing.

I'm sure there's a reason for it, and I would text her and try to meet for coffee and have a conversation, but right after she left the party I dropped my scroll. I dropped it right into a puddle of beer someone had spilled on the floor. The scroll was soaked and her number illegible.

I'm trying to shake off my interaction with her as I head toward the cafeteria for a snack when my phone starts to vibrate. I dig it out of my pocket.

Mom.

Smiling, I find a bench nearby and pop my headphones in before picking up.

"Hi, Mac," my mom singsongs—one of the reasons I love when she calls. She's like a blanket of joy, dampening whatever else I've got going on with her cheerfulness. "You're on speakerphone with me and your father."

So much for a cheerful phone call. I don't usually talk to my dad in between visits home unless my mom is on the call, so it must be important. Some kind of announcement. Dad and I don't have a bad relationship; we just have nothing to talk about unless we're talking about sports, and since I quit soccer a year ago we've had even less to discuss. I don't mind. The less I have to hear him wax poetic about the Baldwin name, the better.

"Hey, Pops," I say. "Hey, Mops."

"How's my Mackers?" Mom asks.

My dad and I may not have a lot to talk about, but my mom and I have never had the same problem. In fact, she has a great relationship with me and all my brothers. She ended up with four sons and never complained once about being the only girl in the house, or that she didn't have a daughter to dress up and play dolls with. My brothers and I all have something special with our mom, but for me it's baking. My mom loves to bake, and she passed that love on to me. I'll forever associate the smell of flour with her. Even now I text her pictures of all my bakes, and she helped me troubleshoot my sourdough starter a couple years back.

"Not too shabby. Sorry I missed your call. Everything okay?"

"Everything is great. We just wanted to share some news about Michael."

"Is he okay?" I ask, concern growing in my mind.

"Yes, he's fine," my mom says.

"Oh." Like dust in the wind, my concern is gone. "Why didn't Michael just call?"

Michael is the second-eldest child in the family, and he's spent the past seven years playing in the NFL. He got recruited right out of college. He and his college girlfriend got engaged last year. Maybe this has something to do with their wedding...

"So he's retiring from the NFL," Mom explains, ignoring my question. "He was accepted into a program. What's it—?"

"Artists and writers' program," my dad cuts in, but he sounds annoyed. He doesn't really believe in things like artists and writers' programs, and I'm aware of how hard Mom must've had to work to convince him to be on the phone right now as a supportive presence.

"Yes! You know he's always done photography on the side, and he'll be going to Antarctica to do photography there. Amelia will be working there too, doing some travel writing."

Antarctica? Damn.

Michael's photography side business has landed him in *National Geographic* multiple times. He and Amelia are always traveling when his schedule allows, and his photography hobby turned semi-professional just a couple of years ago. Of course he's leaving the NFL for something just as epic. This is what the Baldwin boys do.

That is, all the Baldwin boys but me.

"Wow, that is...great for him. Still confused why Michael didn't just call and tell me."

"Oh, we're having a surprise dinner for him in a week—a congratulatory dinner. I know you're coming home for Thanksgiving, but we wanted to make sure you could make it to this too. Big occasion, and we want the whole family there, of course."

"Of course I'll be there," I say.

Celebratory dinners are a big deal in our family, and they're never a surprise. Mom always plans them as a surprise, but no one is ever surprised.

My eldest brother Rob got one when he graduated from this college as valedictorian, and another when he was accepted into Yale Law

School; another when he passed the bar exam; when he got engaged; and his most recent one was for being the youngest person at his law firm to make partner. This is Michael's third dinner, as he also graduated valedictorian from MPC, and of course we celebrated when he was drafted straight out of college into the NFL. Noah, the brother I'm closest to in age, has had two dinners: valedictorian, and acceptance to NASA.

I've had one.

When I made the college soccer team and got a full ride here to play soccer, I got a celebratory dinner.

But I didn't get one when I made captain my sophomore year, and I most certainly didn't get one when I quit soccer after last season, because Baldwin boys don't quit.

But I'm on track to be valedictorian—or at least I'm as close as I can be with Jessie Matthews on campus. I know for a fact that would earn my father's approval and get me a celebration dinner.

Gun to my head, I couldn't explain why I care so much about my father's respect, but I don't know how to be anyone else. I was raised to be a Baldwin Boy and learned from a young age what it meant to be proud of the family name. My dad is a self-made man, and we've all heard the story of how he made his money and how he did it with integrity. Being a man of honor is important to my dad, so it's important to all of us too.

"How's school? Your grades?" my dad asks, almost right on cue.

"Top of my class, Pops."

"Like a Baldwin boy should be."

"Robert," my mother chides in a half-whisper. My mom has always been a "your best is what counts" kind of parent, and my dad a "live up to our name" kind.

"Well, this has been fun," I say. "I've got to get some studying done, so I'll talk to you guys later?"

We say our goodbyes, and I launch myself off the bench, making a beeline for the library.

Any other time after a phone call with my dad I'd be plagued with thoughts of my brother, his accomplishments, and what I need to do to live up to the Baldwin name. I'd go to the library and study for an hour, dead set on acing my next test, but I'm distracted today, and as soon as my parents are off the phone my conversation with them is gone from my mind.

All I can think about is last night.

Jessie in those leather pants.

Jessie's hands on my neck, my shoulders…the way her fingers dug into me.

The little noises she made when I kissed her neck.

Just thinking about it now, my body heats up, my cheeks and toes warm despite the chill in the air. I know I'm not the only one who felt that insane spark between us. But if that's true, why did she act so weird this morning?

Girls are fucking weird.

Hopefully, some time in the library will help get my mind off Jessie and what happened, and next time I see her I'll just talk to her about it.

Simple as that.

"FANCY SEEING YOU HERE," I say to Jessie as I approach Professor Gold's office. Of all the people to run into, in all the places, Jessie is here, at almost exactly the same time as my meeting with Ava Gold, my advisor. A delightful surprise.

"Small college," she says, but she doesn't look up from her phone.

I hum the tune to "It's a Small World" and do a full-body wiggle/dance to match. She smirks, and even though it's not a full smile, just the faintest upturn of the corners of her lips, it feels like a win.

It's Monday afternoon and it's the first time I've seen Jessie since our class together Friday. I spent all weekend thinking about her, about the Halloween party. Whatever small, insignificant crush I had on her before last Thursday has transformed into a very real, I-get-butterflies-when-I-think-about-her crush. It occurred to me at some point this weekend that maybe she's mad at me for not texting and all I need to do is apologize so we can move forward.

I check my watch: two minutes until our meeting.

"Hey, Jessie, I just wanted to—"

"Mac, Jessie, hi." Ava Gold opens the door to her office early.

Damn it.

Ava adjusts her oval glasses on her face and gestures for us to come in. Jessie puts her phone away without so much as a glance at me, and I follow her into the office. Ava gestures for us to sit in the two chairs across from the desk.

The chairs are surprisingly comfortable—something I don't normally expect of vintage furniture. Being in Ava Gold's office reminds me of being in an antiques shop, and I only ever visited those with my grandmother, my mom's mom. She loved antique everything; her house was covered in treasures. It bordered on cluttered, much like this office. Everything is vintage or antique in here. Old newspapers and funky wallpaper cover the walls. Quirky, unique items sit next to books on various shelves. There's a mix of decades—the forties, the sixties, the eighties—and it totally works for Ava, who regularly dresses like she lives in the 1940s. My family is more modern and minimalist, and that style has extended to me. My apartment is mostly neutrals and sparsely decorated. It's a calming vibe, and I can't really say the same about this office.

"Thanks for coming in, you two. I have an opportunity I wanted to present to both of you, so I hope you don't mind that I made this a joint meeting."

"Not at all," I say as Jessie says, "Totally fine," in a pitch she only uses with teachers.

"There's a scholarship opportunity for seniors that is typically associated with valedictorian—"

"The Walden Senior Scholarship?" Jessie says, straightening in her chair and leaning forward. It sounds familiar to me, and if my memory serves, one or two of my brothers must have won it when they were here. They all graduated valedictorian.

Because that's what Baldwin boys do.

"Yes! And I have the application just...here... One moment—I seem to have misplaced it."

She starts rooting around on her desk for the applications, lifting a pile here and checking under a pile there. She opens and closes drawers in her desk, but to no avail. She stands to check the piles of papers on a shelf behind her and then moves to a filing cabinet when the shelf search proves fruitless.

I glance over at Jessie, who's playing with the ends of her hair while her leg bounces violently. It gives me the sudden urge to reach out and place my hand on her leg to steady her. I don't because unsolicited touching is weird. Instead, I clasp my hands together in my lap to keep from reaching out. Her eyes dart around the room, looking at everything except me. Even nervous and ignoring me, I find Jessie almost overwhelmingly adorable.

I must be staring too hard, though, because Jessie's eyes finally land on mine. Instead of looking away like I expect her to, she mouths the word "what," her expression pinched.

But I don't get a chance to respond because Ava Gold finds the papers.

"Here they are!" she announces and hands a shiny green folder to each of us.

Jessie opens hers, devouring the words on the pages within. I set the folder on my lap unopened.

"There's a sample application in there, but you'll fill out the application and submit your essay online. You can find the web address for that at the top of the first page. The winning student is awarded a generous scholarship their senior year, and I assume you both know almost all the valedictorians here at MPC are Walden Scholars. There's a prize for second and third place as well, and the details of that are in the packet."

"Thank you so much, Ava," Jessie says, her voice wobbling a little.

"Yes, thank you for thinking of me for this," I say. I don't need the money, but this could certainly earn me a celebratory dinner with my family. I imagine the smile on my dad's face when I tell him I've won, the handshakes from him and my brothers. The Walden Senior Scholarship may come with money, but more importantly, respect from my father.

"When is this due?" I ask.

"December first. They'll review the applications and send out an email a week later or so."

December first is a month away, which is a year in college time, and although I won't know the results by the time I go to dinner with my family, or even by Thanksgiving, just knowing I have this in my back pocket is fortifying.

"This is great. Thanks again, Ava," I say.

I glance at Jessie. Her eyes are glossy, and she's stopped jiggling her leg. I thought her constant movement was concerning, but her stillness is even more unsettling. I stand, but when Jessie doesn't follow suit, I give Ava a nod before heading out of the office.

"Do you have an extra minute, Professor Gold?" Jessie asks, her voice growing distant as I close the door behind me.

Obviously, that meeting was not the place for me and Jessie to discuss what happened last Thursday, but the way she wouldn't look at me is confusing... Is she really that mad at me? Or is she embarrassed about that night?

Fuck, maybe she regrets what we did and now she doesn't want to face me. Maybe she wasn't as into it as I was.

But the way she pressed herself against me; the way she clung to me... She was definitely into it.

This is ridiculous. I'm obsessing over it like a detective following a serial killer. I might as well have a corkboard covered in evidence and strings with the way I've been analyzing this. A simple conversation will clear it up, and since I don't have any more classes today I have no problem waiting for her.

While I wait, I consider texting my parents to let them know about the scholarship. I even take out my phone and compose the text, but end up deleting it. Better to share it in person, where I can see their faces. Better even, I'll just share when I've won.

I don't have to wait long for Jessie, because just as I'm tucking my phone back into my jacket pocket she emerges from Ava's office. She swipes her hand under her eyes and sniffs. My chest feels tight seeing her red-rimmed eyes, but I bite the inside of my cheek to keep from saying anything. We're not close like that.

Or are you automatically close like that with someone after you've had your tongue in their mouth?

Jessie freezes when she sees me, narrowing her eyes. Is she finally realizing we have to talk about last Thursday? That we can't dance around it? That we could do it again if—

What the hell, Mac? Chill.

"May the best scholar win," I say with a smirk.

"Why are you even going for this scholarship? It's not like you need it," she practically mumbles, brushing past me.

Her question feels rhetorical, so I don't answer. Her tone is tight like it normally is with me. This is the Jessie I know, sort of fiery and maybe even annoyed by my competition. But if she doesn't like it, why does she always ask about my GPA and how I do on exams?

"Scared of a little competition, Matthews?" I follow her. She's at least a head shorter than me, so I keep pace with her easily.

She makes her way to the elevator and presses the button, waiting.

"Jessie," she corrects me without looking at me. "And no. If it scared me to compete with you, Mac, I'd never get anything done."

"Should I list all the times I got a better grade than you? Beat you to an opportunity?"

She stiffens, pinching her lips, tight and frustrated. I recognize this look: I see it when I get a better grade than her. I try to fight a smirk.

The elevator arrives, dings, and the doors open for us. We step inside.

"It would be a short list. Don't waste your breath," she says.

A fire roars to life in my chest. Does she feel it too? The heat of competition. Is that what was between us that night? Or was that heat something else entirely? I've never felt like that with anyone, and I have no idea how to name it.

"Maybe a better use of your time would be partying less and studying more," Jessie says as she exits the elevator, keeping a brisk pace. Is she referring to the Halloween party?

This is my opening.

"Speaking of partying, I was hoping we could talk about the ATZ party."

"Or we could...not." Jessie stops abruptly and looks me dead in the eye. There's a tight smile painted on her face, and her head is cocked to the side.

And then it dawns on me.

Jessie is playing The Game.

Not talking about that night, not acknowledging what happened between us—it's part of our game. The sarcasm, the banter, exciting. If we acknowledge the party, our dynamic might change. Maybe she's just not ready for that. Maybe I'm not ready for it.

Jessie raises her eyebrows at me as if to ask, "Agreed?" And then she nods, tight smile and all, and walks away.

I nearly lost the game bringing all this up, and she knows it. The smug satisfaction on her face is enough to make me zip my lips.

So who will it be, Jessie Matthews? Which of us will break first?

CHAPTER FOUR

JESSIE

Apparently, there is a layer below rock bottom.

I thought losing my full scholarship for senior year was rock bottom, but as it turns out, spending an entire week researching more than one hundred scholarship opportunities, only to find out I qualify for just ten of them, is either rock bottom or whatever comes after it.

Is it hell? Does hell come after rock bottom?

I rub my eyes. They're dry and achy after all the extra screen time this week. I roll my shoulders, sitting up straight for the first time in hours, and wince as something in my back spasms. Maybe I should stop by the student center this week. They do free ten-minute massages for students, which I take advantage of at least once a month.

I drag myself out of my seat to start making some food, but every movement is a gargantuan effort. My limbs are heavy, my chest perpetually caved in from the weight of my financial situation. I was just barely treading water with my classes before this, and now I'm struggling to come up for air.

Jade waltzes into our dorm suite, startling me, and drops her tote bag on the floor. She flings herself onto the couch, draping an arm over her eyes. My stomach growls, prompting me to eat. So for the first time in hours, I leave the table in search of food in my freezer.

"Long day?" I ask and grab a frozen chicken tikka masala microwave meal. I pop it in the microwave and lean against the counter while it cooks.

"Just exhausted from this weekend. I barely slept," she says.

"How's your mom?"

Jade's grandmother called Friday afternoon saying Jade's mom had been left by her most recent boyfriend and Jade went home immediately. She got back late on Sunday, and for the rest of the week we've been like ships in the night. Even when we've seen each other, we haven't had much time to catch up.

Jade only drops everything to go home when things are bad with her mom. I don't know all the details. Jade doesn't like to talk about it. I do know her mom drinks a lot when she's been dumped, and there's been more than one incident with her drinking getting out of control.

"Same as always after a breakup. Reckless. Dramatic." Jade's tone is clipped and distant. Seeing her mom do this to her breaks my heart and makes me grateful for my relationship with my mom. We're close. We have the kind of bond most parents probably wish they had with their kid. I trust my mom, and she trusts me. I don't take it for granted.

I can tell Jade doesn't want to talk about her mom right now, so I won't push. My instinct is to fix it, to make Jade smile, but it's not what she needs. I hate seeing her like this, a muted version of herself, like someone turned down the volume on her personality.

I stir up my dinner and take the microwave tray to our two-person dining table, of which every square inch is covered in books, notebooks, index cards, and various writing utensils. Gingerly I rearrange everything to make room for my meager meal.

What Jade needs right now is a distraction, and since I can't fix it, I'll distract.

"By the way…" I say, blowing on a forkful of rice and chicken before shoveling it into my mouth. "If you think you're going to escape giving me every juicy detail about last Thursday night, you're dead wrong."

Jade sits up halfway. "You do need to get laid."

I scowl at her. "No, I'm just too vanilla to have a threesome, so obviously I want all the sordid details."

"Or you could just…try it yourself and stop being so vanilla," Jade says with a wink and a smirk.

There she is.

"Or…you could just tell me and let me be vanilla."

"Wait, are we not going to talk about your financial aid meeting?"

I texted Jade the details after the meeting. She promised we could talk about it later that night but then ended up going home, and since we haven't talked much this week I hoped she'd forgotten, because talking about it means reliving it. And reliving it means all the heaviness will come back.

"Do we have to?"

"Yes, we have to, because your brooding is polluting the energy in our apartment."

"Hey! You were brooding too!"

"Ugh, you're so right. I'm going to have to energetically clean the fuck out of this place." Jade launches herself off the couch, disappears into her room, and returns with a bundle of herbs and a lighter.

"Spill," she says, lighting the bundle, gently blowing out the small flame, and waving the herbs around. Jade wafts the smoke toward the single window and the door.

The smoke swirls, dissipating into the air. My shoulders droop a bit from my ears, the scent of jasmine, lavender, and a bunch of other things I can't totally identify relaxing me.

As Jade makes a loop around the room with the smoky herbs, I tell her everything, repeating the conversation with Cheri, explaining the list of scholarships, and showing her the ones I circled, how I only qualify for ten. I tell her about the Walden Senior Scholarship, that Mac is applying too, among other students. I only cry a little, and when I do Jade stands next to me and rubs my back.

"You're going to figure this out. I know it's a lot, but literally no one is as smart as you or as resourceful, and it doesn't need to be mentioned, but I'm going to anyway—*no one* has as great of an ass as you do."

A snort of involuntary laughter bubbles out. Smiling, I wipe my tears and lean my head against Jade's side, giving her ass a playful tap.

"So do you, Jade."

"This is really what connects us as friends, our rockin' bods." Jade plants a loud, dramatic kiss on the top of my head and goes to the kitchen, where she finds an empty jar for the herb bundle. She rejoins me at the table, taking the seat next to me. "This is a lot, Jessie. Your plate is overflowing, and all this"—she taps a finger on the scholarship list—"is going to take a lot of energy and time that...I don't know if you have. I know it's a privileged thing for me to say this, so feel free to tell me to fuck off, but why not just take out a loan?"

"I don't know. My parents have always seemed really opposed to it. They have a lot of medical debt and it's a big burden for them. I don't really want that. I don't want the debt hanging over me in grad school and later."

"But if it's between a year of partial tuition coverage in loans or—"

"Or leaving college, yeah..."

When I was in middle school, Miss Julie would sometimes ask me in the middle of a conversation, "Where do you feel that hurt?" or "Where is that sadness in your body?" I still try it sometimes, to find exactly where my emotion lives in my body. But I'm searching now, and nothing. I feel heavy all over and numb.

"No rich relatives leave you money?" Jade asks, leaning back in her chair.

"That only happens in movies and books, I think." I rake my fork through my rice. Jade is probably right, and a loan is an option I might need to be more flexible about. But I'm tired and I don't want to talk about this anymore. The numbness won't last; eventually it'll turn into anxiety. And I don't have time for anxiety.

"Anyway, your turn now," I say. "Tell me all about your raunchy adventures."

"Can I put on my face while we do this?" Jade bounces out of the chair, her face lit up in a way it only does when she's talking about theater or makeup.

I follow her to her bedroom, food in hand. We lucked out getting one of the two-room dorm suites instead of a four-room unit in which we'd have to split the common areas with two other people. Most juniors are in off-campus apartments, so we got first pick, but it's still not ideal. I know Jade would rather be in an apartment, but she says she likes the intimacy of dorms. Really, she's just here because she's loyal as hell. She knows I can't afford to live off-campus, and I would never let her pay for both of us.

"Are you going somewhere?"

"WE are going to the ATZ party round two to see if we can find Sexy Shakespeare."

"We're doing what now?" I ask.

"Oh, stop. I know it's killing you that he hasn't texted. We're going to go back and see if he's there. He's probably a pledge or a brother and most likely there tonight."

It's been exactly a week since that off-the-charts make-out session with Sexy Shakespeare, and I haven't heard one peep from him. With the week I've had, I've basically written him off, but leave it to Jade to convince me I should spend a Friday evening searching for this guy.

"How are we going to find him? It's not like he's going to be in costume."

"He might be," Jade says. I give her a flat look.

"We'll look for a guy his height with the same hair. And when we find them, we'll ask him if he likes to moonlight as Elizabethan playwrights."

"Easy peasy," I say.

I shouldn't go. My pile of homework and projects and things to study for—not to mention the scholarship list—is daunting. I need the full evening to concentrate. I assumed Jade would go out and I'd have the place to myself to put my nose to the grindstone. I push my food around on its tray.

But.

Even now, thinking back to the masked stranger, his hands all over me, his soft lips, the way he kissed me...it sends a signal to my lower belly and then through all of me like a firework—light the fuse and watch it travel down, down, down, until *POP*, *PPPFFFF*, explosion of color and light. All of that inside me warring against the "shoulds."

The firework wins.

"Okay, fine. Fifteen minutes, and then I'm coming back."

Jade squeals, clapping her hands, and settles into the seat in front of her vanity. She slides a headband on her head to pull back her hair, turns on the mirror lights, then starts to open up various eyeshadows, picking out the brushes she plans to use and setting them out in a row.

"Deal! Okay, so! Threesome details, my little vanilla cupcake... One of the people is someone I've hooked up with before. Do you remember Greg?" Jade asks, squeezing some foundation onto the back of her hand.

"Football Greg?"

"No, the other one."

"Greasy Greg?"

"Why would I hook up with him again?"

"Girl Greg?"

"She graduated last year."

"What was her actual name?"

"Georgina." Jade smirks, probably in memory of Georgina.

"Who else is left?" I take another bite, then remember one last person, nicknamed for his resemblance to Mr. Clooney. "George Greg?"

"Yes! Okay, so, I find George Greg at the party last Thursday night randomly and we start to dance, right? It was super sexy, and it turned into kissing, and it's all fun and games, and then this girl walks over, okay? And she starts dancing with us, sort of like on the side, you know. Like she's trying to work her way in, maybe. And I was like, okay, I can get behind this. And then she finally kind of gets in the middle of us and starts to make out with him, and I was like, um, no, bitch. Like, you're not going to steal my dance partner, make-out buddy—no. We're not doing that. So I, like, back up, and then grab her arm and spin her around, so now she's facing me, and I start to be like 'what the fuck,' like, I'm ready to fucking fight her. But then! She takes my face in her hands and literally starts to make out with me too."

"Oh my god." I hide my face as best I can with a fork in my hand. "Am I stressed, am I into this? I don't even know."

"We're into it."

I give her a thumbs-up and a skeptical look. She throws her head back and laughs.

Jade's stories used to make me clutch my pearls, but I'm used to it now. It helps that she's an amazing storyteller, and once I got past the content I started to enjoy Jade's tales of her rendezvous a lot more. But sometimes she still has me clutching my pearls.

"I knew you'd react like that. Anyway, we do the dancing/making out thing for a while, just, like, taking turns, and then she invites me and Greg back to her place."

"What's her name?"

"Anna."

"Okay, Threesome Anna. Got it. So you go back to her place."

"We go back to her place. And it was..." She fans herself.

"I have questions."

"Of course you have questions." She dips a brush into an eyeshadow palette and brushes it onto one of her eyelids. She's gone for a fiery red look, no doubt with an outfit already planned out to match.

"Logistics, specifically," I say.

"Go on."

"Who was on top?" I ask.

"It changed."

"So there's a lot of position shifting?"

"Well, sure—"

"Does anyone get left out?"

"Not that night, they didn't," she says with a smug grin.

"And going forward?"

"We have no plans to make this a regular thing."

"Would you?"

Jade considers, pausing mid-blend. "Maybe. Could be a fun little fling."

"But no feelings, right?" I tease, knowing damn well Jade's motto is "Under no circumstances should you catch an STI, a wedding bouquet, or feelings."

"It was just sex, Jessie."

"Of course it was," I say without a hint of sarcasm.

I haul myself off her bed to look through my closet for something to wear tonight. Jade really does live by her motto. She generally doesn't sleep with the same people twice, and she hasn't dated anyone or had a partner since I've known her. Nor has she attended any weddings and she gets STI tested regularly.

I throw on clean jeans and a long-sleeve shirt, braiding my long hair to one side and donning a beanie. Vowing to come back in fifteen minutes, we walk the same path tonight to the ATZ frat house, but this time I have less anxiety. Well, I have less anxiety about whether I should be studying, but my stomach churns when I think about trying to find Will. Needle in a haystack.

Everything in the basement of the frat house is the same as last week. The lights, the music, the stench of sweat and beer, the large crowd of dancing bodies. It's going to be a nightmare trying to find him again.

I start on the edges of the crowd, looking as closely as I can at people without getting too much in their personal space. As I venture through the throng, I politely decline offers to dance with the people grinding against me. That's something I need more alcohol for and have no plans to indulge in tonight. I push up the sleeves of my shirt, too warm in this sea of bodies. There's no sign of long sandy-blond hair, and it's too loud to hear any accents.

When I get through the crowd to the other side of the room, I find Jade chatting someone up.

"Any luck?" I yell to her.

She shakes her head, abandoning her conversation. With a gesture she asks if I found him, and I shake my head as well.

"I don't think he's here," I say once we've made it outside. "If he is, his hair is different. Or, I don't know, maybe my memory of him isn't very good. He was wearing a mask. I couldn't even tell you what color his eyes were."

"Your only option is to make out with everyone that vaguely resembles him until you find him again," Jade says with a casual shrug, deadpan.

"Ha. Ha. No, I'm done. He has my number. If he wanted to talk to me he would have texted by now. There was a snowball's chance in hell I was going to see him here again tonight. Let's just go."

"Boys are dumb." Jade pulls me in for a hug, and I hug her back. It feels like such a stupid thing to be disappointed over, but I can't ignore the way my heart clenches.

Between this and realizing my prospects for scholarships are dwindling, I'm feeling pretty low. This year had a promising start, and after attending the Halloween party and letting loose a little I thought I could maybe be slightly less vigilant. I could let my guard down some. But little by little I'm seeing how wrong I was. I have to stay focused. I don't need some stupid boy to get in the way of school or my scholarship work.

—————

CHAPTER FIVE

MAC

Brody Jacobs is always fucking late. Our court time for racquetball was set for 8:00 p.m. It's already 8:15 p.m., and now he's not picking up the phone. Most likely he'll do what he always does, which is ignore my calls and waltz up in ten minutes, nearly half an hour late.

I hang up, rolling my eyes. We've lost our court time so many times because of this. I'd stop making plans with the guy, but he's a great racquetball player and we've been friends since high school, and besides never being on time he's not so bad.

I'm about to go in and just get started myself, but I see a familiar figure down the road and do a double-take.

Is that Jessie?

There's another girl with her I don't recognize initially, but as they come closer I realize I've seen Jessie with her before. She has auburn hair and carries herself with the kind of confidence that would intimidate or challenge most men. She's gorgeous, but my eyes don't land on her. Not when she's next to Jessie. Her presence is a magnet and I'm a mere scrap of metal; if Jessie is nearby, some unseen force will always draw me to her.

"Jessie?" I say when she and her friend are just a few feet away. I watch as she registers who said her name. Confusion and surprise cross her face.

Jessie gives me the once-over, and I roll my shoulders a little, knowing the way my shirt hugs my body. Hopefully she likes what she sees. I know she liked it at the party.

"Hello, Mac," Jessie says and slows her walk as she approaches.

"Mac?" her friend asks, looking at Jessie and then back at me. "Mac! Hi. I've heard so much about you."

Has she?

"I'm Jade, Jessie's roommate." Jessie's friend extends her hand, a wide smile on her face.

I dart a glance at Jessie and take Jade's hand, giving it a firm shake. "What has she been saying?" I ask.

"Nothing," Jessie says at the same time Jade says, "If I told you, I'd have to kill you."

Jessie cuts her roommate a glance I recognize, full of daggers and poison. It's refreshing to see Jessie is like this with everyone. I sometimes wonder if maybe I take our games too far; if I'm too harsh despite the fact she dishes it out just as hard back to me. Growing up with three brothers has distorted my view of what banter crosses the line, but Jessie seems to have a healthy roast-to-banter ratio with everyone.

"A bit early to be done with partying," I say, nodding toward The Row, where they just came from.

"We weren't partying," Jessie says. She crosses her arms and glances at Jade, but Jade's not looking at Jessie; she's texting.

"We were looking for this guy Jessie made out with last week. Sexy Shakespeare—"

"Jade!" Jessie cuts her off, slapping her arm.

My brain short-circuits. That makes no sense. Jessie's seen me multiple times over the past week—why would she go looking for me?

"Sorry, did you just say you went looking for him?"

"Yeah! They made out, she gave him her number, and the guy didn't text her. Normally I'd be like, fuck that noise, but—"

"Seriously, Jade." Jessie cuts her off again through gritted teeth, but this time she's gripping Jade's arm. And she's still not looking at me.

Holy shit, did Jessie not tell her best friend she made out with me? Is she seriously that embarrassed? Is that why she's referring to me as if I'm not...?

"Hang on, did you say Sexy Shakespeare?" I ask.

Confused as I am by this conversation, I'm equally taken aback by the realization Jessie thinks I'm sexy. I want to fixate on that for a second, but Jade starts to talk again.

"Yes, isn't that great? He was dressed like—well, I thought he was dressed like a king, but Jessie said it was Shakespeare. And she would know, she loves Shakespeare. But it's like the guy wore the costume knowing Jessie would love it."

"Oh my god," Jessie says and rolls her eyes, covering her face. "Jade." She picks her head up out of her hands. "I'm one hundred percent sure Mac doesn't want to hear about this."

She could not be more wrong. I want to hear all about what Jessie thinks of my costume and our make-out session. Under the light of the streetlamp I can see the way a blush paints her cheeks. She's cute when she gets all red like that, but why would she be embarrassed by this? Something in my chest pinches, and I clear my throat to try to get rid of it.

"So we'll just be on our way," Jessie says. "Nice to see you, Mac."

Except it doesn't sound at all like it was nice to see me.

"Wait—maybe Mac can help us," Jade says, grabbing Jessie's arm and pulling her back.

Jessie flails and then stills at Jade's side.

"Mac, were you at the ATZ party? Did you see a guy in a Shakespeare costume? And a wig. He had on a wig, right, Jessie?"

Jessie nods, but she still won't look me in the eye. That pinching in my chest intensifies, and my phone feels like it weighs ten pounds. I open my mouth to say something, but someone's phone rings and Jade yelps, startling Jessie.

"It's him. It's George Greg," Jade says.

George Greg?

Jade is holding her phone as if it's hot to the touch. She's about to drop it when Jessie grabs it, swipes the answer button, and holds the phone to Jade's ear.

I step away, pretending something on the sidewalk has completely captured my interest. I was going to admit that yes, I was at the party, and I was dressed like Shakespeare because I thought it was clever. It didn't occur to me that Jessie might be there, but as soon as I saw her I knew she'd appreciate the costume. We had an English class together sophomore year, "Shakespeare as an Influencer." Jessie did way better than me in that class. Old English is not my strong suit.

But I can't out myself like this. Jessie looks like she'd rather crawl into a hole and hibernate until spring rather than talk about this with me here. I thought girls always talked to their best friends about stuff, but what do I know? I have brothers. It's clear Jessie hasn't told Jade, or if she did, Jade is in on the game and she's playing it too.

But maybe if I could talk to Jessie alone...?

I check my phone to see if Brody has texted me. He hasn't. When I look back up at Jessie and Jade, they're staring at each other intensely, Jessie with her hands on Jade's shoulders like she's giving her a pep talk. Jade nods and then turns and heads back to The Row.

"Well, I'm heading back to my dorm, but I'll see you around," Jessie says, starting to walk past me.

"Wait," I say and reach out. My fingertips graze her skin, and my perception narrows to this. All my other senses dull like some kind of superhero montage, my sense of touch powering up tenfold. Like making contact with a hot stove, all I can feel is where I grazed her arm.

When the world goes back to normal, I try to read Jessie's face. *Did she feel that too?*

"Listen, about the Shakespeare—" I start.

"Can we not?" She holds up her hand. "I don't want to talk about it."

"Jessie, it's—"

"Seriously. Stop."

"Sorry," I say, and she must hear the sincerity in my voice because she looks up at me with apologetic eyes.

"No, I'm...I'm sorry. There was no reason to snap at you."

"It's fine. I didn't mean to push."

"It's just, like, if Will wanted to text me, he would have done already, right? He got my number. It's been a week. It kind of...hurt my feelings. And I don't love talking about that." She mumbles the last words and averts her eyes again.

"Will?"

"Yeah, his name was Will. Sexy Shakespeare is just...like a me and Jade..." She waves her hands around, vaguely gesticulating.

"Will...as in...Will Shakespeare?"

She obviously doesn't want to talk about it, but if I can lead the horse to water, maybe it'll figure out the stream is for drinking.

"Oh my god," she says as it dawns on her. "He gave me a fake name." She whispers those words, hiding her face in her hands. "I swear if you're laughing at me, Mackenzie Baldwin, so help me god..."

I pinch my lips together, trying to hide my smile. I gave her the fake name because I thought it was clever. Her costume didn't hide her identity, and I didn't think my mask or wig was that good, so I thought the fake name was a clever idea.

Apparently, it was too clever.

"Okay, well, that is exactly the amount of embarrassment I can handle for one day, so I'm going to go now," Jessie says with a groan as she drags her hands down her face.

"No, wait. I—"

"Hey, bro!" Brody yells at that exact moment, jogging up to the gym. "I'm so sorry." He slaps me on the back in greeting.

When I turn back to Jessie, she's already gone.

BY SOME MIRACLE our court is still reserved despite it being forty-five minutes past our time. I guess most people don't care about playing racquetball this late on a Friday night, but Brody and I have had a weekly standing racquetball appointment on Fridays since I quit soccer. I play a few times a week by myself but enjoy the time with my friend.

"What held you up this time?" I ask. "Grandma need help with her Nintendo Switch again?"

"That was a real thing that happened. Nana really likes *Animal Crossing*, okay?"

I raise my eyebrows at him as we collect a ball and racquets from the front desk.

"Nah, I was talking to my girl."

"How is Mandy?"

Brody has always seemed like the kind of guy who sleeps around, but he's been with his girlfriend Mandy since our junior year of high school. He started looking at engagement rings about a month ago.

I'm jealous of what they have. I had a couple of girlfriends in high school, and I've hung out with a few girls since being at Middle Penn, but most of them didn't like coming second to soccer, so no one stuck around long. Now that I don't play anymore, my dating life could look a little different, but I don't see a lot of girls being as interested when they realize they'll be second to studying.

Except maybe someone like Jessie.

"What about you? What happened to that girl you were talking to this summer?"

"Back at home? The one who worked at the ice cream shop on Main?"

"Yeah, the brunette. She, uh... What was her name?"

"Candice."

"Yes! What happened there?"

"Just fizzled out," I say.

"I saw you talking to a chick when I walked up—who was she?"

"Jessie Matthews. We..." *How do I describe Jessie?* "We have a few classes together."

"That it? You had puppy eyes, bro."

"It's complicated."

"I got time."

We don't waste any time getting into the game, and I explain, as best I can while playing, about the Halloween party and the way Jessie acted the next day in class, like she had no idea it was me. Like the previous night didn't happen at all. I give him the rundown of the conversation with her and Jade.

"I don't know," I say. "We've always been competitive with our grades, we always had banter, but tonight, the way she acted...I can't tell if she's just messing with me or not."

"One hundred percent, dude. She is playing the GAME."

"You think she knew it was me and is just...doing a bit?"

"Yes, one hundred percent. This is how girls are. They play the game."

Thinking it in my head is one thing, but now that I've said it out loud and heard Brody agreeing with me...I'm not so sure anymore.

"Why would she do that?" I ask. I'm processing it more than asking, but Brody sees it as an invitation.

"Because she likes you. She likes your dynamic. She thinks it's a game and she's playing."

Brody doesn't know Jessie, and what he's saying doesn't settle right with me. But truthfully, I don't know Jessie that well either. Definitely not well enough to know if she's playing The Game and we're just doing a bit or if she truly doesn't know it's me.

"What if...?" I pause, propping my hands on my knees, the ball bouncing behind me, ignored. "What if she didn't know it was me?"

It wasn't that dark and my mask and wig weren't THAT good. She looked into my eyes. She's looked into my eyes hundreds of times, so she would have recognized me. She's seen my face a billion times over the past two years. She would have recognized me. I'm usually really sure of myself, but the way Jessie is acting has me questioning everything.

Brody pauses too, hands on his head, breathing heavily. "Listen, I have two sisters."

"I know, dude."

"I know a thing or two about girls. They are complex. Nothing is straightforward with them. My sister Lily once pretended she was into emo music for a guy."

"Okay...?" I bounce the ball a few times, catching my breath.

"She didn't just pretend to be into the music. She got into that emo-punk culture. Dressed the part, got a couple piercings, dyed her hair, changed her makeup."

"Did it work?"

"Of course it did. She got him hook, line, and sinker."

"But she didn't like the music?"

"Hated it. But played the game until they broke up."

"Was it worth it?"

"Dude, I don't know. My point is that girls do crazy shit for guys they like. They play games. Games with layers. Serve it." He gestures to the ball in my hand, so I do. I start another round for us.

I'm not inclined to believe him, but what if he's right? What if Jessie likes our dynamic so much, likes our game so much, that she wanted to sort of...add this as a layer? It certainly keeps me on my toes. And if I'm being honest, it's kind of hot. It's like we have this little secret we're not telling anyone else, not even each other. She obviously didn't tell her best friend if they went to The Row to search for me. Maybe she thinks it's hot to keep it a secret too.

The idea that she likes me is enough to distract me, and I play my worst game ever. Brody wins by leaps and bounds because my mind is elsewhere, circling the drain. Is it a game? And if it is, how do I know how long to play if we don't eventually talk about it? We can't do this forever—mostly because I wouldn't want to. If I could have kissed Jessie again tonight, I would have. I want to kiss her again. And take her on a date and get to know her outside of the academic context. The door wasn't really open for any of that before, but now I've stepped a foot over the threshold, and I don't really want to go back out.

CHAPTER SIX

MAC

I'm going to need more champagne.

I probably shouldn't have taken such a large sip for the last speech, but it was the fourth speech tonight, and it was lengthy, and I'm going to need more than baby sips to get through the rest of this evening.

I gesture to the waiter on standby for our family. We're in a private room at our family's favorite Italian restaurant in Lancaster. They know us here. We come often and always pay for the private dining suite on the top floor of the restaurant. Despite the fact it's an hour away from my parents' home, this is where and how the Baldwin family celebrates.

The waiter tops me off just in time for Amelia, Michael's fiancée, to stand. Mom, Dad, and my other two brothers, Rob and Noah, have all given speeches, and I'm hoping this is the last one so I won't have to speak. Amelia smooths out her wrinkle-free dress, clears her throat, and launches into a speech about how proud she is of her fiancé and how she can't believe how lucky she is to be marrying a Baldwin.

I bite back a joke. Time and place and all that.

We raise our glasses. Again. Michael thanks his fiancée, giving her an entirely appropriate kiss, and we all drink for him. Again.

I shoot back my champagne as if it's something a lot stronger and pray this is the end of the speeches.

"Mackenzie, did you want to...?" My mom leans over, nudging me with her elbow.

"Nah, I feel like the last five speeches really captured it."

I know she won't accept that for an answer, and she doesn't, elbowing me until I stand. Everyone turns to me as if they knew I'd stand to give a speech too. It's part of the whole song and dance of these dinners. Almost everyone gives a speech. It's our time to honor each other, Dad likes to say.

I grab my water glass, wishing I hadn't finished off my champagne. "Best for last, huh?"

Everyone smirks, and I wink at Amelia, who shares a smile with me and then with Michael. He gives me an approving grin.

"All I have to say is, what took you so long, you lazy piece of—?"

"Mackenzie." My mother cuts me off. My brothers cackle. I crack a smile. I don't bother to look at my dad. He doesn't usually like my jokes.

"I mean, seriously, if it were anyone else, they would have at least won the Super Bowl before quitting."

Everyone at the table is giggling now except my parents, although my mom is giving me a good-natured smile. My dad forgot how to smile in the sixties.

"And Antarctica, really? Is it because no other continent wanted you? And by the way, that only applies to Michael. Amelia, the President of Antarctica probably called you personally to come down, so obviously that comment wasn't for you, sweetie."

She blushes, and she and Michael share another adoring smile. Rob and Noah are still snorting with laughter.

"Look, personally, I'm glad you're going. It means more Christmas presents for me."

"Hear, hear," Noah says, raising his glass.

"Okay, but seriously, congrats. I have a lot to live up to." I gesture to all my brothers now with a middle finger, landing on Michael. "So, thanks." I lift my glass. "To the second-favorite Baldwin son. We all know I'm the first."

There's another ripple of laughter, and everyone takes a sip as I sit, satisfied I did my job. No one signed me up to be the court jester of our family, but it's the role that comes most naturally to me. I'm not the responsible one—that's Rob. I'm not the smart one—that's Noah. I'm not the sporty one—that's Michael. I learned at a young age making people laugh was the only way to stand out among my brothers. Unfortunately, it garners no respect from my father.

Everyone but my parents gives me a nod of approval or thumbs-up for my speech.

My mom doesn't mind my humor. My dad merely tolerates it. Generally speaking, he seems to merely tolerate me and doesn't hide his preference for my brothers. He sits at the head of the table, Rob on his right, Michael to his left. In my dad's eyes, my brothers have all earned their right to be celebrated. They bring honor to the Baldwin name.

I'm hoping the scholarship will be enough for me to do the same in Robert Baldwin Senior's eyes.

Our salad plates cleared, small plates are placed in front of us, and much larger plates packed with appetizers are set on the table: small slides of toasted bruchetta piled high with cherry tomatoes, caprese salad with bright red tomatoes and fluffy mozzarella chunks, rich brown and green olives marinating in a decadent olive oil, and mini mushrooms stuffed and topped with golden breadcrumbs. It's a feast before the actual feast, and we all fill our small plates.

"Now, how did you meet again?" My mom leans forward, engaging Charlotte in conversation. Charlotte is Noah's girlfriend. Apparently, they've been dating for months, and in typical Noah fashion, he didn't tell us until about a week ago when we found out he'd be bringing his girlfriend to dinner. She's sitting across from me tonight—a distinct pleasure, because not only is she beautiful, but she's also absolutely brilliant.

She reminds me a little of Jessie.

Someone I am trying desperately not to think about.

"Noah and I are coworkers," Charlotte says with a sweet smile. She has bright hair so blonde it's practically white. It goes down to her waist and it's stick-straight. She has on a very classy gray dress, fitting in well at the table with the other partners.

Rob's wife Lori is a lawyer and a partner at her firm, and she dresses the part. She always looks like she just stepped off the set of the TV show *Suits*. Amelia freelances as a writer and editor for several highly regarded travel magazines. She grew from a travel blogger to an expert in the industry. She dresses as well as Lori, but less lawyer-chic, more "traveling first class to Paris"-chic.

Somehow, all my brothers snagged gorgeous, smart women despite being absolute Neanderthals. I hope to do the same one day.

"Oh, that's wonderful," my mom says. "How many women work at NASA?"

"Not enough," Noah says. "But the prettiest one is sitting right here."

Charlotte looks at Noah then, and the adoration in her eyes is enough to make me look away.

Has anyone ever looked at me like that?

I consider the girlfriends I've had, all casual, short-term relationships that didn't make it past two months. Except one girl I dated my freshman year of college. We were together for eight months, and we even said we loved each other, but looking at the way Charlotte and Noah look at each other, I don't think what Melissa and I felt was love. It was puppy love at best. Just two people who preferred to be together rather than alone, but my soccer schedule was too much for her. In the end she wanted to date someone with more time in their schedule. I couldn't fault her for that, but it still hurt. I've kept most of my relationships casual since then. It's easier for everyone.

Our appetizer plates are cleared, replaced with dinner plates. The picked-over serving plates are cleared too, and large bowls of noodles and sauce take their spot on the table. At the other end of the table, house-made spaghetti noodles drown in a hearty, rich red sauce. Near my end of the table, a bowl of thick, flat noodles covered in a creamy Alfredo steams in front of me, the garlic and rich cream sauce making my mouth water.

We all fill our plates, passing around the bowls. Wine glasses are topped off, bread baskets are emptied onto our plates, and the waiters disappear again.

"So, Mac, what's the update? How's your dating life? Anyone special?" Noah asks before taking a huge bite of bread.

Jessie's face flashes in my mind. Her delicate snow-white skin, her long dark hair, her gray eyes piercing me with that annoyed look she gets on her face right before she cracks a smile.

"No, I'm not dating anyone," I say, but a smile fights its way onto my face. I try to control it, but I don't think it works.

"Come on—there isn't anyone?"

"Well..."

"I knew it," Noah says with a grin.

"Knew what? You didn't even know what I was going to say."

"Spill." Noah claps and rubs his hands together like I've got a good story.

"I mean, there isn't much to spill. There's this girl that I've kind of had a crush on for a while, just from a distance, you know. And we…" I glance at my mom, who actually seems interested in my story. I mentally apologize. "We made out at a party on Halloween, and it was great. There was a ton of chemistry."

"Ooh, are you talking about a girl?" Amelia asks, leaning our way.

I eat a forkful of spaghetti and nod, remembering why we like this place so much. The tomato sauce tastes so fresh it's like someone hand-squeezed it earlier today. The seasonings are perfectly balanced, and the chewy noodles make you forget you're in Lancaster, Pennsylvania, and not in a small Italian village eating at a hole-in-the-wall restaurant.

"So, what happened?" Charlotte asks.

"Well, my costume had a mask element, but it wasn't that good—she would have known it was me. But the next day and ever since then, she's been acting like she had no idea it was me. Just the other night she said she didn't know who the guy was. It's a whole long story, but basically, I tried to tell her that guy was me, and she wouldn't let me say the words. If she does know it's me, she's too embarrassed to talk about it."

"That makes sense. I'd be embarrassed if I'd made out with you," Noah says.

I flick him off. He throws his head back and laughs, and my mother slaps my hand playfully.

"If she's acting like she didn't know it was you, then she probably didn't know it was you," Charlotte says.

"That's kind of what I thought too, because my mask wasn't that good, and I was wearing a wig, but that doesn't change my eyes or my voice. Well, I did put on an accent…"

Charlotte just raises her eyebrows as if to say, "My point exactly."

"But! But…we've been competing for years with school stuff, and it's like our vibe to sort of snub each other and make a game out of everything. I was just talking to Brody about it and he said—"

"Brody doesn't know shit, Mac," Noah says.

Since Brody lived down the street from us, Noah knows exactly who he is and what he's like. Thinking about Brody's words now from my brother's perspective makes them a lot less certain in my mind.

"Even so, there's just this, like, playful dynamic between us, and it feels like maybe she's just doing that... I don't know."

I was pretty convinced by the whole "we're just doing a bit" thing until I started saying it out loud to levelheaded people. Now I'm feeling a little dumb.

"What do you mean by 'playful dynamic'?" Amelia asks.

I explain our relationship, the banter, the competition. How things are always kind of spicy between us but good-natured. If anyone can understand that, it has to be my brothers. This is our relationship. Sarcasm, banter, insults—it's a whole language of love we speak with each other.

Noah nods, understanding, and the knot forming in my chest loosens. "I could see it," he says. "She's probably not dumb, your costume was probably not that good, and I think I agree with you. She knew it was you and is just doing a bit like you guys always do, probably because she's too embarrassed to actually talk about it."

I feel justified. I'm about to thank him when Lori pipes up.

"Noah, that's ridiculous," she says. "Sorry, I was eavesdropping." She practically leans across my mom to interject. "She's not playing a game. Even if you guys have a bit going on for school things, when it comes to this kind of stuff, girls are way more serious."

"Are we?" Amelia says. "Lori, you're telling me you didn't play any games in college with boys? With Rob?" Amelia asks like she knows the answer. And she probably does. They were sorority sisters at MPC, so they've known each other for a long time.

"Withdrawn," Lori says. She, like my brother, thinks it's clever to use lawyer jargon casually. It was funny the first year they did it.

"Girls are stupid when they're twenty-one. We're still playing high-school games 'cause we don't know any other way," Amelia says.

"Is that what you did with me?" Michael asks.

"No, of course not," Amelia says with a sly smile.

Michael shifts in his chair, straightening his back, and his mouth falls open a little. "Wait, what did you do?"

Amelia clears her throat. "You know that guy I took to the sorority formal sophomore year? And how you ended up going with my friend Sophie?"

"Ugh, yes. What was his name? Mike? I couldn't stand seeing you there with him."

"Mike, yes. Exactly. You asked me out the next day, didn't you?"

"Yes. I didn't want Mike to snap you up. I would have asked you at formal, but I didn't want to be a total dick to Sophie."

"Yeah, Mike was gay. We had no intention of being together, I just needed you to get your ass in gear."

Nearly everyone at the table laughs at this. Lori looks especially tickled, and even my dad half-smiles between bites of pasta.

"Oh, damn. I've been bamboozled," Michael says, glancing around with sort of vacant eyes.

Amelia placates him with a kiss, and they stare longingly at each other again.

"Get a room," I whisper-yell at them, and my mother playfully slaps my arm.

Everyone starts eating again, but I don't want to lose the conversation just yet. I still can't tell if I'm being an idiot by thinking Jessie and I are playing some unspoken game or if I'm in the clear.

"So, okay. The consensus is that we all think she knows it was me and this is just...banter. And also, maybe she's just a little embarrassed?" I ask, surveying the table.

Amelia, Noah, and Lori nod. Charlotte shakes her head in dissent.

"What if she really just didn't know it was you?" Charlotte asks, emphasizing her earlier point.

"It just seems so unlikely—"

"More unlikely than her playing an elaborate game of 'don't talk about the Halloween party' as banter?"

Charlotte makes a good point. I glance around for someone to back me up, to help me argue with her, but they've gone back to their pasta and started new conversations. Even Noah is giving Michael his attention. It's just me and Charlotte dissecting my love life now.

"Yes, way more unlikely. I'm pretty sure she likes our dynamic as much as I do. Maybe she doesn't want that to change."

"Did you know it's unlikely there's life on Venus? The planet is inhospitable, hot enough to melt lead, but it doesn't stop scientists from believing or testing for life. There are people who dedicate their whole careers to Venus, searching for any signs of life on such a volatile planet. The odds aren't in their favor and they'll likely never find what they're looking for, but they never stop trying," Charlotte says.

"What are you saying?" I ask, chewing on her planet metaphor.

"I'm saying just because something is unlikely doesn't mean it's not worth pursuing."

"Still not following."

"Find a way to tell her it's you. Even if it's unlikely, even if it's impossible, say it. Because if you're wrong, this is not going to end well for you." Charlotte gives me a meaningful look and then turns her attention to Rob when he taps her on the shoulder.

I hate to admit it, but Charlotte is right. I like Jessie. I'd like to ask her out, spend more time with her. I'd like to kiss her again. But I can't do any of that if we don't talk about that party. I have to have a conversation with her about it. Even if she knows and we're just playing The Game, I have to end it.

Long after I've left my family and driven back to campus, the planet Venus lives on in my head. An inhospitable planet with all evidence pointing toward "no life," and there are scientists out there still holding onto hope? Still researching? Trying despite everything?

If someone can dedicate their entire career to Venus, I think I can get a girl to talk to me about a party.

CHAPTER SEVEN

"You've got to be kidding me," I mumble to myself as I stroll up to the student labs for my first day as a research assistant to Professor Campbell, only to find Mac sitting in the lobby, one leg casually crossed over the other, watching something on his phone.

I wasn't going to say yes to Professor Campbell's ask, but losing my scholarship has me rethinking all my financial aid plans for undergrad and graduate school. I'd hoped to get a scholarship or fellowship to cover the cost of grad school, but now I've seen how easily things like that can be lost and I need to pursue other, maybe safer avenues. Like getting an assistantship and being a research assistant. Having experience with Professor Campbell could look really good on my résumé. It's a backup plan agreed to out of fear, but it's safer than not preparing at all.

"What are you doing here?" I ask, trying to keep my voice semi-casual, attempting friendly.

Mac looks up from his phone, a wide smile appearing on his face, his eyes practically sparkling. The way his face brightens when he realizes it's me standing there sends a flutter through my ribs.

"I'm a research assistant for Sara," he says.

"What? No, I am. She specifically—"

"Jessie, hi. Mac, good to see you." Professor Campbell emerges from one of the rooms, holding a stack of papers. "You two must have figured out you'll both be research assistants for me for the next six months or so. How about we get started with a quick rundown before our first group shows up?"

I follow Professor Campbell and Mac into the experiment room, quietly letting out something between a huff and a sigh, because of course the universe has conspired to pair me up with him. We already share two classes this semester, he's going for the scholarship I need to stay in school next year, and he's the only person in my way for valedictorian. Everywhere I turn, Mac is there. And now he's here. And we'll be spending the next six months observing experiments, coding data, and having meetings with Professor Campbell about the experiments. It's a lot of time I'll be spending with someone whose presence is a constant reminder I don't quite measure up.

Maybe I should back out or see if another psychology professor needs a research assistant. I don't want to turn this into a competition; I need this to be the easiest thing in my schedule. My head starts to hurt as if my brain is being inflated and pushing against the sides of my skull. I rub my temples and close my eyes for a moment.

"...a study of self-compassion among college students. I'm measuring outcomes when students are given validating, compassionate words or none at all. This is my third year, and although I have two more years, the data is fascinating..."

I stifle a yawn as Sara tells us about her work and eventually transitions to explaining our responsibilities within the experiment. I'm trying to listen, but with a headache coming on and with how little sleep I've been getting, it's all I can do not to put my head in my arms on the table and just take a quick nap.

All my professors wanted to give out big projects and final assignments and tests this week. It gave me very little time to apply for grants and scholarships, but I still knocked out about half the list. It took me days to complete since I only had a stolen hour or two every night. Even when I get into bed, I'm not sleeping; I'm scrolling social media, looking for photos from the ATZ party. For photos of Sexy Shakespeare. Nothing's turned up, though. No pictures of guys in masks with sandy-blond hair.

It's tempting to give up, free up some brain space, but, *goddammit*, I want to kiss him again.

Professor Campbell finishes her explanations and passes over release forms for when the students arrive. Then she leads me and Mac back into the lobby and disappears.

An uncomfortable silence spreads through the room like lava. I'm not sure where to look, but my eyes keep landing on Mac. The beige walls don't hold my interest. Or his—he's typing on his phone, the ghost of a smile on his lips. From this angle I can see his nose is a little crooked. Maybe a sports injury? He did play a sport, I think. I vaguely remember him wearing jerseys freshman and sophomore year. Crooked nose and all, Mac is undeniably handsome. His skin is sun-kissed, and his hair is messy in the kind of way that makes me want to run my fingers through it and smooth it down.

Whoa. Why the hell am I thinking about running my fingers through Mac's hair? Maybe Jade is right. I do need to get laid.

Remember how annoying he is, Jessie. He can't be attractive and annoying.

He can be, actually. And he is.

"Did you volunteer for this?" I ask, crossing my arms. Maybe if he says something annoying I'll stop thinking of him...like that.

"Sure did," he says, glancing up. His smile widens, taking over his face, and I dig my fingernails into my arms. That smug smile drives me nuts.

"For your résumé?" I narrow my eyes at him.

"Well, it does look good on a résumé, but I'm interested in Sara's work around self-compassion. Did you volunteer?"

"She asked me to be on the project," I say, straightening a little.

"Nice," he says. His face reads impressed, but it's never that simple with Mac. "Did you get your grade from that psychology quiz on Friday?"

I did, as Professor Campbell emailed them out earlier today. I didn't do well, though, given the stress of my life right now. Leave it to Mac to know exactly when to ask about something like this.

"Yes," I say, squinting as if to ask, "What's your point?"

"I got a ninety-nine. What did you get?"

"A ninety-seven," I mumble, and he raises his eyebrows at me, his face radiating superiority. It boils my blood, and I clench my teeth, pinching my lips together.

I would make another comment, but a student arrives for the experiment and Mac gets up to hand them a form. After that, more students trickle in, and we have to hand out and collect release forms while my blood boils the whole time. I'm practically lightheaded from the anger. I direct the students into the experiment room, a fake smile plastered on my face, and when everyone on the sign-up list has arrived, Mac and I take our places in the observing room.

Professor Campbell walks in and starts the experiment. She asks everyone to draw a self-portrait and gives them time to do so. After this she'll collect the portraits and pass out a short quiz with math and vocabulary questions.

The quiz is hard—I looked at it myself. The math is advanced, and even I don't recognize a lot of the words in the questions for the vocabulary portion. Sara will pass it out without saying much, just letting them know they have five minutes to complete as much as they can. She'll start a timer and let them go.

The sessions are being recorded, so we don't really have to watch, but I pretend it's the most riveting thing ever. I need to cool down, but Mac's grade on the psychology quiz still feels sour in the back of my throat. The air in the observation room is absolutely stifling. I wish we could prop open a door or something because I'm too warm. I remove my cardigan, but it doesn't help. It's not the temperature; it's sharing the space with someone who annoys the ever-living hell out of me. If the silence between us in the lobby was uncomfortable, this is downright torture.

I fiddle with the ends of my hair and bounce my leg, but it does nothing to dispel my frustration. I steal a glance at Mac, but he looks perfectly content.

Of course he does. *Ugh.*

"Did you do the statistics homework yet?" he asks, cutting through the silence.

This is the other class we share this year besides social psychology. I'm not doing as well in there as I am in psychology, which means his grade is no doubt higher than mine. *Is that why he's bringing this up?*

"I did." I lean forward in my chair, trying to show I'm more interested in observing the experiment than chatting with him. Especially if he's just in the mood to compete. Normally, I am too, but I feel like I might snap at any moment, and I try not to snap at people I barely know.

"It was kind of hard, wasn't it?" he asks.

"I guess...?"

"Do you like statistics?"

What the hell?

"Why are you asking me if I like statistics?" I peer at him, brows knitted together.

"Gotta be better than silence."

"I don't know. I kind of like the silence."

That's not entirely true, but I've still got lingering slivers of annoyance under my skin, and I'm not in the mood for small talk.

"If you really wanna know, I'd rather be trying to get to know you a little bit."

"Oh," I say, knocked sideways by his honesty.

"We see each other all the time, but we don't really know each other. I thought maybe while we had the time..."

"We should be paying attention to the experiment," I say, crossing my arms over my chest.

"Well, yeah, but it's—"

"Plus, this is not a date."

He scoffs. "I hope not. This would be the weirdest first date ever."

I snort and try to fight a smile, but it tugs at the corners of my lips. "Nothing says romance like creepily watching other people through a two-way mirror," I say before I can stop myself.

"I usually wait until at least the third date for the two-way mirror."

I don't even need to look at him to know he's smirking. I'd know the sound of his "I think I'm clever" voice anywhere.

"Sounds like you're into some weird stuff." I lean back and squeeze my arms tighter in front of me, fighting my growing smile.

"You have no idea."

When I look over at him, his smirk has spread into a full-blown smile.

"Tell me what you're into," Mac says. His eyes are intense, like he's trying to look through me. Like maybe he is actually interested in getting to know me. But his voice is low and his tone suggestive.

I gulp hard as my face heats, warmth spreading down my cheeks to my neck. I shift in the chair. "Um..."

"Oh my god, not like that," he says, horrified. "I—I just meant more generally. Like...what kind of stuff do you like to do for fun?"

My face is still warm, but a half-laugh bubbles in my chest. I cover my face with my hands, feeling really stupid, but I'm laughing. In fact, I'm laughing hard enough my shoulders shake. I groan and cross my arms in front of my chest again.

"Oh my god, that was...really embarrassing," I say, and I realize all those slivers of annoyance are gone. I still can't look at Mac, but I'm lighter and my chest feels more open. Being here with him doesn't feel like being suffocated. At least not right now.

"Okay, what do I do for fun? I don't know. What is fun?" I ask.

"That is your vibe, isn't it?" Mac says, but his voice is teasing. "All work and no play."

"My idea of fun is just different than yours."

"What is your idea of fun?" he asks.

"Practicing my handwriting." I shrug and face him so he can see my smirk.

"Is that a joke...?"

"Sort of. I got really into fountain pens a couple years ago when my grandfather gifted me his collection, and I like to write with them." I look down at my hands. Faint outlines of ink still cover my fingertips from inking up my pen the other day.

"Do you have any with you?"

"Nah, I keep them in my dorm. I don't want to lose one or have something happen to it."

"You'll have to show me sometime. That's really cool, actually."

He really sounds interested, which is kind of sweet considering we're practically enemies. His sincerity actually makes me a little uncomfortable. I don't know what to do with it. I shift in my seat and clear my throat. Sarcasm is a much safer territory.

"Yeah, well, thank you for your stamp of approval. Are you, like, the 'fun police'?"

"I am," he says. "It's my duty to protect and serve and make sure people have appropriate amounts of fun in their life."

I make a noncommittal noise and roll my eyes. This time when there's an extended silence, it's not uncomfortable.

"So you never really answered... What are you into?" he asks, breaking the silence again.

"I did. I said my fountain pens."

"That can't be all you do for fun, is it? Write with fancy pens?"

His question rubs me the wrong way, and I bristle. Is it the way he mocks me? "Fancy pens"? It was friendly and fun a minute ago, but now I'm wondering if he was making fun of me. And why does he care what I do with my free time? Is he trying to figure out how much time I spend doing stuff besides studying so he can brag?

"I spend most of my free time studying." I keep my tone clipped and try to ignore the knot forming in my stomach.

"I study a lot too," Mac says.

I roll my eyes at the brag. I knew it. I knew this was why he started this conversation.

"But I do other stuff sometimes too," he says, "like I—"

"Some of us can't afford to be here unless we keep our grades up," I interrupt, but I cringe inwardly, all my insides shrinking. I've been snippy with him before, but I don't think I've ever been rude.

Too ashamed to check the look on Mac's face, I go back to pretending like the experiment is the most interesting thing I've ever watched.

All the students have handed their quizzes back to Professor Campbell, who hands them another blank sheet of paper and asks them to draw another self-portrait, after which she'll hand out another quiz, but this time she'll let them all know it is a really hard test and most students really struggle with it, so to be patient with themselves.

Mac leaves to collect the papers from Professor Campbell and brings them back to the observation room. He sets them aside as we can't do anything with them quite yet, but I wish we could. I need to do something with my hands besides just play with the ends of my hair.

My knee bounces up and down as I replay our conversation in my head, realizing Mac was actually nice for most of it, and I was a bit of a jerk.

"Jessie, I'm sorry if I—"

"It's fine," I say, my voice way too high-pitched. I need to apologize, but the words feel stuck in my throat. I try. I form the words in my head and open my mouth, but when I try to say them everything inside me coils up with resistance, like a cat being put in a bathtub full of water. My throat gets thick and all my muscles tense up as if I'm about to be pushed off a cliff. I don't have a history of being good at apologies.

The air between us is thick like cotton candy, the silence acrid and unpleasant.

"I bake," Mac says.

"What?"

"I bake. That's what I do for fun."

"You bake?" I shift in my chair, angling my body toward him. *Is this an olive branch from him? Even though I should be the one apologizing?*

"Yep. I've got a sourdough starter named Frodo that I've had since freshman year. I make a loaf pretty much every weekend."

I let that information simmer between us for a moment. His sincerity makes me wobbly, like one of those punching bags that bounces back to you after you hit it.

"I...like *Lord of the Rings*." My brain has short-circuited and come up with the stupidest sentence known to man. "And bread. I like bread too," I say.

Actually, THAT was the stupidest sentence.

"I could bring you a loaf sometime."

"That would be nice."

I nod and shift back, facing the experiment room again. That interaction was...pleasant. There wasn't anything biting or sarcastic. He didn't bring up my rudeness and throw it back at me. Is Mac...nice? I've always seen him as confident, a little arrogant, but he's actually kind of fun and...sweet?

That's fine. That doesn't change anything. There are plenty of nice people that I'm not friends with. There are plenty of attractive guys out there who are fun and nice and smart and who bake and smell like oranges and clean laundry and...

"Hey, actually, Jessie, I—" Mac interrupts my thoughts, but the students filing out of the observation room interrupt him. We rush to them outside the classroom, collecting the rest of the papers from the students and Professor Campbell.

We have a fifteen-minute break before the next round of students. Mac leaves, but I take a seat in the lobby and pull out a bag of chips I packed. Being annoyed with Mac is the easiest thing in the world, but I found myself sort of enjoying his company for a bit today, and I'm not really sure what to do with that.

It was easy, a few years ago, to interpret Mac's competitiveness as friendly and fun. He's generally always smiling, so it never seemed malicious. I was naïve, though. I thought he was a good guy. But after The Incident, I knew the truth. Mac showed himself as selfish and malicious, and even though he kept smiling, I saw his smile for what it was.

But today he was sincere and genuine. I don't know what changed, or if he's actually changed at all. I'm wary of him still, but at the very least his good behavior shined a spotlight on my bad behavior. I didn't need to be rude when he was being kind. Since The Incident I've had the moral high ground and I gave that up today. The scales are unbalanced now, and not in my favor.

When Mac returns, he's carrying two water bottles, one of which he holds out to me. The gesture is so authentically considerate my insides freeze up. My jaw goes a little slack.

"I'm sorry," I say. My voice is strained, and inside I'm screaming. I brace for his reply, something scathing, averting my eyes to the floor.

"For what?"

"For being rude to you earlier."

"Oh. It's okay," he says like he's already forgotten about it, and when I snap my eyes up from the floor his face is painted with the calmest, kindest smile. He doesn't seem mad at all.

My racing pulse calms and I loosen my gripped hands. *Why isn't he mad? Does he not hold a grudge?* I keep mine like pets.

He moves the water bottle just an inch or so closer to me, and I take it, careful to avoid brushing my fingers against his. I still feel frozen, my eyes glued to him. I watch him open his own water bottle, taking a seat and drinking nearly half of it in one go. His Adam's apple bobs as he gulps, his biceps barely working to hold the bottle to his lips. There's a stirring in my chest. It's not quite a flutter, but there is movement.

I ignore it, tearing my gaze away from him as the door opens. The first student of our second group walks in, followed closely by a few more students. Once everyone from the second group has filed in and gotten settled, Mac and I are back in the observation room, back to our silence.

There are two quizzes and three self-portraits per person in the pile of papers from the last group, which we'll sort and start to code. Today there's another group of students coming in, and over the next six months we'll come in for a smattering of other experiment days. I start to sort the papers out, enjoying the quiet of the observation room, but it doesn't last long because Mac starts humming. I glance over at him, hoping maybe he'll get the hint and stop, but he's got headphones in and is lost in his own world. I roll my eyes, that familiar pinch of annoyance around my ribs. If I'm all work and no play, this guy is all play and no work.

I reach over and tap his leg. He looks up, yanking a headphone out of his ear.

"You're humming."

"Oh, sorry." He cringes and pops his headphone back in.

I return to the papers on my lap, but it only takes a few seconds for him to start humming again. I turn to tap him once more but realize I recognize the song.

He notices me half-turned to him, hand frozen in the air. "Am I humming again? Sorry."

"You are, but—I know the chances of this are slim to none, but are you listening to Black Phantom?"

"Yes!" His whole face lights up. "You know them?"

"Yes! I love them. They've been my favorite since, like, middle school."

"Me too!"

I'm at the edge of my chair, clutching the back of it. I can't believe this is happening. Of all the people, of all the bands! Mac's smile is as big as I've ever seen it, and he's at the edge of his seat too, leaning forward. My face is stretched to the max, and I feel like I just took a shot of espresso.

Black Phantom is an indie folk band out of Norway, so they're less popular in the States than overseas and it's hard to find other fans. I've introduced so many people to them, but I've never actually met someone who was already a fan.

"Favorite song?" he asks, ripping out both his headphones.

"'She Wrote My Murder.'"

"God, that one is so good. When they do the instrumental..." He jumps up, doing an air guitar. I jump up too, dropping the papers on the ground and reaching out to grab his arms.

"Yes!"

And then I remember who this is, so I yank my hands back, but I still cannot believe how cool it is to meet another Black Phantom fan. I clutch my head, grabbing my hair.

"The interlude, oh my god, it's like my own personal soundtrack," I say.

"*She didn't mean to, she didn't mean to...*" he sings, and I join him.

"*But she wrote my murder when she wrote me out of her life.*"

We're both contorted into performance-like positions, half-screaming the lyrics. I'm weightless and warm and I think my chest might burst open.

"Wait, wait." I interrupt our mini-concert. "What's your favorite?"

"'Black Heart.' Has been for years."

"Oh my god," I say, slapping my hands over my heart.

"*Could you love me, would you love me...*" I start to sing, and he doesn't hesitate to join. "*With your black heart...*"

Neither of us is a very good singer, and we don't sound anywhere near as good as their lead singer Ingrid Jorgenson, but it feels so good to be singing with someone else who knows my favorite songs that I don't really care.

There's a profound silence when we've stopped singing. We're both breathing more heavily than normal, mere inches from each other, and when a strange sense of familiarity sweeps over me I step back, clearing my throat and smoothing out my shirt. Deja vu always makes me so uncomfortable.

Self-conscious of my singing and that wild display of excitement, I gather the papers off the floor, kneeling on the ground. Mac kneels to help me, but his proximity sends another wave of deja vu over me. My head spins and I feel nauseous for a brief second, but it's replaced with an ache in my chest and the eerie sense that I've been here before. But I have never knelt on the floor of an observation room with Mac, high from the discovery we share a favorite band.

"Have you been to a concert?" I ask in an attempt to get rid of the deja vu, and also not totally ready to be done with the Black Phantom conversation.

We find our way back to our seats, and I clutch the papers, my body relaxing as the sense of familiarity disappears.

"As many as I could since I found them. You?"

I shake my head, twisting my lips to the side. A luxury in my house was going out to eat at Chili's, which we only did once a year on my birthday. A concert ticket was so far beyond imagining paying for that the idea still feels as foreign to me as traveling to China.

"Hopefully one day. Are they as amazing as they seem? I've seen some clips on YouTube," I say.

"I have some videos too. You wanna see?"

"Yes!"

Mac digs into his pocket, but at that moment, the door to the observation room opens and Professor Campbell gestures for us to come out and collect the papers. We scramble out of the room, my cheeks heating even though I know I haven't done anything wrong.

Mac and I collect the sheets as the students trickle out, and after the last one leaves Professor Campbell dismisses us for the day. Mac keeps pace with me as I walk out of the building.

"So I guess you know about their album coming out in, like, three weeks," he says.

"Obviously."

"We should listen together."

"Yes!" I say without thinking. "And you'll have to show me those concert videos sometime."

"Definitely."

We stand outside the science building, neither of us making a move to leave, yet neither of us really having a reason to stay. His brown eyes dance with the same feeling that's floating around in my chest. When our silence starts to get a little awkward, I open my mouth to say bye, but Mac speaks first.

"Sooo...what are you writing for your Walden Senior Scholarship essay?" he asks.

Of all the things he could ask about, it was going to be the one thing that would send me straight into a spiral.

"I don't know."

And it's true, I don't know. I haven't even thought about the Walden Senior Scholarship. I've been so busy applying to the rest of the list of scholarships and grants, the ones that don't require essays and just need a transcript or a quick application, that I haven't even looked at the packet from Professor Gold since she gave it to us. It sends a fresh wave of anxious nausea through me.

But if Mac has already started on it, that means whatever his essay is, it's going to be more polished than mine, and ultimately better, meaning he'll get picked over me.

I try to swallow, but my mouth is dry. I stuff my hands in my pockets.

"I've been tossing around a few ideas," Mac says unprompted. "Probably something with my brothers or my family, and being the youngest, having to live up to expectations—it's still sort of shadowy in my mind."

I make a noncommittal noise because not only do I not care what Mac is writing his essay about, but truly, how hard could his life have been? Must have been so tough to grow up rich, your family having enough money to get a building named after them on campus, while my family didn't have enough money to keep the electricity on some months.

Whatever little voice in my head suggested a few minutes ago maybe Mac wasn't so bad—well, it's gone now. He obviously only cares about competing with me, and that's fine. I'd rather play that game anyway.

"Hey, I gotta get going," I say and pull out my phone and headphones. I breeze past Mac. "I'll see you around."

I don't hear if he says anything; Black Phantom is already blaring in my ears.

CHAPTER EIGHT

MAC

I'll be eighty years old and still remember what Friday night football at Middle Penn College smells like. There's a distinct smell to a cold night, and Friday night football is that cold smell mixed with beer and sweaty college students and body paint and fried food.

MPC is small, but there's a lot of school spirit, especially since we're in the playoffs now and that playoff game is at our home stadium. It feels like the whole school is here, although I doubt the entire student body, small as it is, could even fit into our stadium. We're damn near trying, though. The stands are packed, with barely a seat to spare, and the food lines are long.

After spending twenty minutes in two separate lines waiting for concessions, my arms heavy with food and beer for my friends, I make my way back into the stands where my friends and I usually sit: front row. My friends are all from the soccer team, and sitting front-row for sports events is important for our group. We support our own.

I can't push through the crowd without spilling all the beer I'm holding, so as I wait patiently for everyone to move, I glance around the stands. The normally empty student section is packed to the gills, and I follow the crowd all the way to the guest section, which is also packed but partially taken over by MPC students.

The crowd moves an inch, and I try to see if there's anyone in the stands I know. A pair of laughing girls catches my eye. *Is that Jessie?* I squint and stand in place for far too long. I still haven't figured out if it's her when someone prods me. I move with the crowd, but as soon as my friends have their drinks and food I search the crowd again for her.

"Whatcha doin', man?" Xavier asks me, his beer already halfway gone. "Looking for someone?"

"Kinda."

"Is it that chick who's way smarter than you and kicks your ass in every class?"

"She doesn't—" I don't even bother to glare at him. I know he's just antagonizing me. "Yes. Her."

"What's her name again?"

"Jessie."

I crane my neck to try to see around the crowd, straining my eyes like I can see through people.

"Does she have any friends?"

"She has friends. Whether she has any single gay male friends is anyone's guess." I sip at my beer, eyeing Xavier who asks me this every time I'm talking to a girl.

"Damn. If you find her, can you ask for me?"

"Thirsty, much?"

"Says the guy searching the crowd at a football game for a girl who pretended not to know who he was after—"

"Okay, okay, that's enough of that," I say, and Xavier snorts into his beer. I knew I shouldn't have told him about the party.

I let my eyes wander over the crowd one more time. If I don't find her this time, I'll stop looking. I just saw her earlier today in class, but we didn't talk. I thought after finding out we're both Black Phantom fans we might be able to properly start up a friendship. That I might get a chance to explain about Halloween night, how I lost her number to a puddle of beer, and that at least once a day I wish I could text her and ask her to grab lunch with me so we could just talk. I just want to spend time with her. Apparently my hopes were too high.

But I am nothing if not persistent, so when I actually spot her in the crowd, I don't hesitate. I tell Xavier I'll be back and take my liquid courage with me to go say hi.

I weave through more crowds, and by the time I get to her I'm sweating a little despite the temperature.

"Hey, Jessie. And Jade, right?"

Both girls turn to me, wide eyes paired with smiles. *Smiles?* Over the years, Jessie has had many reactions to seeing me. They usually involved rolled eyes or a "Why are you talking to me?" face, or the ever-classic "I made a better grade than you and I already know it" look.

Xavier always tells me I fall for girls who are mean to me. Which isn't strictly true, but when banter and sarcasm are a love language growing up, it's hard not to be excited by a girl who can dish it out as well as it's dished out.

But now she's smiling at me. Her cheeks are pink and her eyes are bright, which could be the cold or the alcohol. I'm just optimistic enough to believe it's a little bit because maybe she's happy to see me.

"Yes!" Jade lights up. "You remembered. I'm impressed."

"Hi, Mac," Jessie says. She's got a half-empty beer, and I can't help but wonder if that's her first drink. It would explain the lack of eye-rolling.

"You guys excited for the game?" I ask.

That was so fucking lame.

"Yes," Jade says at the same time Jessie says, "No."

"Not a football person?" I ask.

"Not a sports person," Jade says, leaning across her.

Jessie shrugs, the movement slightly muted by the fleece blanket wrapped around her shoulders. "More of a library girl, really. Want to sit?" She scoots a little closer to Jade, and I accept her invitation, warmth spreading through my chest.

"How very un-American of you," I say, and Jessie smirks.

"I'm sure you're the poster child for American college students. Plays seven sports, gets all As, graduates top of his class," Jessie says. There's a playful tone in her voice. It's exactly the kind of banter I've come to expect from her—the kind that defines our relationship. The kind that makes me even more confident I'm right about why she won't talk about the Halloween party. It's all just part of the game we play.

"Jury's still out on graduating top of my class. Got some fierce competition." I wink at her and she looks away, trying to hide a smile as she takes a sip of her drink.

"Want some candy?" Jade holds out a fistful of Twizzlers.

"My favorite," I say and happily take two.

"Is it really your favorite candy?" Jessie asks, sounding surprised.

"Why? Do I seem like a Snickers guy?"

"Yeah, kinda."

"Should I be offended by that?"

"Snickers are a respectable candy. There's a lot going on. I think a Milky Way is way worse. What does that have? Caramel? Nougat? Boring."

"Wow. Should I ask how you feel about Twizzlers?"

She grimaces, and it's something between a smile and a guilty face. It's adorable.

"Yikes. We'll skip the Twizzler opinions. All right then, what's your favorite candy?"

"Not really a big candy person, to be honest."

"Those are some hot takes then for someone who doesn't even like candy."

"I can have, like...one piece of candy and then it's too much."

"That makes sense. You're already so sweet," I say. I wouldn't normally use a line like that on a girl, but I want to push our game into different territory. Plus, it might be just dumb enough to earn me a smile.

It does, and I could punch the air. It feels like a victory. She rolls her eyes, granted, but it's affectionate. She's not annoyed.

"Sweet? Jessie? More like sour. Like a Sour Patch Kid that's only ten percent sweet," Jade says.

"Wow, Jade. Wow." Jessie turns to her, and though I can't see her face I'd bet money I know exactly what expression she's giving Jade.

Jade cackles.

"You drag me here and then drag me again. I think it's time to go home." Jessie looks at her empty wrist as if there's a watch there, which there isn't. "Look at the time—I've got an appointment to hang out with my actual best friend." She starts to stand up, but Jade throws her arms around Jessie and pulls her back to sitting.

"Noo. I'm sorry. I didn't mean it. You're sweet like a, um..."

"Candy necklace?" I offer. It's an obvious toss-out, but maybe it'll open a door.

"Ew, those are so gross," Jessie says, scrunching her nose. "They're like chalk."

I guess it wasn't that obvious.

"Like a jar of honey," Jade says, finally finishing her statement.

"Okay, now you're just being obnoxious," Jessie tells her. "We all know the truth. I'm more like a bitter chocolate, like, eighty-five percent dark chocolate."

I open my mouth to protest. Bitter? No. Jessie is fun and sharp and witty and smart. God, she's smart. "Dark chocolate is my favorite kind of chocolate," I say, low enough that only Jessie can hear.

She glances at me, her gray eyes drinking me in. I hold her gaze, watching her understand what I'm saying. Her eyes dart away from me for just a second but then she brings them back up to mine, biting her bottom lip. That small movement sends blood straight to the lower half of my body. I remember those lips. They were so soft and knew exactly how to move against mine. I thought about kissing Jessie about a million times before that night, and none of it compared to the real thing. What I wouldn't give to just lean over right now and...

"Are you here with friends?" Jade asks, breaking the spell.

"Yeah, they're way down that way." I point. "Bunch of my soccer buddies."

"You're welcome to sit with us as long as you like," Jessie says. Her eyes dart to my lips again and back to my eyes. *Holy shit. Is she thinking about kissing me too?*

"Only if you make a beer run," Jade says, and I tear my eyes away from Jessie to give Jade a nod and a thumbs-up.

"You got it," I say and jump up. I feel a hand on my arm and turn back to see Jessie discarding the blanket she's wrapped in. I stare at her hand, the warmth from her touch radiating through my whole arm. I almost reach out and put my other hand on top of hers, but she pulls away before I can.

"Wait. I'll come with you. I'm too cold just sitting here."

It takes me a second to register her offer. I fully expected to go alone, but this is much better. This is perfect, actually, because now I'll have my chance to say something about the Halloween party.

The crowd has mostly settled, everyone crammed into seats or standing in the bleachers since the game has started. I know Jessie isn't bummed about missing it, and truth be told, I'm not either. Not because

I don't like sports, but the prospect of getting some time with Jessie is a more intriguing pull than the game.

"Bring back nachos!" Jade yells after us, and I give her another thumbs-up.

I step to the side and let Jessie go in front of me. It only takes me about ten seconds to feel good about my choice because somehow Jessie manages to step strangely on the bleachers and pitches backward. I reach out, catching her under her arms before she slams her head on the metal bleachers. Her back is against my chest and she's close enough that I catch a trace of vanilla, Jessie's signature scent. We both stay perfectly still for a second that feels like an hour, Jessie's breathing and my thudding heart tuning out the roaring crowd, the football announcer, the cheerleaders...

"Thank god you were there," she says, half-whispered between breaths. Being this close to her again is making me a little lightheaded, but I've got to keep it together since I'm the one holding her steady.

"Are you okay?"

"Your reflexes are so good. I think I'm just startled. I'm not injured."

I help right her, and as she descends the steps I hover my hand behind her just in case. Even when we've cleared the bleachers and made it to the concessions line, I stay close, keeping my hands loose despite the cold, in case she trips again.

The lines for beer are long, and we have a little time to kill. I'm about to bring up Halloween when she turns to me.

"So why don't you show me those Black Phantom videos?"

I don't hesitate, pulling out my phone to show her the videos I took from a concert a couple years back. I hand the phone to her—it's easier with our height difference. Jessie's head comes up to about my shoulder. It would be so easy to stand behind her, prop my chin on her shoulder, and hold her while we watch videos together, and the thought of doing all that makes my heart beat a little faster. I hold my hands behind my back, though, the model of self-control.

"Were you in the nosebleeds for this?" she asks, visibly confused.

"I was."

She makes a surprised noise but says nothing, just watches the video, mouthing the words and bopping around a little. I stop looking at the screen and just watch her. The unfiltered joy on her face and in her movements is the kind of joy typically reserved for things like Christmas Day and birthday-party surprises.

The video ends and she hands back my phone. "Do you have more?"

"I have so many that eventually you'll stop asking."

"Never," she says with the widest, most gorgeous smile.

"Here—I've got your favorite," I say.

She claps her fingers together and jumps up and down a little. She is so cute. What I wouldn't give to kiss her right now.

I find the video and hand her the phone. This time as I watch her I think back to the Halloween party, the feel of her beneath my hands, the electric current when we kissed. I want to feel it all again so bad.

But if we never talk about it, it could take a long time to get there. Plus, this is just a formality. She knew it was me. And when I tell her I was—what did she call him? Sexy Shakespeare?—she'll laugh and say, "I knew that, silly," and then I can ask her to go on a proper date with me where we sit across the table from each other and talk about nothing and everything.

"Jessie, I need to tell you something," I say.

She looks up with wide eyes, concern stitched on her face.

"It's not bad. I mean, I don't think it's bad."

"Next!" the guy at the counter calls.

Fuck.

Somehow it became our turn without either of us realizing it. We step up and grab our drinks, plus another for Jade. Jessie digs into her purse to pay, but I've already handed my card to the guy.

"Mac, you didn't have to..."

"You guys let me crash your hangout—it's the least I can do. Should we grab Jade some nachos?"

"If we don't, there'll be a riot in the stands."

"Wouldn't want that," I say with a smirk.

"Can you imagine the guilt you'd carry around with you if you were the sole cause of an actual riot? The body count, the blood on your hands... You'd never sleep again," Jessie says.

"I'd have to become Catholic specifically to confess and atone for my sins."

"There are probably worse reasons to become Catholic." She takes a sip of her beer, peering at me over the edge of the cup.

"Such as?" I ask.

"To try to fuck the priests."

I chose the wrong moment to take a sip of beer because my laugh is more like a snort, and somehow I inhale beer up through my sinuses, which causes me to sputter and spew my beer everywhere. Luckily, I snap my head to the side, where there are no people passing by. This causes Jessie to nearly spit out her own drink, and she covers her mouth, and then we're both doubled over in stitches trying to regain control. We both eventually straighten and catch our breath. I finally wipe my face and give her an incredulous look.

"Jesus, Jessie!"

"You didn't know I was funny?"

"I didn't know you were irreverent."

We haven't started walking again, and I know we should get back to the stands, to her friend Jade, but I don't want this moment to end. The way she's smiling at me right now creates a Jessie-size crater in my chest that I'm never going to recover from.

"Did that offend you?"

"Not in the slightest," I say, and Jessie bites her bottom lip, breaking our eye contact and starting the walk to a concessions booth.

"I guess you don't know me that well," she says, more observationally than anything.

"I don't, but I'd like to. I already know your favorite band. And that your only hobby is fountain pens."

"And reading! I read."

"Nerd," I say, but she smiles.

"I bet you read too. I bet you read nonfiction, like sports memoirs or something."

"I do read, but I'm more like a sci-fi and fantasy kind of reader."

"Oh, like *Game of Thrones*?"

"I did read *Game of Thrones*," I say.

"And watch it?"

"Of course."

"Season eight?"

"Sorry, the show ended after season six, so I don't know what you're talking about."

Jessie nods approvingly with a smirk on her face, and our conversation veers into other TV shows we like, books we've read, and similar things we have in common. Which turns out to be just enough to surprise Jessie and delight me.

The food line is shorter, and we get nachos and more candy quickly enough that Jade won't riot, but not slowly enough for me. Jessie lets me pay without a word, but she does scowl at me.

Before climbing the bleachers to rejoin Jade, she pauses, placing her hand on my arm.

"Hey, didn't you say you had something to tell me?"

This is it. This is my chance. But looking into her eyes now, it suddenly feels like the wrong moment, our arms full of beer and nachos. Smiles linger on both our faces and bubbles of joy are still popping in my chest. What if I tell her now and she doesn't just laugh it off? What if she's annoyed I'm bringing it up here? Maybe she didn't know, and if that's the case this definitely isn't the right way to break the news.

There's still time to tell her. And I'm going to. I just need to find the right moment.

This...isn't it.

"Just that I...saw Black Phantom is releasing a single on the album this coming week and I'm really excited."

"Oh my gosh, me too!" Her face lights up, eyes practically glowing, cheeks nearly touching her eyelashes. She asks me what I think the album will be like, more pop or folk, and we walk back up the bleacher steps to rejoin Jade.

I spend the rest of the first half of the game with Jessie and her friend, rejoining my friends after halftime. Xavier gives me a hard time, but I'd do it all over again if I could rewind and redo the night.

There isn't a doubt in my mind tonight was the wrong night to confess to Jessie I was Shakespeare. She didn't seem annoyed by me all night, and I got a glimpse of what it might be like to be friends with her. Real friends. Maybe even a glimpse of what it might be like to date her.

I didn't know she had such a silly, playful side, but seeing that side of her tonight only made me like her more. Sarcastic, smart, playful, irreverent, gorgeous—she's the total package.

I'm not a praying man, but I ask whatever god is listening for more time with Jessie, and soon.

'Cause I've got it bad.

CHAPTER NINE

"Excuse me, you'll need to sign in!" I yell at yet another student who tries to walk right past me.

The science building is open twenty-four-seven, and my job is to sit here from six in the evening until midnight, making sure students sign in and out and recording what rooms and equipment they'll be using. It's a pretty ideal work-study job seeing as it's usually quiet, and I can use the time to get homework done.

Except tonight all I've done is scroll social media and check for more photos from the Halloween party at ATZ. It's been almost three weeks, and people have long since stopped posting Halloween photos, so I'm having to do some private investigator-level snooping just to find them. It is without a doubt a waste of my time, but I can't seem to stop myself. It's almost compulsive. Every time I think back to that night, to our connection, to the way he made me feel, I'm breathless and transported to a version of myself that was relaxed and free, and I find myself doing the only thing in my control to get that feeling back: searching social media for any sign of him.

I want to be that girl again, and if I find Sexy Shakespeare, maybe I can find her too.

But it won't happen tonight. I set down my phone with a heavy sigh. I really need to get started on the Walden Senior Scholarship essay, seeing as I haven't even touched it and it's due in two weeks. I still have a couple scholarships left to apply to from my list, but I need to prioritize this one. Not only is it the largest sum of money, enough to cover the rest of my tuition, but if I win this one it comes with the bonus prize of beating Mac.

Mac started on his essay at least a week ago. I should have started two weeks ago.

I rummage through my backpack for the paperwork, and when I find it I follow the instructions to access the online application. At first glance it's like most scholarship applications: a résumé portion and the essay portion. I'll fill it all out later, but I should try to draft the essay now.

Opening a blank Word document, I read through my essay options.

Option 1: How will this scholarship help you?

Option 2: Tell us about a time when you had a belief or idea challenged.

Option 3: Who do you admire the most?

I twist the ends of my hair around my fingers, staring at the questions. My knee bounces under the desk, and I chew on my bottom lip.

Option two is out immediately. I've answered it on essays before, and although I should just reuse my essays from those scholarship applications to save time and energy, I don't actually like this question. I never really connected to it, so I just faked my way through an answer. This application has to be perfect, so faking my way through it isn't going to cut it.

Which leaves *Option 1: How will this scholarship help you?* or *Option 3: Who do you admire the most?*

Option one is almost too obvious. This scholarship will help me finish college. *Duh.* Although the challenge becomes writing it in a way that doesn't induce pity. And I'm familiar with pity.

Pity is the look in my high school best friend's eyes when I tell her that no, I've never been on a plane or a cruise or a ride at Disney; I've never even been on a vacation. Pity is the cashier at Walmart watching me put back a box of Cheez-Its because my mom told me there was a little extra grocery money this month, but not that much. It is the opposite of what I want from the judge of this scholarship. I want to win on merit, not pity. Besides, pity always comes with a side of shame, and I only want to feel pride when I get the email that I've been chosen as the winner.

And that leaves option three. The people I admire the most are my parents. I can't pick between them. My mom has spent her life working multiple jobs so we can keep our home heated and have food on the table. My dad, who has been on and off disability his whole adult life for his Ehlers-Danlos, taught me how to cook and clean. Whether by accident or design, they bucked against gender norms and made my childhood rich in all the ways money couldn't.

Maybe this is what I want to write about.

A text on my phone pulls my attention from the essays. It's a selfie of Jade in a full face of gorgeous makeup.

Stunning

Do I also text one to George Greg?

Yes, obvi.

And Threesome Anna?

Oh shit...are y'all talking?

There isn't much talking involved

I smile and click my phone off, trying to focus on my essay again.

My leg starts to bounce and I chew on my bottom lip. If I'm lucky, this essay will take me the rest of my work shift to finish. I have four hours left, and for a good essay that should be enough time, but I should probably get it proofread by one of the school-sponsored tutors, and then I'll need to spend at least another hour or two tweaking it. The résumé portion might take a half-hour to complete, and then I have to do it all over again for two more scholarships that I qualify for. It's so much work on top of everything else.

My leg stops bouncing and I drop my head into my hands. There has to be another way.

No rich relatives to leave you money?

Jade's question weaves through my mind, touching on a long-forgotten memory. My mom's aunt had a little money—if I remember correctly—and when she died my freshman year of high school, she requested that a small sum be set aside for my college.

It's too much to hope it'll cover what I need for next year, but a small sum of money would take some of the pressure off. I burst out of my chair, manic energy pumping through me. My heart is racing as I stick a little sign on the desk to inform students I'll be back shortly, slipping out the door and clicking the call button before the door has fully shut behind me.

"Hey, chicken." My mom's voice fills my ears, comfort and anxiety dancing in my stomach. "How are you?"

"I'm okay. How are you? How's Daddy?"

"He's okay. Tripped coming up the basement steps last week and he's banged up real bad. He came down hard on his bad knee, and you know how it is. He can barely walk right now."

While most people can hurt themselves with a normal recovery time, it takes my dad twice as long to heal. He had knee surgery a few years back, and while most people might heal up in 6–12 months, my dad took 12–18 months and even now still wears a brace for support. Tripping up the basement stairs is no small injury for him.

"Why didn't you call and tell me?" I ask, my voice dropping. I know she can hear the hurt in my words, but I know something she doesn't. I'm a hypocrite. I didn't call and tell her about my lost scholarship, and I know she'll wish I had. But, like mother, like daughter, I didn't tell her for the same reason she didn't tell me.

"I didn't want to worry you," she says, and I mouth the words silently along with her.

Of course she didn't. Just like I don't like to worry her.

"Tell him I said I hope he feels better."

My heart aches for him the way it has since I was a child. Growing up watching my dad deal with chronic joint pain, sometimes spending more days in bed each month than out of it, taught me the difference between empathy and sympathy long before other kids my age learned it. I never feel sorry for my dad—he would hate that. But I hated to see him hurting then, and I hate to hear about it now.

"He'll be happy to hear you called. Everything okay?"

"Well, um…" I swallow. Maybe I shouldn't bring it up. Stuff with my dad sounds really heavy, and my mom sounds extra tired. I don't want to put more on anyone's plate.

I glance around, but there's no one out here. I forgot my jacket and it's getting cold. I need to either go back inside or have this conversation now, while I still have an iota of courage.

"I know this is random, but how much did Aunt Betty leave for me? Remember? She died when I was, like, fifteen and set a little bit aside for me for college, but I can't remember how much. And I know we haven't used it 'cause I got the scholarship and a job, but…yeah. Um, how much was it?"

My mom is silent for so long I actually start to worry she hung up.

"Mom?" I check in.

"Still here, sorry. I, um— Why are you asking, chicken?"

I swallow hard. "My scholarship is changing next year."

"What happened? It's not your grades again, is it?" She sounds both disappointed in me and afraid for me. It's one of many reasons I was trying to avoid this call. I can't stand hearing my mom's disappointment. The fear in her voice riles up dormant fear in me. I'm the first person in our family to go to college; what if I'm also the first one to drop out? I'd be disappointing myself, my mother, and the Jessie who cried in Miss Julie's office that day. I don't have any other dreams for my life besides being a child therapist. Dropping out ruins The Plan. Without The Plan, what future do I even have?

My throat constricts.

"No, my grades are good." I push the words out. "I'm still top of my class, or toward the top. But they're canceling the full scholarship program. I'm okay this year, but for my senior year I'll only be getting half the tuition. I'll need to cover the rest of it myself."

"What about other scholarships?" she asks.

It's a familiar question. When I was applying to undergrad, she and my dad encouraged scholarships, grants—anything but loans. They were always upfront with me about how much medical debt they had and made it clear they didn't want me to have to carry the same burden with student loans. I applied like a madwoman to as many things as I qualified for and fortunately got the school tuition I needed. It was a relief for us all, but if the scholarships don't come through this time...

"I've been applying for them, but I'm tired, Mom." I wouldn't admit this to anyone but her, and it's hard to ignore the stab of guilt in my ribs at complaining to her of all people about being tired. "I'm stretched to my limit. I've applied for so many. And I thought maybe that money from Aunt Betty could help take some of the pressure off, even if it can't cover everything."

The silence that follows is even worse than before. A light breeze kicks up, throwing my long hair across my face. I wait for my mom to reply, raking my fingers through my hair to try to tame it, and to give me something to do with my nervous energy.

"Mom?" I can't wait any longer.

"That money is... We had to use it, chicken."

"For...for what?" My mouth is working faster than my brain, which now feels like maybe something got thrown into the cogs of the operating system. I'm rooted completely to the sidewalk. A hurricane couldn't pick me up, so frozen are my limbs and feet.

"We needed it to pay for the knee surgery and physical therapy. You know my insurance isn't very good, and we were still paying for the physical therapy and the bill from when he twisted his ankle. We had to— We couldn't—" Her voice is tight and strained. She sounds small, and I register the remorse in her tone even if she hasn't said any apologetic words. "We used the money from your great-aunt. All of it."

The initial shock wears off quickly and I'm left with the void of disappointment that comes after a sliver of hope. It's short-lived, though. I can't be mad over something I barely knew existed. I didn't even know how much it was. It couldn't have been much, seeing as my parents still carry their burden of debt.

"I'm sorry, Jessica," my mom says, but there's more to her words than just an apology. There's pain laced in her tone and a question: *Why did you ask for something you know I can't give?*

Tears well in my eyes. The shame of asking for money burns on my cheeks, on my chest, and in my belly. I feel dizzy and a little weak. I don't mind crying out here in the dark beside the science building where anyone could walk up and see me, but letting my mom hear me cry? No. I won't make her feel bad for what she can't give.

"That's okay, Mom. I'll figure it out."

We say our goodbyes and I hold my phone in my hand, staring at the cracked screen until the light goes off. It's hard to be mad at my mom about this. I'd forgotten about the money until now, so my expectations for secret family money were low, but they were there. And when it comes to family finances, for being twenty-one, I know a lot more than the average kid because my parents have always emphasized the importance of Clear is Kind.

But none of this makes my financial situation any less stressful, and the knot in my stomach feels like a thousand knots all tangled together.

"Hi."

I whip my head toward the voice approaching me. A tall figure and the vague scent of oranges and laundry detergent solve the mystery: Mac.

The memory of how I behaved the last time I saw him burns on my cheeks. It's dark out, so he can't see, and I'd stay out here and keep it that way, but I'm freezing.

"Hey. I'm just heading back in." I turn and walk into the building, composing myself as Mac follows me.

I'd only had one drink at our dorm before the game last Friday, knowing I'd need something to get through it, but I didn't eat much that day—I was too busy—so the beer went straight to my head. I was overly friendly with him, maybe even flirty. And the worst part is, I enjoyed every minute of it. I learned two things on Friday night. One, I need to eat more before I drink. Two, Mac is really fun to be around.

"You can just sign in here." I tap on the clipboard with the sign-in sheet as I round the desk. "Name, student ID number, and what room and equipment you're using. If there's not enough room, you can continue on the next page—just lift that one." I gesture to the stray pens lying nearby.

I avoid eye contact as I'm not sure how to act around him now that I feel like we have this tentative friendship. Something about sharing a favorite band and being a little drunk can really create a bond, but I'm not ready to say that to him, nor do I know what to do with it.

"I'm...not here for the labs," Mac says.

"Oh. Why are you...?"

"Black Phantom released a song from their new album." A knowing grin appears on his face, and a smile cracks open my own. All the tension leaves my shoulders, all the worry about my financial situation temporarily gone with that one sentence.

"I thought we could listen together," Mac says tentatively, holding up his headphones.

Two weeks ago I might have thought he was crazy, but right now nothing sounds better than listening to a new song by my favorite band. Music has that unique ability to transport me out of all the things I'm feeling into a more peaceful place. I could use some of that right now, even if it is with Mac.

"Yes! Absolutely. How did I miss this? When did it drop?"

"This morning. Can I...?" He gestures to where I'm standing, asking if he can come to my side of the desk. I wave him over, and he steps around and leans against the desk. I lean on the desk next to him, peering over his shoulder at his phone. He's got the song pulled up and holds out one of his Bluetooth earbuds.

I hesitate just a beat before taking it. It's kind of intimate to share headphones, isn't it? Beyond the hygiene factor, this tiny technology will tether us. As I place the earbud in my ear, I can't help but feel there's some invisible string connecting us now. His citrusy laundry smell is much stronger here, but not in a bad way. It smells nice, actually. Clean. Have I never noticed how nice Mac smells before?

A dizzy familiarity washes over me, and I'm not here anymore; I'm at the ATZ Halloween party, but it's just a flash, and then I'm back. I shiver, trying to shake it off.

"Ready?" he asks, and I check over my shoulder to make sure no one has walked in. I give him a thumbs-up.

He presses play, and piano, guitar, and synth all hit my ears in a familiar Black Phantom style, upbeat and relaxed all at once.

"What's the name of the song?" I try to lean in more without touching him. I'm not successful. His shoulder is warm against mine, but to my surprise the touch isn't entirely unwelcome. It's oddly comfortable, like we've done this a million times. Like we always listen to Black Phantom together, practically cuddling at my work-study desk.

He tilts the phone so I can see the name of the song: "Fire." The lyrics play on the screen, highlighted in white as they're sung. Ingrid Jorgenson's voice, clear as glass, croons in my ear.

"You light me on fire
from inside I burn
When you're near I desire
to be lit on fire
When you're far it's too cold,
it's too cold..."

I sneak a glance at Mac, delight splashed across his face. He's moving with the music, bopping his head a little. The movement creates a ripple effect, and his shoulders are moving too, just slightly, against mine. It causes me to sort of bop along with the music as well, and then I'm not thinking about Mac at all but the way the song strikes my soul, the way it feels like the notes originate from somewhere deep inside and they're traveling through me, bursting out of every cell, sweeping through the dusty, long-neglected corners of myself. Eyes closed, waves of emotion swell up and out of me, stress and frustration, until my chest feels lighter. I'm not as heavy as I was three minutes ago.

I can tell the song is ending, and I open my eyes to find Mac looking at me with a wide, enthusiastic grin. I blush, self-conscious all of a sudden. I can get lost in music sometimes, especially if I've got a lot of feelings just floating around. Black Phantom has always helped me process those feelings, and having someone witness that makes me want to hide under the desk.

When the song is over, I hand back his earbud and quickly take a seat. I wiggle my mouse now that the monitor has gone black. When it illuminates, my essay displays on the screen. I click it closed like I've been caught doing something I shouldn't have.

"So?" he asks.

I panic for a second, darting a suspicious glance at him. Is he about to ask me about my scholarship essay again? Didn't I make it clear the first time that we are competitors and I have no interest in discussing—?

"The song. What'd you think?" he clarifies, and instantly I relax.

Of course he's asking about the song and nothing about the scholarship. He probably didn't even see the computer screen.

"Um..." I think for a second, formulating that cellular-level reaction into words. "It reminded me a lot of their first album. Like it's more 'them' than some of their more recent stuff. Which I love, but this feels like they went back to their roots."

"Yes! I totally agree. Getting back their original guitarist—what's his name? Gunnar." He snaps and points at me. "Probably had something to do with it."

Talking about Black Phantom this way with a fan gives me an appreciation for Mac that I don't know I would have had otherwise. He knows the band's history, he knows their names—he adores this band the same way I do, and if for no other reason than this, I decide I wouldn't mind spending more time with Mackenzie Baldwin.

Someone walks in and tries to pass by the desk. Mac slips out from behind the desk but stays nearby.

"Excuse me," I say and give them the same sign-in instructions I give everyone else.

When the student is gone, Mac slides back up to the desk, back on the other side, and leans across the top, hands clasped loosely in front of him.

"So you work here, huh?" he asks.

"It seems like maybe you already knew that." I give him a suspicious smirk. "How *did* you know I'd be here?"

"I've been here before while you were working," he says without a joke in his tone.

"Really?"

"Really. It was freshman year, so I don't expect you to remember, but I've always known you worked here. It's a pretty sweet gig."

I nod, trying to think of something to say while my brain short-circuits. *Freshman year?* I don't remember anything Mac was doing freshman year except annoying the ever-living fuck out of me. I feel the tickle of annoyance but shove it away.

"It is a sweet gig. I get lots of homework done. And I also get to scold college students for not remembering the most basic rule of this building: Sign. In. Which is my favorite part."

"I have a feeling that's not sarcasm."

"Absolutely not. The only job better than this is librarian. All that shushing? That's my jam."

Mac is full-out laughing now, head thrown back. His laugh is bold and big, exactly like him. That annoyance from moments before is gone.

Hanging out with Mac is like an internal roller coaster. I can't decide in any given moment if I want to laugh or roll my eyes.

"Do you work anywhere on campus?" I probably know the answer to this, but I'm making an effort, and if I'm being honest with myself, I'm not quite ready for the conversation to end yet.

He shakes his head. "Nah. I played soccer my first two years here, and I quit because I wanted to devote more time to school. I wasn't getting the time to study that I wanted. Soccer kind of consumed my life. I don't think I could balance a job and school. I don't know how you do it."

"Not much of a choice. You figure it out." I try to keep my voice light, but he touches on a nerve.

"Well, it's obvious you work about ten times harder than I do, and it shows. You're an incredible student."

The sincerity in his voice catches me off-guard, dissipating any brewing resentment. That was a real compliment. I don't quite know what to do with it after years of sarcastic jabs and compliments disguised as jealousy.

"Thanks," I say, fiddling with the ends of my braid. I come up with a thousand things to say back. *You're a good student too, and you make me a better student. Let's be friends, like for real.* But the moment passes without me saying anything, and Mac raps his knuckles on the desk twice.

"Well, I'll let you get back to it," he says and heads out before I can speak up.

Goddammit, Jessie. Could you be more awkward?

As he's walking out the door, Jade walks in. She does a double-take, realizing who she's seeing.

"Was that Mac?" she says, her face lighting up.

"What are you doing here?" I ask, avoiding her question. She knows who that was, and I don't want her making a big deal out of it. Since the football game she's been relentless about how Mac has a crush on me, and I can't get her to shut up about it.

Her face is still made up, fancy from the design she put on. "I thought I'd stop in on my way to see Anna."

"Anna?" I ask.

"Anna," Jade says suggestively.

"Threesome Anna?"

"Threesome Anna," she confirms with a wolfish grin.

"She invited you over? It's past nine o'clock. And I thought you were texting George..."

"Okay, Grandma. Yes, she invited me over for a movie," Jade says with a giggle. "And I was texting both of them."

"Your middle name is Trouble."

Jade cackles at this, and I realize she's not wearing a movie-watching outfit. Jade and I have watched a hundred movies together. She's strictly a pajamas kind of girl when it comes to movie-watching. It's one of her quirks. She's gone to movie theaters in full pajama sets. But Jade is wearing Ugg boots, black workout leggings, a crop top, and a lavender puff jacket. Comfy, but also not "movie comfy." She carries herself with so much confidence that everything she wears looks incredible on her, even leggings and a T-shirt.

"Soooo, were you and Mac hanging out? Because I thought he was your sworn enemy and you were one thousand percent sure he didn't have a crush on you." She mimics me as she works to open the tiny candy jar on the desk filled with jelly beans. She pops two into her mouth but immediately regrets it, spits them out into her hand, and comes around to my side of the desk to chuck them in the small trashcan.

"I could have told you those were ancient," I say.

"They taste like wax. And regret." She spits into the trashcan a few more times as I cackle. "Do you have any gum?" she asks. "I cannot go make out with Anna with wax taste in my mouth."

I dig through my purse to find the gum I know is in there.

"Okay, so Mac likes Black Phantom, he's hot, he is obviously crushing on you. I mean, he came to visit you at work. Clearly, this man has INTENTIONS."

I roll my eyes, but it's hard to ignore the truth in her statement. He is...good-looking, and he did come to visit me at work. He also found me in a crowd at a football game. Would he really do that if he didn't like me? Friends do that kind of stuff, right?

"Remind me why you hate him?" she asks when I don't respond.

"I don't hate him. I never *hated* him. We are casual rivals at best. I just...see him as my archnemesis and we're bound to forever compete until one of us wins, a.k.a. becomes valedictorian, and then we'll graduate and I'll never think about him again."

Jade snorts. "Very casual."

"The most casual." I hand her a piece of gum.

"So what did he do to you again?"

"Don't you remember? Freshman year? The trip to D.C.?"

"Ohhhhh yes. Aw, yeah, that was not great. But maybe time to let it go?"

First semester of freshman year, Mac and I were among a handful of students to apply for a student ambassador role on a spring trip to Washington, D.C. They were choosing three ambassadors, but the top student would have the trip paid for. Mac and I were both chosen along with a third student, but Mac won the top spot, which meant the third person and I had to pay our own way. My school scholarship wouldn't cover the trip, and I certainly couldn't afford it, so I had to back out.

But Mac could have paid for the trip on his own. He could have told the program directors that he was able to pay his own way and didn't need the school to sponsor him. So why did he take that top spot from someone who wasn't able to pay? Another student ended up taking my place, and I had to see photos of the trip in the school newspaper.

Until that moment, I thought Mac and I were friendly school rivals, having a laugh about being top students and competing in the kind of way you compete with your friends when the stakes aren't high and the fire of the competition fuels you. But I knew when I found out who the top spot went to that Mac was out for blood, and I swore I'd never forgive him. That I would beat him ruthlessly and without mercy at everything we ever competed for again. So far I've kept my promise to myself. But the Walden Senior Scholarship is taking me back to freshman year all over again, and this new friendship thing with Mac is muddying the waters for me.

I've always kept my grudges the way a knight keeps an oath, death before deserting. But what would happen if I abandoned my post? Would the world as I know it crack and crumble? Or would I—like I caught a glimpse of tonight—find my irritation is as soluble as sugar when I loosen my grip on those grudges?

Maybe I'll never get an apology or acknowledgment from Mac, but I can get a little peace for myself.

CHAPTER TEN

JESSIE

I am not a rule-breaker. I am not the kind of person who does things she isn't supposed to do. I don't defy authority on any kind of regular basis. So when I check the status of my federal student loan application again, knowing my mom has explicitly refused to cosign for a loan, knowing she'd wildly disapprove, I shove all my discomfort deep down inside, because I don't have time for guilt. I'm losing sleep over this financial aid situation. My mind is a tornado of circling thoughts: what if I don't get any scholarships? What if I have to drop out? How will I finish my degree? Neither of my parents finished college because neither of them went to college. I know I'd be letting them down by not finishing. I'd be letting myself down.

And I'd be letting down an entire future generation of kids who need access to mental health resources. Who need more Miss Julies and Mr. Greens. What would my own life have looked like without them—without a counselor to help me?

I've learned the art of not wanting. Through middle school, when all my friends were wearing the trendiest outfits and newest accessories? Didn't matter, I didn't want it. Everyone in my orchestra class had a shiny new instrument and mine was thrifted and somehow always out of tune? Wanting a new one wouldn't buy one, so why bother? It was easier to convince myself I didn't want these things than to let myself hope.

But this dream of being a therapist for kids? It's one of the few things I've let myself long for. I can't let it slip by just because my mom won't cosign for a loan. She tells me all the time "Debt is a burden you don't want, chicken," but it's my life, and I'll take on a couple thousand dollars of loans if it means I can achieve my dream.

Which is why I submitted my application for a loan earlier this week.

I just need her to cosign for it. But that's a problem for another day.

Stiff and achy, I finally stand for a stretch break. It's almost five o'clock, and I've been at the library since after my eight o'clock class this morning. Which isn't what normal students do on Fridays, but I needed to finish scholarship applications, get this loan application filled out, and start studying for exams, because those are in two weeks, right after Thanksgiving.

Mid-November until after my exams, a time I fondly call "Exam Season," is the stretch of time that I basically live at the library, but especially now I've got the extra burden of my financial aid situation and I'm in a statistics class. Math isn't my strong suit, and even though I spent most of the morning doing practice worksheets and reviewing every assignment from the semester, I'm still not sure I understand any of it. I took a break for applications, and now I need to get started on my psychology paper.

Sighing, I slump, leaning against the table for support. I allow myself thirty seconds to be tired and box breathe my way through it.

Inhale…1, 2, 3, 4… Hold…1, 2, 3, 4… Exhale…1, 2, 3, 4…

And then I pocket my phone and head upstairs to the stacks.

I've always loved the library. I didn't own a lot of books growing up, so nearly all my reading material came from the library. Until I could drive, Mom would take me to the library like clockwork every three weeks to return a stack and find a new stack of books. Even when I started driving, she'd go with me when she could because she liked being surrounded by books too. She'd check out big coffee table books full of art and stare at the pictures while she ate dinner between work shifts.

I still find the most peace in the instant silence of walking into a library. It's just you and hundreds of stories. Lives lived and never lived, spines waiting to be cracked, and words ready to be consumed. Even a school library is a sanctuary, a place of reverence. What some people find in a church I've found in the library. This is holy ground.

I climb the stairs to the third floor and stroll through the aisles of books, taking my time to get to where I need to go. While the first floor has a few rows of shelves, it's mostly tables, cubbies, and study rooms. The second, third, and fourth floors are just shelves of books. And, of course, the odd couple making out, but even they can find better places on campus. Less dusty places, anyway. My throat is already dry.

I finally end up in the aisle I need to be in. I take out my phone and pull up the email I sent myself in class the other day with a list of titles I thought would be helpful for the psych paper due at the end of the semester. I should have started earlier, but a month will be just enough time.

Of course the book I need is on the highest shelf, so I have to find a stool, which takes way more time than it should because no one puts them back at the end of the aisle when they're done like they're supposed to, so I have to weave in and out of a few aisles of shelves before I find one. I'm so frustrated that, as I finally reach for the book I want, I don't notice there's a person behind me—until their arm stretches up next to mine for the exact same book. It startles me, and I lose my balance.

I yelp and try to lean forward to catch myself, but I've already started to fall.

Strong arms come around me, and the fall is over no sooner than it started.

"This again, huh? You're a hazard to yourself, Matthews."

Irked as I am to be called by my last name, relief sweeps through me at being caught. And of course the person who caught me is none other than the only person at this school who occasionally calls me by my last name.

"Thank you," I manage to say through gritted teeth. He just saved my ass—no need to correct him on the name.

Mac holds onto me as I step off the stool, a steady hand on my back and the gentle brush of fingers against my arm. His hands are gone the second I'm steady. My gaze lingers on them, though. He reaches for the book I never grabbed, and I watch it in slow motion. The library is dimly lit, but I can still make out the veins climbing the back of his hands up his forearms, the ridges of muscle that appear with the extension of his arm, the size of his hand—large against the thin book he holds. Like a fire across a forest, heat rolls through me, a slow, uncontrolled burn I fear I'm not going to be able to contain.

He hands me the book, our eyes meeting, and the slow drag of my fingers across his sends a shiver like a release up my arm and then down my spine.

I swallow hard. *What the hell just happened?*

"I'm a little surprised to see you at the library on a Friday night," I say, clearing my throat as I tuck the book under my arm. I take a small step away from Mac, trying not to be obvious. I look at almost anything but him—the shelves, my old Converse, the worn carpet, Mac's stylish boots that kiss the hem of his straight-leg jeans.

"What else would I do on a Friday night?" he teases.

I bring my eyes back up to his to find his ever-present smirk painted on his face. It only annoys me a little bit.

"Racquetball?"

"Brody went home already for Thanksgiving."

"You don't play by yourself?"

"I prefer a partner." He winks at me, and my cheeks heat.

"Well, Olsen is taken." I read the name off the spine of the book I'm holding. I'm not bold enough to flirt back, so I sidestep the flirting but try to keep it playful.

"Olsen is a hot name. Maybe we could make it a group date?" His tone is suggestive, and the heat on my cheeks fails to cool.

"I could find you your own. I think Friedman, Burnbach, and Eisenhall are available." I read off authors' names from the email I sent to myself.

"I'd only really want to do a group thing if you were involved."

Oh. My. God.

I avert my gaze again, trying to focus on the shelf in front of me, not really seeing anything. My sweater starts to feel like too much material, and Mac feels way too close even though he's almost a full arm's length away.

Maybe Jade was right. Maybe Mac does like me...like that. *Who says something like that to someone they aren't interested in?*

"What are those names again?" Mac asks, his tone shifting from playful to curious. He cups his hand around mine, turning my phone screen toward him, and my heartbeat picks up pace. This close to him, I can smell the mint on his breath. I couldn't turn my head without my nose hitting him, so I let my eyes drift over him and to our hands. His hand engulfs mine entirely, and my stomach isn't in my stomach anymore; it's in my throat.

"I need that book too, actually," he says, leaning away from me. "Is this for your psych paper? What are you writing on?"

"The bystander effect."

"Great minds," he says with a smirk.

"Damn it," I say, a rush of frustration bringing me back to reality. *Of course* Mac chose the same subject for his psychology paper. I spin on my heels and head back to my desk. I have to figure out a new topic now.

"Do you want me to choose a new topic? I don't mind at all," he offers.

"It's fine."

It's not fine, but it's also not worth my energy. I hadn't started the paper yet.

He follows me all the way down the stairs and to my table, where I toss my now useless book. I guess Mac can use it. I swipe my finger over the trackpad to wake up my laptop.

"I'm just over there." Mac points to the table next to me. "Can I sit with you? It's more economical that way."

"Right, because it's practically *The Hunger Games* in here for a table," I mumble, but he still hears me. I don't particularly want Mac to sit with me. I'm still annoyed with him.

"My kingdom for a table," Mac says, his voice loud and booming.

A loud "Shhh!" comes from someone in another part of the library.

I duck, covering my face instinctively at the secondhand embarrassment. The blatant rule-breaking.

Both Mac and I look around but don't see where the shushing came from. He goes a bit sheepish, grimacing then covering his mouth with a hand.

"You just got shushed quoting Shakespeare in a library," I whisper-yell at him.

He shrugs with a bright, tight smile and walks away to get his things.

While Mac gathers his things, I organize my table. I line up my pens, arrange my book just so, and place my water bottle in front of me, aligned with the pen ends. The order feels right. It's a microcosm of control and organization. Small things like this are important to me because growing up there were no systems of organization. The kitchen table was always covered in unpaid bills and the house littered with piles of clutter, because you never knew when you'd need something and you couldn't just go out and buy it. It was a pantry and fridge stuffed with jars that had about one spoonful left of something, because if it wasn't scraped clean it wasn't empty, and you used every drop of everything because grocery day was once a month after food stamps went out.

But my room was always immaculate because it was the one thing I could control. And right now I can't control my tuition, or if I'll win any of my scholarships, or that I chose the same psychology paper topic as Mac. But I can control this space right here.

Mac reappears with his backpack slung over his shoulder, laptop cradled in his arm. He stands behind a chair like he's waiting for something before he sits. It occurs to me I never told him that he could sit with me.

"Yes, okay, fine," I say, waving to a chair. My dark cloud of annoyance has passed. A moment here, a moment gone. I'm getting better at this "letting go" stuff.

He smiles like he knew I'd say that and sets up his stuff.

I try to conjure some ideas for a new subject for my psychology paper, but I find I'm distracted. I'm not used to studying with someone else, and just his presence in my peripheral is hard to adjust to. He's put headphones in, and even though he isn't humming this time, he is sort of dancing to the music. Just a little, swaying his body back and forth.

This is exactly who Mac is, I realize as I watch him. Someone who dances to music no one else can hear in a public place. I scan the area around us. The library isn't empty, and people could see him if they looked up. I almost tell him to stop because it's really not an appropriate place to dance, but something on Mac's face stops me.

When I was younger, I'd come home from school some days to find Dad dancing in the kitchen, wearing teeny-tiny headphones that he'd had since the 80s. He'd have a rag in one hand and a spray bottle in the other, not a care in the world. It was one of those rare days he wasn't having a flare, and he was younger too.

The pure, unbridled joy on Mac's face reminds me of my dad. Before joint pain and muscle aches consumed him, my dad was always smiling. Now, mostly, his smiles are tinged with pain.

Why would I take that joy from Mac?

I wave to catch his attention. "What are you listening to?" I whisper, gesturing to my ears.

"'*Derelict Heart*,'" he says. His eyes have that distinct brightness of a person talking about something they love.

Derelict Heart is Black Phantom's third album. Their first two albums were strictly folk, but that one was a slight departure with a more indie pop feel. Of course he's dancing—it's such a fun album.

"Want to listen?" He holds out an earbud for me, but I shake my head. Mac might be okay with dancing in the library, but I don't think I'm there yet.

"I'm not humming this time," he says like a child proud of his accomplishments.

"I am eternally grateful." Smirking, I give my attention to a list of ideas I could potentially write my psychology paper on. I'm able to focus this time, and eventually I don't even notice Mac, until my stomach reminds me I need to eat and I check the time: eight o'clock.

How did that happen?

I dig through my backpack to find my mostly unsquished sandwich.

"What's for dinner?" Mac asks, removing a headphone and nodding to my Ziplock bag.

"PB and J. I'm pretty boring." I shrug. "Got some chips too, but I'll save those for later," I say like it's a real treat to have a bag of chips.

"You seem like a salt-and-vinegar kind of girl. Am I right?"

"Sour cream and onion. Should I be offended by your insinuations?"

Mac chuckles. "Maybe, but I mostly just meant you seem like the kind of person who likes a classic chip, nothing fancy." He makes a face like his favorite sports team just missed a goal. "Man," he says, "I usually get that right."

"You have a talent for guessing what kind of chips people like best?" I ask.

"Yes," he says in all seriousness, and then, to my utter surprise, he reaches into his own backpack and pulls out a sandwich wrapped in white paper like they use in the cafeteria deli on his way here. Even if it was made by someone else,the forethought is there. He packed dinner. He really did come to spend his Friday night studying at the library.

For years I've had Mac pinned as a party guy who just happened to be good at school. I saw it in high school—kids who goofed off in class, who definitely got someone else to do their homework, never studied, and aced all the tests. Ultimately, they still did mediocre because tests don't count for everything, but it's still frustrating for people like me who work their asses off to earn their grades. And then I got to college and watched as people balanced partying and school.

I tried it for one semester and failed so spectacularly that my GPA dropped dangerously low for a scholarship student. I don't do balance well. I'm an all-or-nothing girlie. I have always assumed Mac is one of those party people who can balance school and partying.

But my conversation with him from two nights ago at my work-study job floats back to me. *"I wasn't getting the time to study that I wanted. Soccer kind of consumed my life. I don't think I could balance a job and school."*

I think I've been wrong about Mac.

And I hate being wrong.

"Do you spend a lot of nights and weekends here at the library?" I ask.

"About half my weeknights and every Sunday night."

"Why have I never seen you here?"

"Probably weren't looking for me. I've seen you."

It isn't so much what he says but the way he says it that sends something hot from my heart into my stomach and all the way to my knees. I bite the inside of my lip to keep a smile from creeping over my face. He leans in, elbows on the table, voice low.

"We could have been studying together this whole time," he says. It isn't a particularly sexy statement, so why does it send that fluttery jolt below my belly button? Why is my heart beating faster?

Mac stretches a hand across the table, palm up, an invitation. For what? Is he trying to hold my hand? Is he about to say something that's actually sexy? Because I don't think I can handle that. I stare at his hand for so long, unmoving, that Mac finally speaks up.

"I can take your trash for you."

"Oh!"

I hand over my trash like it's on fire. I will myself not to blush, but I can feel the heat on my cheeks and neck. God, I hope he can't tell.

"I could use some coffee. What about you?" he asks, collecting his trash and standing.

"I'm okay," I say too quickly.

"It's on me," he says. "I insist since I stole your psychology paper and all."

"Okay, but just a small one." I relent. "Sugar and cream, please."

He smiles, and with a nod disappears.

What is happening to me? I keep getting into these scenarios with Mac where all of a sudden I feel like we have this crazy sexual tension. Is he feeling it too?

Oh my god, it doesn't matter, Jessie. Stop thinking about Mac like that.

I squeeze my eyes closed and press my palms against my forehead, conjuring Sexy Shakespeare and the Halloween party. Even if Mac did like me and I was…starting to maybe be interested in him in that way too, could we possibly have the kind of chemistry I had with Sexy Shakespeare? Will I ever find that with anyone again?

Or is it time to just accept that it was one really awesome night and that's it? I don't like to give up on things so easily, but if I can let go of my years-long resentment of Mac, I can definitely let go of a barely month-old crush on a stranger.

With food in my stomach and coffee on the way, I try to work on statistics again, but by the time he's reappeared I still don't feel like I'm making any progress. It's just a homework assignment, but I'm only halfway through, and that's after hours of work on it from earlier.

"Are you any good at statistics?" I ask as Mac slides my coffee across the table.

I hate asking for help, but I'm desperate.

"I'm all right, but two heads are better than one." He takes the seat next to me, setting his coffee on the table. I shift my laptop so he can see my screen, and he scoots the chair a little closer.

I don't have to give too much context since we're both in the class and he recognizes the assignment. As it turns out, Mac is really good at explaining things. He doesn't make me feel dumb at any point, and he repeats and reexplains things as many times as I need it.

It's refreshing, participating in schoolwork together instead of against each other. Is this what it would be like to date Mac?

Whoa.

I shake the thought from my head as Mac stands, taking a sip of his coffee and coming around to my side to see the laptop screen better, presumably, but just as he does, that deja vu feeling comes back. It sweeps through me, that sense of remembering, and I get lightheaded. It's overwhelming, such a sense of familiarity being so close to Mac. I stand suddenly, pushing my chair back with my legs and bumping into him, causing him to spill coffee all over himself and a little on the chair. The deja vu feeling finally passes.

"Shit," Mac hisses.

"Oh my god, I'm so sorry." I grab the few napkins he brought back with him and without thinking start pressing them to his shirt, trying to soak up the extra liquid. I'm frantically dabbing, realizing his shirt is white and now it has this horrible coffee stain, and also that his shirt is white and now it's sort of...see-through. *Oh, fuck.*

I pause and lift my eyes to meet Mac's. He's frozen and wears a half-shocked, half-amused expression.

"Sorry," I whisper and hold out the damp napkins for him to finish cleaning himself off, because pressing my hands against his very firm...

Okay, that's enough of that, Jessie.

"It's fine. It's totally fine," he says, not sounding even a little bit mad. He takes the napkins from me and blots at his chest and stomach a few more times.

"Is there any on your laptop?" he asks, wadding up the napkins and tossing them on the table.

My voice is shaky, like I'm on the verge of tears, and I might be because now I'm so stressed I'm spilling coffee on people. "No, my laptop is fine. I'm so sorry."

Mac puts his hands on my shoulders and gives me an intense stare, making sure I'm holding eye contact with him as he talks to me. "It's okay. It will dry. Are you okay?"

"I just, um, I got deja vu and I was just trying to get rid of it. I'm—not going to apologize again." I nod, and then he's nodding with me, but a funny look crosses his face when I mention deja vu.

"What?" I ask.

He looks like he's about to say something but shakes his head and releases me. He plucks at his wet shirt. "I probably should call it a night."

Mac throws a hoodie on over his wet shirt, and we gather our things and walk out of the library together. Distant sounds of partying float toward us, deep basses and the occasional "woo" of a drunk girl. Save a few people wandering the campus, it's as empty out here as it was inside the library.

"Can I walk you back to your dorm?" he asks.

"Even with your wet shirt? Don't you want to go home and change?"

"It's barely wet anymore."

I raise my eyebrows at him.

"I'm a gentleman," he says. "It's practically the law."

"A scoundrel more like."

"You like me because I'm a scoundrel."

"*Star Wars?*"

A huge smile cracks and breaks open his entire face. "I'm surprised you recognized it."

"Me? I've got nerd written all over me," I say as we begin the walk to my dorm. "But you? *Game of Thrones, Star Wars,* your sourdough is named Frodo..."

"You sound surprised."

"Well, yeah. Hot, well-dressed guys don't usually like nerd stuff."

"First of all, that sentence was chock-full of stereotypes we should break down, and second of all, you think I'm hot?"

Oh, shit. I did say that. And out loud.

"I just meant...uh..."

"I know what you meant," he says, teasing.

"No, it's not like..."

"You think I'm hot, it's totally fine. I think you're beautiful. What's a couple compliments between friends?"

I trip over my own feet and accidentally grab Mac's arm to keep from falling. I grip one of his arms with both of my hands, and he freezes so I can steady myself. One of his hands covers both of mine, and he dips his head so he's closer to my ear.

"That's twice in one night, Matthews." His voice is low and smooth. "Am I going to need to carry you home?"

Again that flutter shoots through my lower belly, and I straighten, releasing my grip on Mac. I tug my clothes straight and adjust my bag on my arm.

"I'm perfectly capable of walking," I say primly.

"Yes, obviously. You're in full command of your faculties." He nudges me, and I teeter, but he catches me before I can tip sideways. I gasp, half-smiling, half-gaping at him, and point an accusatory finger.

"That was...!" I'm yelling, but I'm also laughing, and the words don't fully come out right.

"God, Matthews. What's wrong? Were you sneaking drinks at the library tonight?"

Holding onto my arm, he gently pushes me to the side and then pulls me back and does this a few more times like I'm wobbling, but Mac is in control of my movements. I'm laughing so hard I'm not sure I could walk straight even if he weren't pulling me back and forth. Eventually, I wheeze out the words "Okay, stop, please," and he does. He steadies me, and I realize we're at the bottom of the stairs that lead to my dorm.

I straighten and catch my breath, but before I can say anything Mac has closed the space between us and wrapped me up in a hug. I'm still breathing a little heavily, and the press of his chest against mine as it moves with my labored breathing is a new kind of intimacy for Mac and me. It takes my body a minute to catch up with my brain, but I eventually hug him back. I hold my hands as still as I can, but I can feel his muscles under his hoodie. That clean laundry scent is all around me now, and I'm having trouble resisting the urge to relax into his arms, to rest my head on his chest.

"Good night, Jessie," he says, his voice somewhat muffled by my hair.

"Good night, Mac," I say and extricate myself from his arms. As quickly as I can, I run up the stairs to the door, the sound of Mac wishing me good night lost over my shoulder.

As soon as I've closed the door I lean against it, resting my head back and closing my eyes. I let my heart rate slow to a normal pace, holding my hand to my chest. I try to shake the feeling of him, but I can't. He's everywhere, like the scent of sunshine after coming inside on a summer day.

Besides the ferocious pounding, what is that feeling in my chest? That expanding lightness that makes me feel like I'm attached to a hot air balloon and I could take off any minute... Is that—? *Oh god.* Do I have a crush on Mac?

Maybe I do, but what does that mean for Sexy Shakespeare? Surely the kind of chemistry I had with a guy like that is impossible to find with anyone else. Lightning doesn't strike twice and all that.

I walk to my room, questions and doubts circling inside me, trying to land. I let myself go back to Halloween night, an evening that's already starting to fade despite it only being three weeks ago. The electricity I shared with that stranger is starting to feel more like just a small carpet shock. It all feels like a dream and less like something that actually happened.

Can I really keep living in a fantasy, pining for a guy I may never find, when reality is starting to look so much more tempting?

CHAPTER ELEVEN

I've spent nearly all day searching for photos of Sexy Shakespeare on social media. This really is a last-ditch effort, but I could barely sleep last night after studying in the library with Mac all evening. I just kept thinking of him and the mystery guy and how maybe I like Mac and maybe I want Mac to kiss me, but I'm also not ready to let go of this stranger who made me feel so alive.

I'm running out of people I know whose photos I can dig through to find him. I'm just about to give up so I can finish my dinner and get ready for work, but as I inhale a forkful of Ramen noodles, I see it.

A man in a stereotypical Elizabethan shirt, masked, at the Halloween party. It's not a great photo of him—it's blurry and he's sort of in the background, and it's dark and his eyes are closed behind the mask—but it's there. He's there. He's *right there*. I stop breathing for half a second before I panic-call Jade, only remembering to breathe again when she picks up.

"I found him. I found—a photo. I have a photo." My words stumble over each other on their way out of my mouth, but Jade understands me just fine.

"Oh my fucking god. If this is an April Fool's joke I am going to be so mad."

"Jade, it's November. Not a joke. We have to go. Tonight. ATZ. We have to find him. We have to ask around. Where are you?"

"I'm with George. Deep breaths, girl. Or just regular ones. I'm worried for you. Yes, we will go. Don't you have, like, work right now?"

"Shit. Yes. Um…okay, think, think, think. It's a Saturday night, so parties will go late, right? I'll text—um, what's her name—? Someone can cover the last hour, and we'll go at, like, eleven. Okay?"

"Done and done."

I can't finish my dinner now. I shove it to the side and with shaking hands text the person who works in the labs after me, promising to cover them an hour sometime if they'll come in early tonight. They agree, and all I have to do now is make it through the next four hours.

About two hours into my work shift, at nine o'clock, I get a phone call from my mom. She never calls this late, and a knot of worry starts tangling itself in my stomach.

"Hey, Mom. Everything okay? Is Dad okay?"

"Your dad is fine. Everyone is okay." Her words are reassuring, but her voice is tight. I didn't get in trouble a lot as a kid, but when I did Mom was the discipliner. And this is the voice she used.

Am I in trouble? But for what?

"Uhh, okay. What's going on?" I ask.

"What's this email I got about cosigning a loan for you?"

The knot tightens.

"I meant to tell you about that. I've just been so busy." Not a lie, but also not totally the truth. I've thought about calling and telling her every day. I'm more of a coward than anything. "I just thought a loan would make everything easier. I've applied for the scholarships, but I don't want to take any chances. I AM going to graduate from college." I consciously lower my voice, realizing I was steadily raising it while speaking. No one is here, but I grit my teeth and continue. "It's MY future. It's me that will have to make the payments. I should get to decide if I do this."

"You're right. You should be able to do that. Which is exactly what I said to my dad," my mom says.

"But you didn't end up going to college, and I—"

"I lied," my mother says so quietly I almost don't hear it.

"What?" My heart races, thudding in my chest, my ears. I try to swallow, but my throat feels like sandpaper.

"I did go to college for two years. I went to a very expensive art school for two years and took out loans for both years. It was a hundred thousand dollars in loans, and it has been over twenty years, chicken, and I am still paying on them. I'll tell you how much, if you really want to know." Her voice shakes, and I know she's probably crying. My mom is one of those people to whom tears are very accessible.

Maybe I'm a bad person, but right now I don't care that she's crying. She's been lying to me my whole life.

"Why didn't you ever tell me?"

"I was ashamed. Ashamed of my loans and the debt, and I've always tried to protect you from our...financial situation. But part of the reason we are where we are is because of choices I made when I was eighteen. I know you're twenty-one, and I know this isn't as much money as I took out, but had I gone on to be an art teacher like I meant to, maybe things would be different."

But she didn't go on to be an art teacher because she had me. The way I always heard the story was that Mom couldn't afford college, her daddy refused to let her get loans, and so she started working right out of high school to save up. But she met my dad and they got pregnant with me when Mom was nineteen, she had me when she was twenty, and they got married shortly thereafter. She always said being a mom and going to school would have been too much, and she was already working, so why not continue?

I used to watch my mom paint when I was younger and she and my dad both had jobs. She had more free time then, and Dad had less joint pain. As I got older, Mom had less time, Dad had more pain, and Mom didn't paint anymore. I knew she dreamed of being an art teacher. I had no idea she actually tried to go to school for it.

I had no idea we had more than just medical debt.

A small part of my brain understands everything. Why she wouldn't tell me. Why she wouldn't want to burden her daughter with this. And another, less reasonable, much larger part of me wants to rage.

I swear when I blink I see red behind my eyes. I squeeze my fist so tight my forearm muscles ache, and it does nothing to relieve the searing fury inside of me. I cannot believe she kept this from me. I don't even know what to say to her. Actually, I know exactly what I want to say, but I won't kick her while she's down.

"Jessie?"

"I...I gotta go, Mom."

It's not true. I don't have to be anywhere, but I don't want to be on the phone anymore.

"I want you to remember that you cannot predict everything that will happen in your life, and having a loan makes some of those unpredictable things more difficult. I will cosign the loan if that's what you really need, but I wanted you to have the whole story first. The whole picture. I'm sorry it took me so long to tell you. I love you, sweetie."

"Love you, Mom." I slam my phone down on the desk and cover my face with my hands.

Fuck.

It never occurred to me that we struggled financially because of anything other than my dad's medical situation. And maybe if my mom didn't have the student loan debt, it wouldn't be much better, but every month she's putting money toward a loan that could have gone toward something else. I don't want to let myself think about all the things that extra money could have been spent on.

Worst of all, she's right. Loan money is easy right now, when I'm not staring at the balance due every month on top of whatever other bills I'll be paying as interest accrues, keeping me from ever truly getting out of debt. My mom is forty-one, but her hair is already so gray and she always looks tired. It's aged her. I've watched firsthand what the stress of debt and staying afloat looks like. Of course I don't want that.

But what do I do if these scholarships don't come through?

I loosen my jaw, realizing when it starts to ache that I've been clenching it. I shake out my hands, sore from being squeezed, and try to take some deep breaths. One thing at a time. And right now that one thing is finding Sexy Shakespeare.

I try to focus on homework for the next few hours, but I'm haunted by my mother's words. *"I lied."* Is lying okay if it's done in the name of protecting someone you care about? The answer to me is an obvious and resounding no. Honesty is the best policy, even if it's hurtful. The person I learned that from was my mom, which makes this even more of a slap in the face.

By the time my shift ends and I've met Jade at the ATZ house, I'm dying for a drink. I've almost forgotten why I'm doing this, but Jade insists I show her the picture of Sexy Shakespeare then screenshot and send it to her. She squeals, jumping up and down, and her enthusiasm chips away at my frustration.

Focus on the task at hand, Jessie. Tonight you're just a girl looking for a boy who made her feel like a million bucks.

The house smells like cheap beer and strong vodka, and my ears are already hurting from the cacophony of music and drunken screams. Jade and I split up. I go to the basement and she goes upstairs. I don't have a lot of luck showing drunk people the blurry photo of a costumed man, asking if anyone recognizes him from a Halloween party. I get a lot of "I don't know" and "maybe" and just straight-up "nope." Wasn't expecting much from the basement people anyway.

I head back to the main floor, reeking slightly of smoke and sweatier than I was twenty minutes ago. I don't see Jade, so I wander around, stopping everyone and asking if they recognize the guy. More rejection on top of rejection, and after another half-hour I'm officially discouraged.

On top of everything with my mom tonight this is the last thing I need. I'm about to text Jade and tell her the search is over and my hopes are dashed on the rocks when I realize I missed a room. A few guys trickle out of a door off to the side: the frat study room. Who knows how much studying actually gets done in there? But this room is my last chance.

I steel myself with a deep breath.

The door is cracked, and I push it the rest of the way open. The whole room is so out of place in a frat house. It kind of looks like it should be a sitting room in *Pride and Prejudice* instead of a home that regularly reeks of Bud Light. There's a wall of books, and I think they're actually real. There's art on the walls too, although that is definitely not real. At least I hope it isn't. Four guys sit at the table, but no books are out, and there is definitely no studying going on, mostly just cigar-smoking.

"Mac?" My stomach lurches up to my throat. *Am I excited to see him?*

I haven't finished processing our interaction at the library last night. The flirting, the banter, how his voice would get all low and sexy when he talked to me. And I certainly haven't processed the way I fell asleep thinking about him and woke up thinking about him too. I'm emotionally unprepared to see him right now, but isn't that just my life?

"Jessie? Hey, what are you—?"

"Mac, who's the hottie?" one of the guys at the table asks.

I narrow my eyes, giving the guy an "Ew, back off" face.

He holds his hands up as if surrendering. "Whoa-hoa. Hottie with a 'tude, okay, okay."

"He's drunk—ignore him," Mac says, and the guy stands, announcing to all of us he's going to get another drink. Mac starts to follow him out.

"Hey, I'll be back. Wait here, okay?"

I almost forget my mission, but when I glance down at my phone the photo is still pulled up, so I hold it out to the other guys at the table and ask if they recognize the guy in the photo. They shrug and shake their heads. All the hope inside of me shrivels up.

I need to just go home. This whole night has been a shit show. I start to text Jade, but Mac comes back with a couple of red Solo cups. He offers me one, and when I look into his dark caramel eyes, I know I'm not leaving. I'm going to stay here awhile even if it's just to keep looking into those eyes.

Damn it, he's handsome.

"What happened to your drunk friend?" I ask and take the cup, chugging the contents immediately. I click my phone off and stick it in my pocket.

"Got distracted by a 'hottie.'"

"Oh, so it wasn't just me."

"Sorry to disappoint you."

By the window at the far end of the room there's a small side table and two chairs that belong in a teahouse, not a frat house. I follow Mac's lead to the slightly quieter spot. We each take a chair, but Mac scoots his a little closer to mine.

"Shouldn't you be off studying somewhere tonight?" he asks.

"My favorite place to pick up guys is at a frat house," I say with my own smirk.

"Really? I assumed you picked up guys in the library."

"Only on Fridays," I say, fighting a smile at my own cleverness. Afraid he'll continue this line of flirting and say something that flusters me, I change the subject. "Are you pledged here?"

"Nah, but a lot of my old soccer buddies are, so if I'm partying, which is not very often, it's here. Plus, they have some of the best parties on The Row."

"Is that who your friends are—soccer friends?"

"Basically. What about you?" He moves his knee, knocking it against mine. Until this moment, I didn't fully realize how close we were, but Mac moved his chair close enough that it's almost easier to reach out and touch him than it is to keep my hands to myself.

"Yeah, all my friends are soccer friends," I say.

Mac throws his head back and laughs a big, booming laugh. It's not that funny, but I have a feeling this isn't his first drink. And anyway, it makes my chest feel fuzzy to see him laugh like that at something I said, knowing it's not at my expense.

"No, um…just Jade, really. I've never really had a ton of friends."

I struggled with friendships at school. I'd go to my friends' houses and see all the things they had and realize how little I had. By the time I got to middle school, I stopped inviting friends over to my house, and I said no to a lot of social events because I didn't have much extra cash. Jade is the first friend I've kept for more than a few months, and she never lets a day go by without reminding me we're not allowed to stop being friends, because if I leave her she'll kill me.

I check my phone to see if she's texted me. She hasn't, and I'm guessing she had no luck with Sexy Shakespeare either. I take a sip of my beer and try to ignore the rising disappointment, but it's heavy in my chest. I peer over my cup at Mac and notice his leg is still resting against mine.

"And boyfriends?" Mac asks and drains his cup. He sets it on the floor and then leans on the arm of his chair, his eyes focused intently on me as if I'm the only other person in this room, maybe even the whole house. The way he can make everything I'm worried about just fade into the background when he looks at me should be alarming, but it's not. With Mac there's just fun and laughter, and things don't feel so serious. He's magnanimous. His presence takes up so much space that I have nothing left for stupid boys who kiss me and disappear.

"Just one in high school and one my freshman year of college."

"Anyone serious?"

"Can you really be serious with anyone in high school? Or freshman year. The guy I dated my first semester was a big partier. I tried to keep up but almost lost my scholarship. I wasn't used to balancing a boyfriend and going out every weekend, and college turned out to be a lot harder than high school. The adjustment was hard, and having a boyfriend who didn't care about his grades made it harder."

"You dumped his ass though, yeah?"

"Yeah, I almost lost my scholarship. Scared me straight." I make a noise between a laugh and a huff. Staring into my empty cup, a big part of me kicks and squirms because admitting when things are hard for me to anyone, but especially to him, is uncomfortable.

"You were too good for that loser," Mac says, his truth in humor a soothing balm to my fear.

I flick my eyes up to his, a small smile my only response.

"Another beer?" Mac offers, pointing to my cup. I nod, and he saunters off to get us a couple more drinks.

I scroll through my phone in his absence, checking my texts, social media, and my email—which is mostly junk—but there's something from my mom. A PDF of her most recent loan payment and statement.

I scan it quickly, noting her payment and how much it covered of the principal balance and interest. Her payment is barely making a dent. She's still got over $70,000 left to pay on the loan. My head spins a little and I close the email, setting my phone on the table and holding my face in my hands.

I'm rubbing my temples when I feel a tap on my hand.

"You okay?" Mac asks. He hands me my beer and sits down in almost the exact same place as before, knee against mine. It's just his knee, but my whole body is on as if his touch is a light switch and every light in the house just illuminated, every appliance running.

"I guess. I just…" How much do I really want to share with him? "Found out that my mom has been keeping something from me. It's not bad, but it's not great either. It's just, like, she should have told me years ago. She waited so long, and it's like I don't actually care about the news, I care that she lied."

Mac doesn't say anything, but his face is empathetic. It spurs me on. I pushed all this frustration down earlier, and now that I've cracked the lid I don't think I can stop.

"I'm just, like, what is wrong with brutal honesty? Trying to protect someone from hurting them or whatever is like saying you don't trust them to be able to handle whatever the truth is. And that's shitty. Like, my mom didn't trust me to know the whole story? And then it's like, this guy, the Shakespeare guy from Halloween. I've been searching for him but, at this point, if I found out who he was, I'd be like, fuck you for waiting so long. Like you gave me a fake name and then didn't even— Ugh. I'm sorry. You don't need my angry ranting."

Now that it's out I feel about a thousand pounds lighter. I always forget how good it feels just to get something off my chest. I feel about half as angry as I did earlier today, and all because I let out a little steam.

"Jessie, that's...I'm really sorry," Mac says, but he looks uncomfortable.

"Honestly, it's okay. I just needed to rant. Sorry to be a Debbie Downer." I chug about half my beer. Now that I feel lighter, less frustrated, I don't want to talk about it, and I don't want to give him any room to either. "What were we talking about before? Dating in college?"

"Yeah, and I thought about this." He picks up the conversation quickly. "I'm not sure I agree. I think dating in college could be worth it. For the right person. Who was the guy you dated?"

I appreciate his swift pivot. Mac is good for that, keeping things light.

"Brian O'Toole."

Mac shakes his head. "Don't know him."

"He pledged Kappa Tau. He's always with those guys."

"Ah. And your high-school boyfriend?"

"Because you're definitely going to know his name."

"Where did you grow up again? Maybe I have a friend of a friend..."

"Western Maryland. Basically in West Virginia."

Mac twists his face into a thinking scowl. "Tell me his name," he prompts.

"Drew Cleary."

"Oh my god!" Mac says like he does know him.

"Oh, stop," I say and slap his knee.

He smirks and grabs my hand. I pull it away, playfully slapping his knee again. It's all just a silly excuse to touch each other. Maybe it's the beer or my growing attraction to Mac, but my lips feel tingly and my body feels like it could burst with wanting him to touch me again and more. His knee against mine is such a tease.

"And was there a middle-school boyfriend?" he asks.

"Yes. Stephen...I forget his last name, but that doesn't count."

"It counts if you kissed."

"Oh, are those the rules?" I raise my eyebrows at him.

"Those are the rules."

"Well, me and Duncan Hart kissed in middle school, but he was never my boyfriend. Just my first kiss."

"Duncan Hart. Lucky guy." He says that last thing into his drink.

I blush all the way down to my chest and wipe my sweaty palms on my jeans. "And your first kiss?" I ask.

"Rebecca Bloomingate, seventh grade, after our orchestra concert, in the parking lot of my middle school."

"So was this a one-night stand, or did you and Rebecca have a long, happy relationship?" I ask.

"Oh, no, she used me. She had another boy she was chasing, Chuckie. I don't remember his last name. But the next day she and Chuckie were an item and I was just another dork playing the cello and mooning over Rebecca." He takes a sip. "My first real heartbreak." He says this with a smile, but I have a feeling there's some truth to it.

"My first heartbreak was this kid Matt Tropiano," I say. "He was a little jackass, but fifteen-year-old me didn't know that. I had such a huge crush on him, and he did not notice me. Until we got paired together in a group project."

"Uh-oh."

"And I thought for sure this was it. This was when he would notice me. And for like a week he was so nice to me. I thought he was flirting with me and that we were vibing, but as soon as the project was over he went back to ignoring me. And I did all the work on the project. He didn't do anything but present it."

Mac's expression is the exact right reaction for this story. Pained and understanding.

"I thought he liked me, and I remember I told all my friends. I wrote it in my diary. I felt really dumb. The sting of rejection is not for the weak of heart," I say.

"Is that what's happening here, by the way? Are you hanging out with me because I'm smarter than you and you just need some school help?" Mac asks, smirking. He bumps his leg against mine again, and I gawk at him. I give him another playful slap on the leg.

This time when he grabs my hand, I don't pull it away. He loosens his grip but intertwines his fingers with mine. I pretend to be cool about it, but inside I am on fire. The heat starts in my hand, radiating up my arm and spreading through all of me like lava.

Is he feeling this too?

"First of all, I think my grades speak for themselves as to which of us is smarter, and, um, to be honest, up until, like, two weeks ago I kind of hated your guts."

"Really?" He leans forward, further into my space.

I lean forward a little too. A tilt of my head and our foreheads would be touching. He rubs his thumb over mine, the movement sending chills down my spine.

"Really. I found you very annoying," I say.

"And now?" His voice is low. He's doing that sexy voice thing again, and even though I'm not standing I feel weak.

"Slightly less annoying. And you?" I ask, my own voice low and quiet. "Did you despise me as well?"

His eyes bounce between my lips and my eyes. "No. No, I did not."

My heart rate speeds up and I wet my lips, trying to control my breathing as he tilts his chin, angling his face. I want what he's about to do. I want him to kiss me, so I lean too. I can feel his breath on my lips. There's a hint of citrus—

"JESSIE?" Jade flies into the room, yelling my name. "Oh god, Jessie, there you are. Wow, what is happening here? I am so sorry I interrupted. But unfortunately, I need you. Threesome Anna wants to do the movie on the lawn thing, and she's bringing friends and told me to bring friends, and you're my only friend and I need you!"

I barely have time to grab my phone before Jade is practically dragging me out of the chair. I don't usually mind when Jade drags me places, and typically it's less literal, but tonight I could kill her. I try to wave goodbye to Mac over my shoulder, still holding onto my cup of beer as it sloshes all over my hand.

I think I'm done looking for Shakespeare.

MAC

It's been twenty-three days since I kissed Jessie Matthews and there hasn't been a day I haven't woken up wondering if this will be the day I can do it again. Until she walked through the doors of the study room tonight I'd pretty much counted today as a wash.

I had hope there for a minute.

But now...

It'll be twenty-four days.

I slump back in the chair, downing the rest of my beer and tossing the empty cup on the ground. I drag my hand down my face.

Goddammit.

She wanted to kiss me. I could see it in her eyes. Something is different between us now, and it makes me feel like I'm on fire. It's one thing to have a crush on someone from a distance, and quite another up close. The shared longing glances. Touching them just to feel their skin against yours. Teasing them just to see a smile light up their face. Talking about nothing at all just to keep them around. And they're doing all the same things back to you.

She was doing all those things back to me.

I leave the party without saying goodbye to anyone. The cool night air hits me like a slap in the face.

As if not getting to kiss Jessie isn't bad enough, it turns out I've been an absolute fucking idiot about the Halloween party. She really has no idea it was me. She hasn't been playing a game. She was never playing a game. She was never doing any of it for my attention.

She really had no fucking clue.

I thought maybe it was a stretch. Especially after I ran into her and Jade and she said she'd gone looking for the guy. But I thought maybe her friend was just egging her on and that maybe Jessie just...really didn't want to talk about it.

But tonight. Tonight I saw the very real frustration of a girl who got ghosted by a stranger. She was being so vulnerable, and she would have said something tonight if she knew it was me. But she didn't.

And now it is way too late for me to say something to her.

The pain in her eyes when she talked about her mom lying to her. About her mom keeping a secret from her for years. I've been keeping a secret for less than a month.

But now I'm going to keep it forever.

There isn't a snowball's chance in hell that I'm going to tell Jessie it was me. If I tell her now, it's done. She'll never speak to me again, and all this will be over.

If I didn't like her so much I probably wouldn't care, but I do like her. I like her a lot.

And I think she likes me too.

And I'm not willing to lose her.

CHAPTER TWELVE

Office hours are not supposed to be sexy.

Yet somehow sitting next to Mac at the tables in the student labs is one of the most sexually charged scenarios I've ever been in.

We had a few more rounds of observation with Professor Campbell earlier today and decided to stay behind after to work on some coding. Every so often Mac will press his leg against mine or knock his arm gently against me. And every time, it sends a shock of electricity through me. The touch is never quite enough. It makes me want to lean into him, to feel what it might be like to rest my head on his shoulder. Would he kiss my forehead? Or maybe he'd just kiss me. It's only Monday, but ever since we studied together on Friday at the library, I feel like I've thought nonstop about what it would feel like for him to kiss me.

Even now I'm so lost in daydreaming that it takes me a few minutes to realize Mac is saying my name.

"Jessie?"

"Yes, sorry." I blink a few times.

"Where did you go?" Mac asks, a soft smile on his face.

"Nowhere, I didn't— Sorry, did something happen?"

"Sara said we could go."

We gather our things in silence, and I say goodbye to Mac as we leave the room so I can use the restroom before heading back to my dorm to study and get some lunch. But when I emerge from the bathroom, Mac is leaning against a wall, hands tucked into his pockets.

"Were you waiting for me?" I ask.

"No, I was just waiting."

"In a general sense?"

"Yes. Just general waiting. Waiting for time to move. Waiting for snow to fall, paint to dry, all of that."

We stand there grinning at each other, amused by each other, though I narrow my eyes at him so he knows I'm onto him.

"I thought I'd see if you wanted to get lunch," he says, stuffing his hands deeper in his pockets.

"I'm actually crazy busy today."

"Studying?"

I nod.

"Nerd."

I smile.

"Let me buy you lunch," he says.

"If you insist."

We fall into step together.

"I'm surprised you're still on campus this week," I say. "I thought most people had gone home by now since Thanksgiving is on Thursday."

"I usually wait a little longer. With all my brothers and their partners, it gets pretty cozy."

We walk together through the science building and outside, toward the cafe. I zip my jacket up all the way, and Mac pulls on a beanie.

Handsome as always, but it doesn't irritate me like it used to. Well, only a little. Is it really fair for someone to be that good-looking and smart?

"How many brothers do you have again?"

"Three."

"Wow. I'm an only child. I can't imagine a life with one sibling, much less three."

"It was never a quiet household."

"Your poor mother."

"Poor nothing." He blows a raspberry. "My mother loved being a boy mom and having a house full of dirty, obnoxious boys. I think she wanted at least two more, but my dad felt like four was plenty."

I try to picture a young Mac playing with his brothers, an adoring mother looking on. I bet he was a cute, mischievous child.

The wind bites at my cheeks and nose. It smells like fall, earthy and wet like it just rained. I bury my face into my jacket collar until we make it to the cafeteria.

"Hey, just a couple days until the album release," Mac says as he pulls open the door for me.

"I am so excited."

"We're listening together, right?"

"Didn't you just say you'd be at home for the rest of the break?"

"Ah, shit." He stops in the middle of the lunchroom. "Can you wait 'til we can listen to it together? Or I can— Well, shit. Are you going home for the break?"

"No. I usually pick up some work-study shifts around campus— whatever is open, ya know. Too far for just a couple days off." Plus, my mom will probably be working. My dad would appreciate the company, but I like the quiet of the campus, and it's fun to get to work other odd jobs for a couple of days.

"You should come home with me," Mac says.

I stop breathing for long enough that when I do finally exhale it comes out like a heavy sigh. "What?"

"I just mean for dinner. We can just stay one night and do the album listen on Friday and then come back. There's tons of guest space at my house, and—" He must realize what he's saying because he pauses with an "oh shit" look on his face.

"Can I think about it?"

I already know how I feel about it. I feel it in my gut immediately. *Yes.* I want to spend more time with Mac. It's such a girlfriend thing to do, but for some reason that doesn't scare me. It's a yes that reverberates through all of me.

And *that* is what scares me.

"Yeah, of course. I didn't mean...I was just thinking...for the album, but also you said you're not going home and maybe you wanted a home-cooked meal for Thanksgiving. I don't know what they serve here on campus, but it can't be that good. No pressure. Just let me know by, like, Wednesday night. I'll drive home on Thursday morning."

I nod, pressing my lips together and bringing to mind all the reasons it's a bad idea to go home with Mac for Thanksgiving. His family might not be very welcoming. What if his brothers are mean? What if I'm uncomfortable? I couldn't leave easily.

But most of those reasons feel flimsy. I'd get to spend so much time with Mac—in the car, sitting next to him at a family dinner, listening to the new Black Phantom album together. All the opportunities to be close, to get to know him better... It's tempting.

But that immediate yes gives me pause. I think I like Mac more than I'm ready to admit, and it happened kind of fast. Letting go of the past was the crack of the avalanche, and now snow is tumbling and trees are being ripped up by their roots and I feel about as chaotic inside as a landslide.

We both get food and claim a small table by a window with our trays. We eat in silence for the most part, the crowd of students and professors filling the space around us. Mac grins at me from across the table, his eyes meeting mine. I give him a small smile, dropping my eyes to my bag of chips. When I peek up, he's still looking at me, beaming. A balloon inflates behind my sternum. I feel so light I worry I might float away.

"I got my scholarship application in," he says with a proud smile, breaking the silence.

The balloon pops, the rubber snapping inside my chest. Why does he have to bring this up?

"I know it's kind of early, but I started writing the essay and—"

"Why are you even applying for the scholarship?" My words come out sharp. Staccato. I drop my fork with more intensity than I mean to. I haven't thought about the scholarship in a few days, but it all comes rushing back to me now. My mom's lie. The fact that I'm screwed without this scholarship or any other that I applied for. And the mere mention of it brings all that up with a sour taste in the back of my throat. I may have let go of what happened between us freshman year, but if Mac wins this scholarship over me and I can't stay in school because of it? I see red, and I'm not able to control myself. "You don't need it. You live off-campus. I assume your parents don't have any trouble paying your tuition. What the hell do you even need the scholarship for?"

The smile slides right off Mac's face. *Shit.* I was too judgmental, too mean. When I get angry that quickly I have no control over what I say —I just lose it. And now, seeing the effect of my words, of my tone and my anger, I want to take it all back. I want to rewind and take a deep breath. I might still ask the question, but not with the same venom.

He presses his lips together and swallows hard. A storm of emotions passes over his face, and I can't even begin to name all of them. I lightly touch my fingers to the back of his hand, an offering of apology and peace.

"Mac, I'm sorry, I—"

"I'm the youngest of my brothers. My oldest brother, Rob, is a lawyer, graduated top of his class from Harvard as an undergrad and in law school. He's a partner at a top firm in Philadelphia now. Michael is next oldest. He plays in the NFL, but he also has a biology degree and just announced he's retiring to go to the South Pole science station with his fiancée to pursue photography. Noah is only two years older than me and he started a job at NASA about six months ago." He pauses, taking a bite of a French fry and chewing it slowly.

His whole demeanor changes as he starts talking about his brothers. He tells me about their jobs like he's reading off a menu. There's no pride in his voice, but no envy either. Just facts.

"I was okay at soccer, but never good enough to go pro. I'm okay at school as long as I work hard. You know what I am good at? Making people laugh. But a career in comedy or acting is not something—I could never tell my parents that's what I really want to do. My dad won't even let me take a theater class, one class, because he doesn't believe in arts as a career or some bullshit. Even a psychology major is a bit of a stretch for them, but with a lawyer, scientist, and an engineer already, my parents didn't need me to be great at anything."

I slide my hand over his, covering the back of his hand with mine. My heart breaks for little Mac, whom I imagine at family parties making everyone laugh, no one taking him seriously. I imagine his dad, stone-faced and unapproving as he grows up and does his best. It's hard to imagine a life where my parents didn't actively encourage me and cheer me on. My heart clenches.

"I wasn't expected to do as well as my brothers, but I'm still expected to do well. Going over and above, getting the accolades that come with the Walden Scholarship isn't a lot, but it's something." His fingers curl around mine.

The entire cafe has disappeared, the bustling lunch hour slowing almost to a stop.

"Mac." His name sticks in my throat.

His eyes meet mine and he gives me a tight smile. "I know it's dumb."

"It's not. It's not dumb at all," I say as earnestly as I can, but it doesn't feel like enough. I'm embarrassed for having judged him so harshly, for thinking he had no issues because he had enough money to fix any problems he did have. It was so ignorant of me; so judgmental. I never considered the kind of problems money can't solve. I squeeze his hand, and he squeezes mine back. His eyes hold mine, and I hope I'm communicating everything I can't find the words for.

It never occurred to me Mac might feel the same kind of pressure I do. I don't have siblings, but I understand expectations. When I got accepted to college there was an instant expectation that I'd be the first one in my family to graduate. And even though finishing is the bare minimum, my own expectations drive me to be the best. I won't just be the first person in my family to graduate college; I'll be the first one to do it *and* I'll graduate valedictorian. I carry immense pressure not to let my family down. Even if that pressure is somewhat self-imposed.

For once I feel like I understand Mac in a way that I never have.

It occurs to me for the first time that maybe he didn't take the ambassador opportunity away from me two years ago. Maybe he wanted the opportunity to shine in the already bright landscape of his family. My heart softens, melting a little for Mac. Whatever bitterness lived inside me toward him is gone. That lingering frustration about the scholarship—it's also gone.

The Walden Senior Scholarship isn't any less important to me than it was before, and I won't be giving it up because I know why Mac wants it now. But I will stop seeing him as a villain hell-bent on destroying my academic career.

"Am I interrupting something?" Jade's voice comes from behind me.

I yank my hand out of Mac's and stand abruptly. "Jade, hey," I say and hug her. We're not usually the hugging type, but I feel like I just got caught doing something I wasn't supposed to be doing, and I don't know what else to do to diffuse the awkwardness.

Jade pats my back. "Okay, weirdo," she says in my ear. "I saw that." When I release her from the hug, she asks Mac, "Can I join?"

"Absolutely," Mac says, getting up to grab another chair for Jade. Whatever vulnerability was just there is gone now. It's like he's got a mask of positivity that he's slipped back on, but I wanted more time with the vulnerable Mac.

Maybe if I go home with him for Thanksgiving...

"You two will not believe what just happened." Jade sits with all the gusto of a main character, interrupting my thoughts.

"I probably won't," Mac says.

"I might. Try me," I say.

We both give Jade our full attention, because that's what you do when Jade is in the room. She rolls her eyes at both of us and pulls a protein bar out of her backpack, ripping open the package and tearing off a bite.

"So I'm walking with George Greg to his next class—"

"George Greg?" Mac asks.

"He's a Greg that looks like George Clooney, so we call him George Greg to differentiate between the other Gregs she's slept with," I say quickly so Jade can go on with her story.

She nods at me appreciatively as I take a bite of food, which is getting cold since I didn't eat a bite while Mac and I were talking.

"Gregs? Plural?" Mac asks.

"And we're holding hands—"

"Excuse me?" I nearly spit out my food.

"Shut up," Jade says, taking a breath to launch back into her story.

"No, no, no. What you just said needs more processing time. You were holding hands with someone?" I ask.

"Oh my god." Jade rolls her eyes.

"Wait—is holding hands bad?" Mac asks.

"Holding hands is emotional," I say. "It means something."

"It's physical!" Jade says.

"Do you hold hands with everyone you hook up with, Jade?" I ask.

"No, of course not, because I—"

"Because you sleep with them and then never see them again, and now you've been on many dates with George Greg or hooked up with him multiple times, whatever you want to call it, and you just admitted to holding hands with him."

"Okay, I'm with Jessie," Mac says. "In that case it means something for sure."

"I don't like you." Jade scowls at Mac.

Mac smirks.

"Okay, fine. It meant something. It meant I wanted some part of my body on his, and we were in a public place and had to go to class and I couldn't exactly get my mouth around his dick outside of the computer labs, now, could I?"

A person passes by our table and gives Jade a disgusted look. She flicks them off. I snort with laughter, but Mac shoots me a mildly horrified look, which only makes me laugh more.

"You get used to her," I say and pat Mac lightly on the arm. "Continue," I say to Jade.

"Okay, thank you. So we're outside the computer labs. We're kissing, he cops a feel, and then he goes inside. Great. I'm about to walk away, but literally right after he walked in—I mean, no more than a minute later—Threesome Anna walks out."

I gasp.

"Threesome Anna?" Mac asks.

"Jade had a threesome with Anna and George Greg a while ago. Halloween."

Mac almost chokes on his water. Jade and I ignore this.

"Did she see you guys?" I ask, eyes widening. Listening to Jade's stories is almost as good as reality TV.

"I don't think so, and if she did see anything she didn't care."

"How do you know?"

"Because...she comes over immediately and kisses me. With George Greg's spit still on my lips, Anna kisses me right on the mouth. She tells me I taste good. I just about die right there."

"I think I'm dying right now," I say, my hand pressed to my chest.

"AND THEN," Jade says, emphasizing every syllable, "Anna asks if I'm going anywhere, and can she walk me? I say sure, I'm going to the theater building. What does she do? She takes my hand and walks me there."

"Oh my god, Jade," I say, putting my hands over my face and sinking back into my chair.

"I know."

Jade and I exchange a meaningful look. Mac catches it.

"Wait...am I missing something?" he asks.

"Jade is obviously starting to catch feelings for both of them."

"Oh, yes, obviously," Mac says, his voice thick with sarcasm.

"I don't have to spell this out for you, do I?" I ask.

"I think you do," Jade says around a mouthful of protein bar. "If not for him, then definitely for me."

"It's a public display of affection. Jade, your displays of affection are generally behind closed doors."

"Sometimes they're in shared spaces. Living rooms, kitchen counters..."

"Oh, Jesus Christ," I say.

"I'm not opposed to public—"

"Jade. Let the poor guy get used to you." I turn back to Mac. "Jade doesn't love stuff like hand-holding, soft kisses, touching that doesn't lead to sex, couple shit," I say.

She makes a face like I've just shoved moldy cheese under her nose.

"That's what I mean. If you do that stuff it's never in public. That is a huge deal. Hence, you have feelings for both of them."

"I don't know..." Jade says, but she thinks about it for a few seconds, her face transforming from disgust to despair.

"Yeah," I say. "That makes this all a bit..."

"Complicated?" Mac offers.

"Complicated," I agree.

"Complicated," Jade groans. "I think you're right, Jessie."

"Music to my ears."

"I felt like I was going to throw up at the idea of getting caught with George Greg in front of her. I *cared* about getting caught."

"Feelings," I say.

"Feelings," Mac says.

"Feelings," Jade groans.

"Will you choose one?" Mac asks, invested now.

"What? Choose! No. I mean, nothing is exclusive yet. I'm just going to keep doing what I'm doing, which is not wrong because I haven't promised exclusivity with anyone, and if Threesome Anna or George Greg were with someone else I wouldn't care."

"Mm-hmm..." I raise my eyebrows at her.

"Okay, I might care a little bit. But it's fine. I'm fine, and everything's fine." Jade finishes her protein bar, and just as dramatically as she plopped down, she grabs all her things and stands. "Ugh, I'm going to go do some yoga. Clear my chi or align my chakras or something. I don't need all this confusing energy in my life."

She sweeps out of the cafe, leaving me and Mac reeling a bit.

"Well, that was…"

"Enlightening?"

"I think my chakras need aligning too," Mac says, and I snort.

We gather our things and throw out the trash on our way out the door.

"Your friend Jade is a riot," Mac says.

"She's wild, but she's also an amazing friend."

"You're lucky to have her, and she's lucky to have you."

Mac's smile is gentle, and I recognize the soft vulnerability in his eyes. Strange how little it takes to really understand a person. All it takes is the simple putting to death of every grudge and judgmental belief you've held onto for years.

Easy peasy lemon squeezy.

"You'll think about Thanksgiving?" Mac asks, his voice uncharacteristically quiet.

I promise that I will, and he walks away, leaving me wishing I'd been brave enough to reach out and hug him.

The truth is, I already know what I want to do. But if I'm not brave enough to hug him, how will I be brave enough to say yes?

CHAPTER THIRTEEN

JESSIE

"You're doing what!" Jade practically yells into my ear.

"I know you heard me."

"A month ago you were ready to ruin Mac's life, and now you're going to his house for Thanksgiving break?"

"For the record, I was not really going to ruin anyone's life. I was just feeling a little bitter."

Jade snorts. "A little."

"But Mac and I are friends now—"

"Friends, my ass. When are you two going to get it on already?"

"Jade! God."

"Oh right, sorry. You would have to actually kiss first to even get to that— Actually, you know what? You probably don't even need to kiss. You two have so much fucking tension you could skip right to the good part. It's been, like, a month of foreplay. Years if you count the banter and rivalry that came before this."

"Jade, oh my god." I stuff my toothbrush into my small bag and roll my eyes.

"Tell me I'm wrong."

"You're...mostly wrong," I say without hesitation.

"Ha! I knew it. You want to jump his bones and you're too chicken-shit to admit it."

"I'm hanging up now," I singsong. I'm smiling, and she knows it.

"Just call me when you finally kiss, bitch."

"Byyyyyye."

I toss my phone onto the bed and rifle through my bag, double-checking I have what I need. It's just two nights, and Mac said there's a guest bed and his parents won't mind at all about having a last-minute guest.

I almost didn't say yes. I lay on my bed last night clutching my phone to my chest, pep-talking myself into telling him I wanted to go. I want to spend time with Mac and listen to the Black Phantom album with him. The idea of having a home-cooked meal with a large family puts me in near tears of happiness. Even if it's not my family. When I did finally text and say yes, I threw my phone across the room.

There's a knock at the door, and I walk over to it, unlocking and opening it to find Mac in the doorway holding a holiday cup from a local coffee shop.

"Good morning," he says with a smile and hands me the cup.

"What's this?"

"Coffee. A little cream and sugar. A road trip necessity."

I step to the side and let him into the suite. He remembered what kind of coffee I like. This simple detail takes the wind out of me, and I take a second to compose myself while Mac sizes up our space.

He swivels his head, taking in Jade's living room decor, the kitchen that's nearly always tidy because I clean when I'm stressed, the piles of blankets everywhere because we're always cold. I leave him there to grab my bag, which Mac promptly takes from me, throwing the strap onto his shoulder.

"Shall we?"

"You don't need to carry my bag." I reach for it, but he takes my hand, gently lowering it to my side.

"I actually do. I was cursed at birth by a witch to be a gentleman. So I have to carry bags for damsels and open doors and all manner of gentlemanly things."

"A gentleman, huh? Your curse seems to have some spotty rules."

"The witch was drunk."

I chuckle and shake my head, locking the door behind us as we leave.

The car ride, although two hours, is too short, and we mostly fill it with Black Phantom songs and speculation about their upcoming music. We find other things to talk about too, because as it turns out, Mac and I enjoy a lot of the same things. By the time we arrived at his house, my cheeks hurt from all the smiling and laughing. But as we pull into the driveway, nerves get the best of me. My palms start to sweat and my stomach roils.

Mac's house is huge. It's exactly the same kind of house I saw in the rich neighborhoods near my home. It's at least two stories, and there are so many windows I can't even begin to count them. It looks like two or three houses attached to each other. There's a three-car garage, and I have no doubt three very expensive cars sit in there. Multiple luxury cars are already in the driveway.

I chew on the inside of my lip. This is too fancy. I pluck at my old T-shirt. Jade told me I was welcome to anything in her closet, but I wanted to be as comfortable as possible. Now I'm wondering if I should have taken her up on her offer.

Mac takes my hand in his for a moment and gives it a squeeze. "It's going to be a little chaotic in there, but you'll be okay. And if you need a break, just signal me, and I'll find us a quiet place."

I nod and take a sharp breath in and out through my nose. We gather our things from the car, Mac grabbing both of our bags and his fresh sourdough loaf. I wish he was still holding my hand to ground me, to steady me. But I steady myself, counting my steps and my breaths.

Mac opens the door to his house and we step into a huge foyer with an enormous glass chandelier hanging from the ceiling. My brain can't decide what to process first: the absolutely heavenly smells coming from the kitchen, the noise from a huge family laughing and yelling over each other to be heard, or the grandiosity of Mac's home. A wide staircase twists up along the wall and to a hallway on the upper level. The carpet on the stairs is so white and plush I want to bury my toes in it, and also to avoid it completely. Has anyone ever stepped on that carpet? The hardwood of the foyer is practically shining it's so clean, and in fact everything is so pristine it doesn't look like anyone lives here.

I check to see if I should remove my shoes, but Mac keeps his on, so I do too. We walk down the short hallway right in front of us, ignoring the two rooms off to the side of the foyer. Framed family photos and artwork line the walls, the only sign so far that this house isn't actually a museum. I try to stop and look at every one of them, but Mac doesn't stop for me, so I don't bother. The hallway leads to the biggest open-concept kitchen/living room I've ever seen in person. I've only seen spaces like this in movies.

The room is definitely full with more than just Mac's brothers and partners. There are people here of all ages—some older couples and a couple of young kids. I wasn't anticipating this many people, and when I look over at Mac to ask why he didn't tell me they'd all be here, it becomes clear he didn't know about them either.

"Mac!" someone yells, and the whole room collectively turns and shouts. People start to step forward and hug Mac, slapping him on the back.

I hang back toward the hallway entrance, my hands clasped in front of me, fingers tight. Awkwardness clings to me like a bad odor. I've made a huge mistake. This is too many people.

My heart is beating too fast, and I have to swallow away the nausea. I dig my fingernails into the back of my hand to ground myself. I'm lightheaded and try to lean against the doorframe as casually as I can.

Maybe I can tell Mac I'm sick and that I need to go home. But we're hours away from school and I could never afford an Uber back. Mac would have to drive me, but we just got here, and there's already food on the table. I can't ask him to leave his family just because I don't want to be here anymore. Tears prick my eyes, my face heats, and the room starts to get really small. My breath picks up, and in just a minute I'm going to puke.

And then Mac turns back around to me. He must realize what's happening because he takes my hand and leads me back out into the foyer without a word to anyone else.

"Hey, what's going on? You okay?" He stays close, a hand on my back, his brow furrowed.

I nod even though I'm not actually okay. I lean into him, resting my forehead against his chest. I wrap my arms around him, and he does the same, rubbing small circles on my back.

"It's just a lot of people. And I..." *I feel like I stick out like a sore thumb. In a bad way.*

"They're going to love you, I swear," he murmurs into my hair. "And we don't even have to talk to everyone. Or anyone."

The nausea subsides and my heart slows. How did he know that was what I needed to hear? I lift my head and meet Mac's eyes. He looks at me the way men in movies look at their love interest. There should be music and dim lighting. Other people should be swooning at us right now. *I'm* swooning. Mac is looking at me the way all girls dream of being looked at. My eyes drift to his lips and back up to his eyes. His eyes do the same, and suddenly Mac's house doesn't feel so big. His chest against mine, I feel his every inhale and exhale. We both lean in.

It's nearly imperceptible, but a loud group laugh from the living room breaks the spell. We both blink a few times, shaking off the moment we just shared.

"Should we sneak past the group and get some alcohol?" Mac asks, and as I nod I recognize the absence of any anxiety.

Mac starts to walk away, but I grab his hand and stop him.

"Thank you," I say, and when he smiles, a thousand tiny fireworks explode inside me.

He wraps his hand around mine, leading me to the living room where a bar cart is set up. It's a fancy bar cart, but it's got more liquor than some actual bars I've been in, and it's all top-shelf. No one is there at the moment, and he stands between me and the people as a buffer.

"What's your poison?" he asks, leaning close, his mouth practically against my ear.

"White wine is fine." I point to the bottle in an ice bucket and Mac pours me a generous glass.

He hands it to me as a woman who looks the right age to be Mac's mother approaches. She and Mac have identical smiles, and her blonde hair is styled back in a chic hair clip. She comes up to Mac's shoulder and has one of those sturdy body types that indicates she gives a great hug. Mac hugs the woman warmly and introduces us.

"Anita," she says and grabs my hand before I can offer it to shake. But the shake feels more like she's warmly holding my hand for a moment before she pulls me in for a hug. I was right. She does give a great hug. It's so motherly and kind it brings tears to my eyes. I blink them away. Anita releases me and looks me dead in the eyes. "I am so glad you're here. You are so welcome."

"Jessie, this is my mom."

"Thank you so much for having me. For letting me crash the dinner at the last minute," I say, genuinely grateful.

"Oh, honey, we love having company. Plus, Mac never brings home girls. You must be—"

"And that's enough of that." Mac grabs my shoulders and steers me away from his mom.

I hear her chuckle behind us as Mac guides me to a corner of the room where we can see everything. He stands behind me, leaning in, his mouth next to my ear.

"That is Rob, my oldest brother, and his wife, Lori." They both look like they just stepped out of a J.Crew ad. This must be the lawyer brother. "That's Michael and his fiancée, Amelia." They're just as refined as Rob and Lori, but in a much more relaxed way. They look like they attend expensive sports games, and I remember this is the brother who played in the NFL and is heading to Antarctica. He points out Noah and his girlfriend Charlotte, and then a small handful of aunts, uncles, and cousins whose names I don't remember.

"I'm going to go say hi to Noah," Mac says. His hand rests gently on my lower back, the pressure of his fingers light. "You can stay here or you can come with me, whatever you're more comfortable with. If you stay I'll come right back."

"I'll come with you," I say. Between Mac and the wine, most of my social anxiety has dissolved now.

We approach Noah, who's picking at a cheeseboard on the island. If I didn't know any better, I'd think Noah and Mac were twins, they look so similar. He's got his arm around a very pretty girl with long blonde hair and he's feeding her a piece of cheese. She looks absolutely smitten.

"Get a room," Mac says.

Noah turns from the girl, his entire face lighting up when he sees his younger brother. "You son of a bitch," he says with a loud laugh and leaves the girl's side to punch Mac's arm and put him into a headlock.

I sidestep out of the way, moving closer to the girl, Charlotte.

"So violent, aren't they?" she says to me.

"I can't even imagine what Anita had to deal with raising all four of them."

She laughs and holds out her hand. "Charlotte."

"Jessie." I take her hand with a smile.

"Oh! Jessie! I've heard so much about you." The smile on her face is genuine. She seems really pleased to be meeting me, but I'm so taken aback by what she said that I can't figure out what to say back. *Heard about me? Why was Mac talking about me?* What could he have been saying?

"And who is this, Mackenzie? Is this your girlfriend?" Noah asks.

Mac steps back to stand next to me. He places his hand on the small of my back again, a reminder just for me that he's here. "No, no, she isn't my girlfriend." But he's looking at me as he says this, and the look is loaded and meaningful. Like maybe he wishes I was.

"Just friends," I say, echoing his sentiment by holding his gaze. The unspoken phrase hangs between us in the air.

Just friends...for now.

"Jessie," I say. Noah's face lights up as he shakes my hand like he recognizes my name. He gives Mac a knowing look, and my stomach turns over.

Mac really has been talking about me.

"So, how's NASA?" Mac asks, and I kind of can't believe I'm in a place where that's a real question and not a sarcastic comment made by a drunk uncle.

"Well, that's where I met this gorgeous human, so you can probably guess." Noah gives his girlfriend a sweet kiss. She smiles at him in a way that displays her love for him, and he returns the look. Their mutual admiration for each other is sweet—and the kind of thing that would have Jade running for the hills.

"How did you get hired there again?" Mac asks.

"Har, har." Noah makes a face.

Mac gives him a small shove.

"All right, everyone," a booming voice calls over the noise. "Let's eat."

"You doing okay?" Mac leans in as people file out of the living room.

I give him a nod and a tight smile, but this time I'm being honest. Meeting some people has relaxed me a little, even if it's just three people. Mac's family seems kind, and they're more welcoming than I could have hoped for.

Everyone helps bring food in from the kitchen, filling the dining room. The table is huge and decorated to the nines with beautiful china dishes and a napkin swan at every place. A deep red tablecloth and a gorgeous, seasonally appropriate centerpiece inspire ooohs and ahhhs from every guest. Roast turkey, creamy mashed potatoes, fresh bread, savory mac and cheese, and a thousand other smells compete for attention—it's hard to decide what I'm looking forward to eating the most.

Mac leads me to a chair near his brothers and their partners, and we all sit. I'm between Mac and Charlotte, probably the person next closest to me in age, and also the only other woman here without a ring on her finger.

Food is passed and plates and wineglasses are filled and then emptied. The whole affair stretches on for hours, with rounds of food and refilled glasses. Pie is distributed and consumed, and soon everyone is leaning back in their chairs, bellies bursting. The noise levels have died down, and mostly people are just talking to one other person.

Mac taps my arm to get my attention. "Let's go get a drink."

I don't really want another drink, but I wouldn't mind a moment away from this table full of people.

Mac leads me back into the living room, now quiet and empty. I insist that I'm okay, and he pours himself a small finger of bourbon and knocks it back. While he pours himself another, I take in the living room.

I thought it might be interesting to see where Mac is from. It's no secret he comes from generational wealth. A building on campus is named after his family, he drives a Range Rover that isn't any older than two years, and Jade has, more than once, identified all the high-end brands he wears. I knew Mac's home would be nice, but this is beyond what I came up with in my head. It looks like the spread of a magazine. Effortless, and yet I know someone—Anita or some paid professional—probably spent more than a few hours making this room look the way it does. And it's been decorated for Christmas. The tree is huge and stunning, all the ornaments on theme and matching the rest of the Christmas decor. It all looks so expensive, and I can't believe people live this way. The couch looks like it costs as much as a year of college tuition alone, but the cost of everything in this room combined is unimaginable. The TV, the random decor pieces, the rug under our feet—it's all flashing neon dollar signs. I wonder what it would be like to not have to think about money except to say "However will I spend all it?"

I swallow the bitter taste at the back of my throat and make a conscious effort to be grateful for today. I touch my fingertips to Mac's forearm. "Thank you. I know I said that already, and I am grateful for earlier, but I wanted to thank you for all of this. It's the best Thanksgiving I've had since coming to college. I normally spend them alone, eating mediocre turkey in my dorm. And this is...the opposite of that."

"I am really glad you're here," he says. He draws me into a hug, wrapping one arm around me.

I slide an arm around him and look up at him. "Me too," I say, and I almost laugh, because two months ago I would never have believed someone if they'd said I'd be here in this exact scenario today.

"God, get a room." Noah's voice comes from the doorway. "And quit hogging the drinks."

Mac releases me and finishes his drink, setting it on the cart. "Should I grab my mom? We can show you to your room."

I nod and follow Mac where he leads.

"OH NO," Anita says, one hand over her mouth. "Mac, I didn't realize you'd be bringing a friend and I promised all the guest spaces to your cousins and aunts and uncles."

"I can sleep on a couch," I say, not fully ready to process what the alternative might be.

"Don't be ridiculous. If anyone is sleeping on a couch, it's me," Mac says.

"Yo, those couches are terrible to sleep on." Michael walks by and pats Mac on the back. "Have fun with that."

She just gives him an apologetic look. "I wouldn't have committed to letting everyone stay if I'd known. I'm so sorry."

"Mom, don't worry about it. I should have called." He gives her a hug, and she mumbles something about linens and disappears.

"Let's go get you settled," Mac says with a smile on his face.

"I'm really sorry," I say to Mac, but he dismisses me with a wave of his hand. He ushers me up the stairs, but this time I slow and look at every picture lining the wall. It's almost hard to tell which kid is which —all the brothers look vaguely similar. But Mac's smile stands out in all the photos.

"You were a cute kid," I say, pointing to a photo of him in elementary school.

"I'm still cute."

"That's true," I say with a smile. I take the steps one at a time, pausing to look at the photos. Mac with a trophy from a spelling bee. Mac and his brothers at the Grand Canyon. Proms and graduations for each of the boys. A family photo at Rob's wedding. It's a whole glimpse into Mac's life that I didn't know I wanted. A lump forms in my throat, and I hustle up the rest of the stairs. He walks down a long hallway and leads me to what I assume is his bedroom.

I assumed right.

Mac opens the door and I step in cautiously, like this is sacred space. The room is a bit sparse, and somehow this surprises me. I didn't really expect Mac to be a minimalist. He walks confidently to one corner of the room, illuminating the dark space with a lamp. It casts a soft glow over the navy-blue walls, making the space feel even more intimate.

Bookcases span an entire wall of the room, covered in more books than I've ever seen in one bedroom. It doesn't surprise me at all. In fact, it delights me. I resist the urge to march right over to them and look at every single book. I take in the rest of the room instead. There's a large window that takes up nearly the whole wall directly across from the door, framed by long, flowy curtains. A small desk in front of the window with just a solitary lamp on it is the last piece of evidence that Mac is every bit the schoolboy nerd I'm learning he is.

The room is twice the size of any room I've ever lived in, and the centerpiece is the huge king-size bed. Mac has slept there. Mac has slept there many times. His half-naked body tangled up in sheets flashes through my mind, and the heat in my cheeks spreads through my whole body.

Mac grabs my overnight bag from my hand and sets it on the chair in front of the desk. "So. This is it. The sheets are fresh, I'm sure. If you don't like the pillows, we have more."

"Thanks," I murmur. I'm tempted to wander the room and touch everything as if I could soak in everything I don't know about Mac through osmosis, but I feel frozen to the spot, staring at the bed.

"Well, let me know if you need anything." Mac walks across the room to leave, but I grab his wrist as he passes me.

He pauses, standing beside me, waiting for me to speak, but my throat is dry.

"Stay," I say.

"Stay?"

In my peripheral, I can see Mac looking at me, probably giving me a totally baffled stare, but I can't seem to bring myself to look him in the eye.

"The bed. It seems big enough for both of us. It's silly for you to try to sleep on an uncomfortable couch. I wouldn't sleep if I knew you were uncomfortable. So stay." I release my grip on him, my hand slipping over his.

As my fingers graze his, he flexes his hand, trapping my fingers between his. Only a few of our fingers are touching, but I feel it everywhere.

"Are you sure?" he asks, his voice a near whisper.

It's bold, and if I'd thought about it before I said it I would have talked myself out of it. But we're here now, and the air between us is so tense it's hard to breathe.

"Yes."

The silence between us is so loud, it aches in my ears. My shirt moves with the hammering of my heart. He glides a thumb over the back of my hand.

"I'm going to go say good night to my family, if you wanted to, um," —he clears his throat—"change and such."

He doesn't move for what feels like ten minutes but must only be ten seconds, and when he does, slipping out of the room, the weight of his absence clings to me. His room feels twice as large, and so empty I almost crawl into the bed to hide under the covers until he comes back. But I force myself to change into pajamas, brush my teeth, and braid my hair. When I do crawl into the bed, I push away all the voices screaming in my head about how weird this is. His sheets are soft, and as I settle, the laundry detergent scent surrounding me, it's like being completely engulfed by Mac's scent.

I dig my book out of my bag and try to settle in to read, but it's so distracting being in here, surrounded by Mac. It isn't just his smell; his whole personality is stamped in this room. And when he slips back inside and steps into his bathroom to change, I'm so distracted I can't focus on the words on the page.

All I can think is that any minute now Mac and I are going to be sharing a bed. And two months ago, all this would have been entirely unthinkable. But it isn't just happening—it was my suggestion. Jade is going to implode. She's also going to assume something happened between us.

Which it definitely, one hundred percent, will not.

Mac walks out of the bathroom in a T-shirt and pajama bottoms. I burn a hole through the pages of my book to keep from staring at him, but my gaze slips and the way his T-shirt hugs his body and his pants hang loose on his hips makes me squeeze my legs together.

Fuck, he is so good-looking.

The bed doesn't even shift when he climbs in, and now he's so close I could reach out and touch him. I should get an Olympic medal for resisting the urge to do so.

Does he want me this bad too?

I snap my book shut, turn off the light beside my bed, and move onto my side away from him. It does nothing for my awareness of his proximity, but I shut my eyes and tell myself if I can't see him, he's not there.

He turns off his light, and I feel him settle down for the night. Is he facing me? Is he clenching his fists trying not to touch me the way I am? Is he thinking about all the things we could be doing right now? Because I am. I can't stop thinking about how easy it would be to roll over and find him in the dark with my hands, and then my mouth. To kiss him until neither of us can breathe and then touch every inch of him, clothes not required.

Oh my god, Jessie. Go to sleep. Stop it.

I force all these thoughts out of my mind. This is not the time or place. I tell myself if I can count to one thousand, I can reach out and touch him.

I don't even make it to seventy-five.

CHAPTER FOURTEEN

MAC

I'm in my bed at home and I'm not alone. It only takes half a second for my brain to register the spill of dark hair on the pillow beside me and who it belongs to and the reason why.

I don't know how I could have forgotten she was here, especially as I've woken up with a...situation.

Some of this might have to do with the fact that somehow during the night she found her way into my arms, her back against my chest, my arm slung across her side, and some of it might have to do with the very specific sex dream I had about her.

It started out innocently enough. We were on a vacation in the summer at my parents' beach house, but it was just us. We were on the beach, which is private given the location of the house, and we'd just gone for a swim in the ocean. We were laying in the sand, still wet from the swim, and I rolled over onto my side and we started to kiss. In my dream she was just wearing a bikini, and when I started to kiss her I tasted salt and the sweetness of her skin. She tasted the same as she did at the Halloween party, and in my dream I kissed the same spot on her neck as I did that night. In my dream she arched under me, a small moan escaping her lips, encouraging me to keep going. So I did. I explored her whole body with my mouth, tasting every inch of her, eventually focusing on the part of her that brought her the greatest pleasure, until she finished in the most fantastic way. The noises she made, the divots in the sand where her hands and feet were clutching and clawing at the ground, the sand in my hair from her hands—it was the sexiest dream I've ever had, and when I woke up, seconds after my name was on her lips, it took me a minute to reorient myself to my bedroom.

And the fact that the girl I just dreamed about was lying right up against me.

So of course I have a...situation.

I shift my hips back, trying to create space between us. Having her this close is intoxicating, but I don't think she knows we're cuddling, and I don't want her to wake up and freak out.

Since yesterday, having her in my house with my family has been better than I imagined it would be. She fits right in, everyone loves her, and even with a spot of anxiety she never tried to just run away. I'm not like that. When I'm somewhere I don't want to be I just leave. If my options are fight, fawn, or flight, I am flight one hundred percent of the time. But Jessie does hard things way more often, and with way more grace than I do.

I carefully lift my arm, moving ever so slowly, but she makes a grunting noise and rolls over to face me, burying her face in my neck. It solves the issue with my...situation given that her hips are nowhere near mine and my one arm isn't around her anymore, but my other arm is still trapped under her head and she's using it as a pillow. Her lips are practically on my collarbone, and it's not making my...situation any better.

She looks so relaxed, so beautiful. I push back a strand of her hair, tucking it behind her ear. She moves her head at the touch, and I freeze.

I don't want to wake her, but I'm starting to feel awkward just lying here stock-still. I should try to sneak out. The urge to cuddle her for real is so overwhelming, and if I don't leave soon I might just lay here and let myself hold her.

I would never without her full consent, but I do think she's feeling all the same things I am. I see the way she looks at me. I haven't missed the way we've casually added physical touch to our dynamic, and it isn't just me making the moves. Jessie is feeling this, and it makes me really excited for the listening party tonight.

I wait until her breathing is fully even and deep and slowly start to pull my arm out from under her, but she stirs, so I freeze again. When she's still I start again, inch by inch, moving my arm so as not to disturb her. But suddenly she jolts, inhaling deeply and waking with a start. I snatch my arm out and quickly put it under my own head, resting on it on my pillow very cool and casual-like.

Jessie blinks until she's oriented, and when she realizes how much of her head is on my pillow she scoots back, her eyes closing again, like maybe she didn't mean to wake up and wants to go back to sleep.

"Good morning," she says, her voice adorably crackled with sleep.

"Hi."

"It's Black Phantom album day," she says with a lazy smile. Her eyes blink open, but she squints, the light from the window too much for her tired eyes.

"I know," I say, my own face stretched into a smile. She's so cute I can barely stand it. "I have something special planned for our listening party."

She pulls the covers up to her chin, snuggling in and closing her eyes again. She probably has no idea how beautiful she looks right now. My fingers ache to touch her again. My arms ache to hold her.

"Will there be cake?" she asks, her words slow and languid.

"No cake."

"Then by definition it's not a party."

"Has to be cake to be a party?"

"Mm-hmm. Has to."

"All right. Well, then it's actually a listening meeting."

"Perfect. So what's the plan for today?" she asks.

"Well, the album party—sorry, meeting plans—are later tonight, so I thought we'd just hang out at the house all day and eat leftovers. Most of my family will still be here, so we can hang out with them, watch football. I don't know if anyone is going to brave the crowds for any shopping, but if you wanted to tag along to that."

"I'm okay with just hanging out here. I never do that."

"What? Relax?"

She nods.

"All work and no play," I say.

"That's me." Her eyes squint with her smile, and my heart melts like wax over my rib cage. That smile is my undoing.

I offer to change and get ready in a guest bathroom and scurry out of the room before she can protest. And before she can notice my...situation, which disappears quickly enough once I'm out of the bedroom.

Jessie meets me at the top of the stairs and we walk down together, joining everyone for coffee and breakfast, which is practically another feast.

"Is this what breakfast is always like at your house?" Jessie whispers to me as we stand at the coffee pot.

"Nah, Mom went all out for the family. Usually it's a fight-for-your-cereal kind of breakfast place."

She looks a little surprised but nods.

"What was breakfast like at your house?" I ask.

"Um…" Jessie darts her eyes around and shrugs. "I'm not much of a breakfast person, so I usually just had, like, some toast." She stirs some cream into her coffee, staring intently at the cup, and I eye her plate piled high with a little bit of everything—fruit, a Danish, French toast bake, a hard-boiled egg, bacon, and toast. It's a generous plate for someone who "isn't a breakfast person," but I bite my tongue.

After we eat, I volunteer to do the dishes, if for no other reason than just a bit of alone time, but it doesn't last long, as Charlotte joins me. She picks up a kitchen towel and starts to dry some of the larger dishes that were air-drying on the counter.

"So," she starts, her voice low enough that no one outside the kitchen can hear her, "I assume this is the Halloween party girl."

"Yep," I say, knowing exactly where this conversation is heading.

"And I'm assuming that if she's here it means you did the right thing and told her who you were, and she's here with full and complete knowledge about what passed between you?"

When she says it like that it sounds kind of bad.

"She does not know," I admit.

Charlotte cocks her head to the side and gives me a face that screams, "What the hell?"

"It's not like I didn't try! But…it just…I can't. I can't tell her now. It's way too late."

How do I explain that I've decided never to tell her? That I'm sure I'll lose her if I do and I'm not willing to risk it? I saw how hurt she was after she found out her mom lied to her. If I'd told her right there I would have been stacking hurt. And even now, telling her…I can't. I don't want to be that person in her life. But I don't know how to tell Charlotte all this and make her understand.

"I know I'm butting in where I haven't been asked to, but I have to tell you, Mac. I don't see this ending well."

Her words make me squirm inside. I don't really want to think about that.

Dishes done, Charlotte gives me a meaningful glare and leaves the kitchen. I scowl at her when she leaves and then put the conversation out of my mind. She doesn't understand. If she were in my shoes she would have done the same thing.

I join the group in the living room, where everyone is watching the pre-game football coverage. I take a seat on the arm of the chair Jessie is on, not sure how long I want to linger. Jessie's having no trouble integrating with everyone. She fits in seamlessly with my family, but she also seemed okay yesterday until she wasn't. I try to read her face, but when she looks up at me, the smile she gives is authentic. Maybe she is okay. I rest my hand lightly on her back, just to let her know I'm here and I'll be damned if I sit this close to her without touching her. She leans against the arm of the chair, her shoulder pressing against my leg. We sit like this, just barely touching, until my butt goes numb from sitting weirdly and I wander back into the kitchen to see if my mom wants some help with lunch.

"Oh, I'm just prepping the leftovers. You go watch the games."

"I don't mind," I say. "Plus, the company is good."

My mom nudges me, blushing. She hands me the Tupperware of deviled eggs and a deviled egg plate. I wash my hands and start to transfer the eggs from the Tupperware to the dish.

"Jessie doing okay? Does she need anything?" my mom asks quietly. She's arranging shredded turkey over a tray of slider buns.

"Yeah, she's okay."

"She's quite pretty."

"She is," I say, unable to stop the smile from spreading over my face.

"Do you like her?" she asks.

I don't answer, just give my mom a look that says, "Do you even have to ask?"

"I thought so. She likes you too. You're cute together."

"We're not together," I say, almost defensively. Not because I don't want to be, but because I don't want my mom saying anything to Jessie that might make her uncomfortable.

"What else is new?" my mom asks as she spoons cranberry sauce onto each of the turkey sliders.

"Not much. I—"

"How are your grades, Mackenzie?" my dad asks from behind me, appearing in the kitchen like a magician. He opens the fridge and pulls out a bottle of beer, using one of the fridge magnets to pop it open. He takes a swig and sets it on the counter, not offering to help, just watching as Mom and I prep food.

"My grades are fine."

"Just fine?" my dad asks, unimpressed.

I give him a firm nod and he takes another swig as Mom and I prep in near silence. I was going to wait to say anything until I'd won, but standing there like he is, waiting for me to tell him some amazing accomplishment, it sort of comes out before I have a chance to think about it.

"Did I tell you about the scholarship I'm going for?"

I glance over, but Jessie doesn't seem to have heard me. I know it's kind of a sensitive subject for us, but I do want to tell my parents. They're the reason I'm applying for it.

"You didn't. What is it?" my mom prompts me before my dad can butt in.

"The Walden Senior Scholarship. The same one Rob and Michael got."

I feel almost skeezy for saying it like that, for bragging about something I haven't even won for the merest ounce of recognition from my dad.

I finish with the deviled eggs and start cutting sliced cheese into smaller slices for the turkey sandwiches with the knife and cutting board my mom set next to me. My mom hands me the tray of sliders. I lay each cut piece of the turkey on the bread and close up each sandwich.

"Yep. I thought you should go for it. Glad to hear you've applied," my dad says. He nods approvingly, and it's the closest thing to praise he's given me since I played soccer. I'm still not sure he's forgiven me for quitting.

I thought this moment would feel better. That his praise would lift my spirits, but it does nothing for me.

"Wouldn't that be special?" my mom says. "Four valedictorians in the house. Wow."

"I've got some stiff competition. Jessie applied too," I say, nodding at Jessie.

"No Baldwin boy has lost the scholarship, and I don't expect this will be any different," Dad says like that's the final word on the topic. It has the desired effect: neither my mom nor I say anything else about it.

"Everything else okay at school?" Mom asks, taking the tray of sandwiches away to place them in the oven. She hands me a plate and directs me to grab the blocks of cheese and boxes of crackers to set up a charcuterie for everyone.

I swallow hard. My mom has given me an opening to say something I've been hoping to bring up but just haven't had the courage to do so.

"Yeah, actually. I was looking ahead a little and I'll have some space in my schedule next year. I thought I'd register for an acting class. Just the 101 class. I've done all my foundational classes and just have a couple classes left for my major."

"No," my dad cuts in.

I don't even have to look to know what's painted on his face. I bite back a smart-ass remark and close my eyes to keep them from rolling.

"I have the space in my schedule if I don't take—"

"Take a class for your degree, or you take a business class—"

"I've already taken—"

"Something respectable—"

"Theater is respect—"

"Not some sissy—"

"Hi, sorry." Jessie's voice cuts through the yelling. "I was just hoping to get a little extra coffee." She holds up her mug and makes herself small as she winds her way around us to the coffee pot, half-full on the warmer.

No one says a word while she prepares her coffee. I bounce between watching Jessie, my mom, and my dad. Jessie is a statue in the middle of our family storm, my mother an innocent bystander, and my father the hurricane. No one is comfortable right now. Dad's words linger in the air, weighing on all of us.

My mom makes herself busy with lunch, and I tap my fingers against the counter. My dad sips at his beer and stalks out of the kitchen, back into the living room. My shoulders instinctively relax.

I turn back to my cheeseboard, letting the interaction roll off my back. I got the scholarship out there, I mentioned the class—it's a success by all standards. And I didn't miss the way my mom's eyes lit up when I mentioned the theater class. Even with Dad's negativity, my mother is the brightest light.

"Can I help?" Jessie asks, appearing at my side. Her sweet smile dissolves any remaining tension in me.

"Sure." I slide over the block of cheese and knife to her, grabbing a few bags of veggies from the fridge and starting to arrange them on the tray.

"So, a theater class, huh?" Her voice is low so no one else can hear.

I guess everyone heard everything then.

"You got sick of football?" I ask, nodding to the living room where she was sitting with my brothers and their partners.

"You're avoiding."

I am. I barely had the courage to mention the theater class to my dad, and now, faced with talking about it with Jessie, I don't feel as brave as I did. Not after getting knocked down a few pegs.

"Yeah, I don't know. It seems fun."

"You'd be really good."

I let her words hang in the air between us, hoping they'll sink into my skin the same way my father's words do.

"Can't you take one and not tell them?" Jessie asks, darting her eyes around to see if anyone might be trying to listen in.

"Are you suggesting I break rules, Matthews?"

She smirks, looking up at me through her lashes. It sends a rush of blood to a very inappropriate place given I'm within ten feet of most of my family.

"That's not very like you," I say.

"You're a bad influence."

She nudges me with her elbow, and I nudge her back. She does it again, just a little bit harder, and I do the same, but my nudge is a little too hard and I knock her off-balance. I reach out on instinct and grab her, steadying her.

She narrows her eyes at me, but she's also got a smile that makes me feel like a million bucks. "We both agree that was you and not just me being a klutz," she says, poking my chest.

"You can have this one."

I wink at her, and she bites her bottom lip. I reluctantly release her now that she's steady on her feet, but neither of us moves until someone clears their throat behind us, making us both snap our attention back to our tasks, Jessie on the cheese and crackers; me on the veggies.

My mom squeezes between us, reaching for a drawer we're both standing in front of. She gets what she needs, not looking at either of us.

When we take our place at the counter again we exchange smiles and sideways glances.

I can't wait for the album listen tonight.

CHAPTER FIFTEEN

JESSIE

After we've watched all the sports and had all the leftovers, Mac starts to gather warm layers for us both. He instructs me to stay inside while he prepares the truck, so I wait in the kitchen with Amelia.

"I've never seen Mac like this."

"Like what?" I ask.

"Like, so smitten."

I tug at the neckline of my shirt, averting my eyes.

"I know you guys said you were just friends, but there is clearly something between you two," she says, eyes narrowed, eyebrows raised, awaiting confirmation.

But I don't have to say anything: she reads me like a book. She's been reading me since I walked in the door twenty-four hours ago.

Amelia is giddy. "Oh, Jessie, don't ever play poker. Your face tells me everything. The way you look at him... God, I hope that's how I look at Michael. And don't even get me started on how he looks at you, because frankly, I could drown in looks like that. Haven't you noticed?"

Of course I've noticed the way Mac looks at me, but I guess I didn't notice when it changed from a look full of nothing to a look full of something.

"Ready to go?" Mac leans through the doorway of the front hallway into the living room. He's dressed warmly in a beanie, puff jacket, gloves, jeans, and boots. He's so handsome I have to clench my fists to keep from reaching out to touch him. Inside me, a marching band has started playing their loudest, most rowdy number, cymbals, drums, trumpets, and trombones all blasting off inside. It's an absolute riot in every corner of my body, heart, and mind.

"Ready?" he asks again.

Amelia gives my arm a gentle squeeze, and I follow Mac out to the driveway.

"Whose truck is this?" I ask as I climb in.

"Michael's."

"Where to?" I buckle up.

"It's a surprise." He gives me a devilish grin and a wink and starts the truck.

"Even if you told me the exact place, it would be a surprise. I have no idea where I am."

"Perfect."

"Is it perfect because you're actually going to murder me?"

"Yep. Hope you've lived a good life."

"I had a few things left that I hoped to accomplish. Would you be willing to give me a few more years? I'd go without a fight if we can negotiate this out."

"You convinced me. Should we revisit in five years?"

I suck in air through my teeth. "Gosh, I'm actually suuuuuper busy in five years. Can we make it eight?"

"That seems reasonable. Let me just throw that on my Google calendar."

My cheeks are already aching from smiling. The rest of the car ride is exactly like this, and after thirty minutes, when Mac turns into a campground, my stomach hurts from laughter.

He parks at the camp office and leaves his truck running for me. I text Jade furiously.

> At a campground with Mac for the album listen.

> We shared a bed last night.

> WHAT. WHAT. WHAT. WAHT.

> Yeah all the guest rooms were taken.

> HOT

> It kinda was?

> Anyway, this campground seems romantic.

> Or creepy. Did you consider murder?

> Lol yes

> And you definitely ruled it out?

> I guess it's never really off the table

> Statistically speaking, your partner is most likely to murder you.

> Yeah well he's not my partner.

> Yet.

MAC CLIMBS BACK into the truck and I click my phone off. It vibrates a few more times with messages from Jade, but I ignore them. I'll get back to her later. The rest of the night is just for me and Mac.

It only takes us a minute to drive to the campsite. It's empty, though I half-expected there to be a whole setup. The closest pole light is a few spots away, so our spot is pitch-black, and when he turns off the headlights of the truck it takes my eyes a few seconds to adjust.

The moon is just a sliver tonight, barely lighting up the night. No stars shine quite brightly enough for me to see anything but the outline of some trees and darkness.

Mac turns on his phone flashlight, illuminating the car.

"Wait here," he says, excitement heavy in his voice. His back doors open and close as he transfers the things in his back seat to the bed of the truck. The vehicle shakes with his movements, and I try to twist around to see what he's doing, but it's too dark, so I just wait.

The marching band inside me has dulled to just a solo trumpet, and I jiggle my leg to get out some of the energy, fiddling with the end of my braid. I know I have no reason to be nervous, but something about tonight feels different. There's an anticipation about the evening, and it isn't just because of the music.

Mac opens the door.

"Okay, come on out," he says like a kid eager to get started playing his favorite game. He helps me out of the truck, using his phone flashlight to light the ground for me. Then he leads me around the truck to stop at the tailgate. He holds his hands out as if to say, "Ta-da!"

Four small electric lanterns are placed at each of the four corners of the truck bed, illuminating an air mattress covered in blankets and pillows. It's the coziest thing I've ever seen. It looks like a date idea off a Pinterest board, and it's all for me.

Tears spring to my eyes.

"Okay, so I've got a couple heated blankets up here so we don't freeze. My Bluetooth speaker will be set up momentarily. I've also got warm beverages." He holds up two thermoses. "Alcoholic and non, whatever suits your fancy."

He holds out a hand and helps me climb into the bed, then comes up after me. We both sit, and the warmth of the electric blanket hits me right away, sending chills up my legs and back.

The romance of all this, the thoughtfulness, the level of detail, tells me more than any words Mac could ever say about how he feels about me. He wouldn't have set this all up unless he liked me. My love language is thoughtful details, and everything about this setup—the lanterns, the drinks, the campsite he probably had to book in advance—is a level of thoughtfulness I had no idea Mac was capable of.

"What?" Mac asks, sounding worried. He lays a hand on my arm.

"What?" I ask, confused.

"Your expression, your face. Is something wrong?"

"No, it's...it's perfect. No one has ever done anything like this for me. It's really— Thank you, Mac."

His face is only partially lit by the lanterns, but even in the dim light I can see his smile, the way he beams at my words. The urge to lean over and kiss him has never been so strong, but I resist. For now.

"Did you say you had alcoholic beverages?" I ask.

Mac offers me a thermos. "Hot chocolate and Baileys."

Steam rises from the thermos as I open it. The drink warms me from the inside even with the smallest of sips. I hold the thermos close to my face, enjoying the rich, chocolatey smell and the way it defrosts my nose, which is already cold.

"Is this how you always do album releases?" I ask.

"Not initially. I usually listen alone on the floor of my bedroom, but this one time a couple years ago I was at the lake house when their album dropped. I ended up going out to this spot in the woods where there were no lights, no people. It was just me and a blanket and some headphones and the frogs and rabbits and crickets. I lay there for hours listening to that album."

"Which one was it?"

"*The Sky Will Love You.*"

"That's a good one," I say.

"It's still one of my favorite albums because to this day, every time I listen to it, I'm back by the lake, looking up at the night sky, watching shooting stars."

For me *The Sky Will Love You* is sunscreen and French fries.

I listened to that album nonstop the summer it came out. I was working at the diner with my mom, at one of her jobs, and every day I'd listen to it on the way to work and the way home, as I was falling asleep at night, and during my downtime.

"That sounds amazing," I say.

"It was."

A month ago I would have felt jealousy or bitterness at his lake house memories versus my diner memories, but all I feel is a nostalgia for that time in my life when I was relatively unburdened. I was helping pay for things around the house, but it was my only responsibility.

Mac and I both lie down. He props himself up on his side, and I follow his lead, facing him. He reaches across the small space between us and takes my hand in his, closing his fingers around mine. We lie mere inches from each other, our breath puffs between us, two clouds of white mingling and disappearing, growing smaller and larger with each breath we take.

"I promised myself that one day I'd share that experience with someone. I'm glad it's you," he says.

My heart expands like one of those toy dinosaurs you put in water and watch as they grow. There are so many things I want to say back, and none of them feel like the right thing, so I say nothing and just give his hand a light squeeze.

Mac grabs his phone, releasing my hand, scrolling and tapping until the music starts. He turns the music up just enough that it drowns out the bugs and rustles of nature, until it's just the sound of Black Phantom and our breathing.

The first notes are magical; they travel directly to the quietest corners of my soul. I thought tonight couldn't get any better, and I have never been so glad to be wrong.

"It's beautiful," I say.

"Yes, it is," Mac says, but he's staring right at me, so intently I don't think he means the album.

There's a riot in my stomach. It feels a little bit like I might throw up, and also like I might cry or maybe scream. I pull the blanket up to my chin, burying myself in it to try to control the uncontrollable reaction I'm having to this man.

"Are you cold?"

He's misinterpreted my blanket adjustment, but I don't know how to explain what just happened inside me, so I don't.

"A little."

"C'mere." He tilts his head, inviting me to move closer.

I do exactly that. I scoot over into his space and his arm comes around me, tucking me in close to him. I rest my head in the spot between his shoulder and his chest. The warmth of his body seeps into mine, and in no time at all I'm actually warm. I tuck an arm between us and rest the other on his chest. He pulls the blanket up so it's almost at my chin and takes my hand in his. Mac touches his lips against my forehead in a light kiss.

Between Mac and the music, I lose myself completely to the moment. Every new note, every lyric, feels like a surprise; a present opened on Christmas morning. Before now I didn't believe in magic, but it's all around me here. I can taste it. It's a tangible, living thing, and the way it moves through me makes it so hard to resist the urge to stand up and dance.

I am awestruck by this moment, by the way happiness fills and flows out of me. If I've ever experienced joy like it, it hasn't branded me the way this moment will. When I die they'll cut me open and find bits of stardust from tonight's sky scattered through my lungs. Today's date will be stamped on my bones, Mac's initials etched into my heart. When my soul separates from my body, this album will play, as if by listening now I'm trapping it inside me, only to be released upon my parting from this world.

Between songs, Mac and I give our honest reactions, and he seems to love the album as much as I do, which only makes me love it more. Each time, I pick up my head, propping myself up enough to easily converse. But before each new song, I nestle my head back into the warm spot on Mac's chest, relaxing into the moment and letting the magic of it all sweep me away.

MAC

If there's anything better than listening to my favorite band and cuddling with Jessie under the stars, I don't think I want to know what it is. I feel like I've peaked. The way her warmth and the heat of the blanket mingle, creating a cocoon I never want to leave. Her head fits so perfectly against my chest, her body molding against mine.

And I still cannot fully relax. I've been feeling off since this morning. Between talking with my parents about the scholarship, Jessie's breakfast comments, and the things she's said in the past about work and school, I've got an itch in my brain. We've made it through the first two songs of the album, and I'd hoped it would disappear by now, because it feels like the wrong time to ask. But if I don't do it now...

"Hey, Jessie?"

"Hmm?"

"I know this is random, but I'm going to ask anyway. Why are you going for the Walden Senior Scholarship?"

She doesn't say anything immediately, but she does shift a bit in my arms. She's quiet, and I'm tempted to tell her.

"Actually, I—um...I'm at school on a full scholarship, but it will only be a partial next year. They're canceling the full scholarship program, so it's not just me. Everyone on a full ride is going to half tuition, but I..." She pauses, clearing her throat as if the words were stuck there. "I need the money. I can't finish—" Her voice wavers.

I wait for her to finish her sentence, but the rest of the thought never comes. I know how it ends anyway. For a second I stop hearing the music, the wind in the trees. There's just a faint buzzing and my blood rushing through my ears.

She tenses as she waits for me to respond, and I know every second that ticks by is probably making her feel more awkward, but I can't seem to find the right words to say. Do I thank her for telling me? Do I tell her how much the school sucks? That I don't want to go to school next year if she's not there? That just thinking about it now is making me feel a little sick?

"Fuck, Jessie."

It's the only thing that even closely captures everything I'm thinking. And it doesn't suffice. She's trusted me a lot by telling me this, and my words are way too lame to reflect my gratitude for that trust. I hold her a little tighter and press my lips to her forehead. What I wouldn't give to kiss her right now; to honor her vulnerability with affection.

"I'm sorry. I didn't realize..." I start, but I'm not sure where I'm going with that sentence.

"Why are you apologizing?" she asks. She shifts back, looking up at me. Her brow is furrowed, her mouth pinched in confusion.

"I don't know," I say honestly. "I'm sorry the school sucks. I'm sorry you're in the situation you're in."

I want to apologize for applying to the scholarship, but it feels like privilege guilt, not a thing I'm actually sorry for. I don't think she'd like that.

"If you're feeling guilty because of the difference in our financial situations, don't," she says, reading my mind.

I swallow hard, again not sure what to say. I lack the grace to talk about finances with my peers. Jessie is being braver than I know how to be, and I'm trying to follow her lead.

"It isn't anyone's fault that we grew up the way we did. It's the hand we were dealt, and there's no use feeling guilty or lucky," she says.

"Were you always this wise?"

"No." She chuckles. "And I didn't always feel this way."

She pauses for long enough that I wonder if maybe we've reached the end of the conversation. Should I change the subject?

Jessie clears her throat. "Can I confess something to you?" she asks, but her voice is small.

"Always."

"Do you remember the D.C. ambassador program? From our freshman year."

"Of course. You got second place, right? But you didn't go..." I say, realization dawning on me.

"I couldn't afford it without the scholarship. Which you—"

"I won. Right." If I could crawl into a cave and hide for eternity, I would. I have never felt so much shame in my life. I could have afforded that trip without the scholarship. But my guilt is short-lived because the look on my dad's face when I told him I won pops into my mind. Winning that scholarship won me the respect of my dad. It was right on the heels of me announcing I wouldn't be playing soccer anymore, and I swear I thought he'd never talk to me again. But then I won the ambassador program and he was so proud.

But the pride was short-lived because I had to miss one of my last soccer games for the trip, and he wasn't happy about that.

Jessie props herself up on an elbow, laying her hand on my chest, directly over my heart. I cover her hand with my own.

"I resented you for a long time for that. But I realized not too long ago what a waste of energy that was. It's taken getting to know you to see that you didn't do it on purpose. You didn't know my situation, and even if you did I wouldn't have wanted you to sacrifice something you deserved to win just for me. Just because of my financial situation. I don't want your pity."

"No pity, I promise."

"I..." She pauses for a long time. Long enough that I'm not sure she'll finish the thought. As best I can in the dark light, I watch a whole scene of emotions break out over her face. There's something she wants to say, and she's deciding if she's going to say it or not. "I like you, Mac. I don't care how much money you have. And I don't want you to care either."

"I don't. You could have a penny to your name or be rich enough to send a dick-shaped rocket to the moon and I'd still like you."

A burst of laughter breaks out of Jessie. It echoes into the night, and when the sound bounces back to us I absorb it right into my bones. What I wouldn't give to swim in that sound, to hear it every day and let it be the soundtrack to my life. Her laugh moves her entire body, and she rests her forehead against my chest, convulsing with laughs still. I smile, fully satisfied. If I didn't make anyone but Jessie laugh for the rest of my life, I would still be fully satisfied.

She picks her head back up, her eyes meeting mine, and the music swells over the speakers. The air shifts, and I can't help it—my eyes drift to her lips.

She likes me. She said it, and she knows I like her too. My heart feels three sizes too big for my chest and I'm aching to kiss her, to feel the thing we felt at that Halloween party.

She leans in, and I shove away the guilt of what I'm keeping from her. I'm not going to let that ruin this moment for me.

I lift my head just enough to narrow the space between us. She pauses, her lips hovering inches from mine. I can smell the hot chocolate on her breath.

I close the gap between us and take what I want. I press my lips to hers, and the touch is so light, so delicate, it's almost like I'm imagining it. But I'm not just hungry for her—I'm starving. I cup the back of her head and give her more of me. She accepts it, hungry for this too. Her fingers clutch at my chest as our tongues meet.

It's in this exact moment I realize my memory is a thief, having stolen from me all the details of kissing this woman. The softness of her lips, the way she moves her tongue against mine, her taste, the subtle movements of her body. All of it is familiar and fresh. Some of it lost to time, but here it is again. Like a coin buried in the sand, every sensation, every second of this a treasure that somehow got buried.

It is the most natural thing in the world to kiss Jessie Matthews, and if I could spend every single day doing this I'd never get sick of it. She melts into me, deepening our kiss, and I tighten one arm around her. I want her as close as possible, and that is not nearly close enough.

Jessie pulls away, but not far. Her nose brushes my cheek and I feel her smiling against my lips.

"Would you make fun of me if I told you I've always wanted to make out with someone while listening to Black Phantom?" she whispers, brushing her lips over mine.

"Never. Because me too," I say and sweep the back of my finger down her cheek. Her skin is like silk, and I chase the graze of my finger with a kiss.

She closes her eyes, making a humming noise. I want more of those noises. I want more of her, but I'm not going to push her or try to make tonight into something it's not.

"You know what they say," I murmur against her lips. "Teamwork makes the dream work."

Jessie bursts into a laugh, resting her forehead on my chest. It makes me want to kiss her again, so I hook my finger under her chin and tilt her face to mine. It's bright with joy, and when I kiss her I swear I can taste it.

CHAPTER SIXTEEN

MAC

I never, ever get nervous. But standing in front of the theater waiting for Jessie to show up has me pacing and a little sweaty. I'm not nervous to see her—we've spent nearly every day together this week since Thanksgiving break. So I will my nerves into excitement. It's how I always feel seeing a play. I was only able to see one or two shows over the past two years because of my soccer schedule, but every time I did I felt like this. It's how I felt before soccer games—a sense of rightness, but also the thrill of doing something I like. Eventually that feeling faded for soccer, but I recognize it here, waiting on Jessie. I check my watch. The show starts in ten minutes, and she was supposed to be here five minutes ago.

I peer into the lobby, which is bustling with people, and stuff my hands into my pockets, rocking back and forth. When I turn back around, Jessie is approaching, her hair slightly windblown, her cheeks pink from the cold air.

"Ready?" she asks, a big smile on her face.

I love her smile.

"Absolutely. I haven't seen a play in forever," I say.

"It's not a play, Mac," she says with a chuckle.

"Oh. What are we seeing?"

"One-acts. They're like short plays, and they're student-directed. Jade is in one of them. She does them every year."

"Does she direct?"

"Jade? Behind the scenes? Are you kidding?"

I shrug and nod in a "fair point" kind of way.

"Hey, I'm going to run to the restroom really fast," Jessie says and darts off across the lobby.

While she's gone, I pretend to be really interested in the bulletin board, which is covered in random business cards and flyers for vocal coaches and local shows and old cast lists and random photos, but it turns into real interest when a bright yellow flyer catches my attention.

IMPROV NIGHT
FRIDAY DEC 9TH
EVERYONE WELCOME! AUDIENCE PARTICIPATION
ENCOURAGED!

At the bottom of the flyer are a bunch of random graphics. The flyer looks like it was made by someone who had about ten minutes to spend on it. I snap a picture with my phone. This would be incredible. It's not a class, it's basically after finals—there's no reason for me not to do it. My dad's voice pops up.

Do something respectable. Not some sissy—

"What's that?" Jessie asks, joining me at the bulletin board.

"Nothing," I say, turning away and following the crowd. "Shall we?"

She eyes me, suspicious, but doesn't push.

We settle into our seats and spend the next ninety minutes

watching a series of short plays. We watch Jade absolutely kill it in her play as a ghost summoned by her ex-husband on accident. There are three actors in the skit, but Jade steals the show. We cheer extra loud for her and don't miss another girl at the end of our row cheering just as loud as us.

"I think that's Threesome Anna," Jessie whispers to me, leaning in.

"Is Jade still seeing both of them?" I whisper back.

Jessie nods, raising her eyebrows at me.

I'm about to ask another question about Jade's...situationships, but the lights dim for the next play.

By the time the shows are all over, I find myself wishing there were at least three more. The thing I love about theater, even its micro-format, is the way it evokes every emotion. One minute you're sad, but it doesn't last, because there's usually some glimmer of happiness some-where. And even if there's not, you've still been transported to a life outside your own. More than once tonight I imaged myself on stage in a scene.

"You're absolutely glowing," Jessie says to me as we ascend the stairs back to the lobby.

"That was amazing. It's, like, almost the same high as going to a sporting event."

"I would argue with you, but that's not the hill I want to die on today."

"Is it because you don't like sports or—?"

"It's that one. Whatever you're going to say next is moot. It's that one."

We claim one of the open benches in the lobby while we wait for Jade. We're all eating together after this and promised Jade we'd wait for her.

Jessie leans against me, and I slip an arm around her. I haven't felt this content in a long time. Being in this building feels *right*. I couldn't explain it if I tried, but maybe I need to. Maybe I need to sit down with my parents during Christmas break and explain why this is important to me or maybe I do just need to take a class and not tell them...

With the Walden Senior Scholarship in my pocket, maybe they won't care as much.

But thinking about the scholarship gives me a weird pinching feeling in my ribs. I glance down at Jessie. If I get it, that means she didn't, and what does that mean for her coming back to school next year? I can afford the tuition. She's specifically told me she can't, and that makes the pinching in my ribs transform into a dull ache. Withdrawing my application wouldn't guarantee she'd get it, though. We're not the only students who applied—surely. The most qualified maybe, but there's no way to know for sure that my concession would still benefit Jessie.

But I don't really want to think about this right now, so I stuff it to the back of my mind.

Another day.

For now I hug Jessie just a little closer to me, and when she looks up at me and grins, her eyes sparkling, I know without a doubt that I'd move heaven and hell to keep her.

Scholarship or no.

"You two are actually disgusting. Like, I was Team Mac, and now I'm Team Stop-Looking-At-Each-Other-In-Front-Of-Me." Jade rocks up, her stage makeup mostly gone.

Jessie stands, hugging her friend. "You were fantastic," she tells her.

"You really were," I echo and stand too.

"I was, wasn't I? Let's get some food. I'm absolutely starving."

Jade and Jessie link arms and lead the way to the caf. It's after ten o'clock on a Friday night, and even though the caf is open twenty-four-seven, barely anyone is here but us. I buy dinner for all of us, and Jessie only protests one time before Jade reminds her the best part about taking a lover is when they buy you nice things, to which Jessie mutters, "It's caf food?"

"Better than cat food," Jade says, claiming a table in the near-empty cafe for us. Jessie sits next to me, Jade across from us.

"Are your standards that low?" Jessie asks, pouring dressing all over her salad.

"My standards are astronomical," Jade says.

Jessie raises her eyebrows at her.

"For a partner."

Jessie's eyebrows go to her forehead. Watching them together is better than TV.

"Like, not just a sexual partner. A life partner. It's why I'm never getting married. A chain of casual lovers who don't expect anything from me suits me just fine," Jade says between bites of French fries. "Commitment is for the birds. But I'm glad it's working out for you two pheasants."

"Did you just call us peasants?" I ask.

"Pheasants," Jessie says, emphasizing the "F" sound. "Like the bird?"

I shrug. I genuinely have never heard of a bird called a pheasant. Jessie looks at me like I just announced my arrival from another planet.

"I thought you said he was smart," Jade says.

"I thought he was too," Jessie says. "At least he's cute."

"I can hear you," I say, digging into my burger.

"Good. Your ego could use a knock down a level or two." Jessie nudges me with her elbow.

"You keep me humble," I say, throwing a fry at her face. It bounces off her cheek and lands on the table.

She picks it up with a grin and tosses it back at my face. It misses entirely, hitting my shoulder and bouncing back into my lap. I snap it up and stuff it in my mouth. Still smiling, I lean in for a kiss, and Jessie obliges. The kiss is quick and over too soon, but she tastes every bit as sweet as the first time I kissed her.

"Seriously, guys. Get a room," Jade says.

"Sorry, sorry," Jessie says.

"I'm not," I say, and I watch as Jessie's face turns bright red. I try not to stare, but I can't help it.

Jessie is everything I had no idea I wanted. My crush on her for the past two years was a distant, untouchable thing, our banter, our dynamic, the bright spot in my day countless times. But after the Halloween party, that crush became corporeal. It was smoke in my lungs that turned back into fire and became something I could no longer control. Every minute spent with her, every smile, everything I learned about her, became fuel, spreading a wildfire through all of me with reckless abandon.

When a wildfire eventually dies out, all that's left in its wake are bare trees, charred grass, and ash. Thinking of a tomorrow without Jessie feels like that.

I don't know if it was luck or divinity that got us here, but I'll worship any god who claims a hand in it. Whatever sacrifice I need to make for a forever made of tomorrows, I'll make it. No questions asked.

JESSIE

Mac insists on walking us back to our dorm and all the way to the door. Jade says good night quickly and ducks inside, leaving Mac and me alone. I stand in the doorway, half in and half out of our dorm, and he leans against the doorframe, one arm framed above me, propping him up and boxing me in. I could step back if I wanted some space.

I don't.

"Thanks for coming with me," I say, tugging on the hem of his shirt.

Leaning in, he places a soft kiss on my lips. He grips my hip with his free hand and pulls me against him. His arm comes around me and his kiss becomes more demanding. I let the dorm door shut behind me and lean into Mac—lean into the kiss.

Whatever awe and wonder I thought my first kiss would inspire was completely missing, but I found it here, with Mac. Someone should warn us it isn't our first kiss that's magical, but our first kiss with magic is the first one that matters. Maybe the only one.

We say good night, and I wait until Mac has disappeared into the elevator before slipping back inside the dorm. Jade is waiting for me on the couch.

"I really cannot get over you two. Like, who are you and what have you done with my Jessie?"

"I don't know!"

"Are you officially over Sexy Shakespeare?"

"That is an easy yes. Well—it's almost an easy yes. Mac and I have chemistry too. It's similar to Sexy Shakespeare, but...I don't know. I can't describe it."

"What if it was Mac?"

"What if who was Mac? Sexy Shakespeare? With the wig and the accent?" The idea makes me chuckle. "What are the actual chances of that?"

"You know I'm bad at math."

"I am too. Plus, I think I would have known. The accent was real."

"Are you sure?"

"I guess I can't be totally sure. But if it was Mac...he would have told me."

"That's true," Jade says with a shrug.

I join her on the couch, checking my email as I get settled. I freeze just as I'm about to throw a blanket over my legs.

"Oh my god. I...I won a scholarship!" I gasp, a sharp intake of air.

Jade launches herself at me, crawling all over my legs to try to see my phone screen.

"What! Which one? The Walden Senior Scholarship?"

"No, no, just one of those ones from the list I applied to. They're giving me two thousand dollars."

I know my heart is still beating and I'm still getting breath to my lungs, but I can't feel any of these things happening. Two thousand dollars is something. I won something. It's not nearly enough to cover the whole year, but if I won this one, maybe I could win a few others.

For a moment the initial shock and numbness give way to a sense of security, but it dissolves when I remember how much needs to be covered. The rest of my tuition, books, housing. It's so much money. This barely scratches the surface. My hope crumbles, a forgotten cookie at the bottom of the bag.

Jade reads through the email but stays on my legs, looking up at me. "Hey, that's a good start. You have more scholarships and grants to hear about."

"I've already gotten rejection emails from five. Two for not actually qualifying. I misread the list of qualifications. Two because I just didn't win. And one because they aren't offering any more scholarships for the next school year but said I could 'try again for the following year.' Very helpful."

Jade gives my leg a reassuring squeeze.

"That leaves four, not including the Walden Senior Scholarship," I say.

I drop my phone in my lap and scrub my face with my hands. I want the stress of this to be over. It's the thing on my plate that I want to scrape off because it's touching everything else on my plate. It's mucking it all up like gravy on a slice of pie.

Two things could erase my immediate stress: the loan my mother hasn't cosigned yet and the Walden Senior Scholarship. Since talking to my mom I've been hesitant to move forward with a loan. All that money for the rest of my life? I'd hoped I'd get out of college with the privilege of being debt-free, but it's looking less and less like that's an option.

And as for the Walden Senior Scholarship...winning that would mean Mac wouldn't win it. I know how much it would mean to him. I saw the way his dad was, heard the conversation about the theater classes. The scholarship and maybe even valedictorian would go a long way for him.

And the hardest part is that I want that for him. I both want to win for myself and I want him to feel the pride of winning, to see the look on his dad's face when he finds out. If he won, I'd want to celebrate with him, even though it would mean I lost something I desperately needed.

Would I still want to be with Mac if he won the scholarship and I didn't?

Yes.

A resounding yes echoes around my chest. Even though my brain knows we need the money, somehow I also know I'd be okay if I didn't get it. That I might be stuck with a loan, but if my parents found a way to make it work, so could I. Maybe a few smaller scholarships like the one I just won could offset the cost.

Whatever it is, there's a strange peace about the whole situation for me. Strange because a few weeks ago I couldn't bear the thought of losing to Mac. And now I can't stand the thought of losing him.

CHAPTER SEVENTEEN

JESSIE

I adjust the strap of my backpack and stare at the front door of Mac's apartment. He bribed me with a homemade dinner if we worked on data coding for the research project at his apartment instead of the library. I didn't need to be bribed, but he doesn't need to know that. I haven't been to his place yet, and I'm curious about where he lives.

But now I'm nervous. Seeing the inside of someone's home is intimate. Even having been in his bed at his childhood home feels different than being in his personal living space. The kitchen he cooks in, the couch he lounges on. The implications of being on that couch or being alone with him in his apartment. There's a wave of butterflies in my stomach.

My phone dings.

Have fun. Make bad choices. 😉

Jade.

I send her back a smiling devil emoji and tuck my phone away. When I knock on the door it opens almost immediately. Cinnamon, clove, and that glorious onion-garlic combo hits my nose.

"Whatever you're cooking smells amazing," I say.

A bright smile lights up his face. "If you wanted to show up here every day and compliment me as soon as I opened the door I wouldn't be mad about it."

I take one step into the apartment and Mac cradles my face in one hand and kisses me like I'm made of glass. He doesn't linger, though, taking my bag off my shoulder and setting it on the couch.

"Come in, come in. Snoop all you like. Dinner will be done soon."

Mac disappears into the kitchen, leaving me to take everything in. Besides the smell of whatever he's cooking, the apartment smells clean and nothing like a stereotypical college student living space. It's freshly vacuumed and there's a candle burning on his tidied countertop. It's a small apartment, without much space between the living room and the kitchen, but it's cozy. Long curtains cover the windows and tastefully framed inspirational quotes and artwork are all over the walls.

"Did you decorate this?"

"It was mostly my mom, but I contributed some."

It's so different from what I expected. I don't know what I did expect—maybe something more sparse and bachelor pad-like—but this apartment feels like a home. On a college campus, that is something special.

"You okay?" Mac chuckles.

"It's so...clean."

Mac barks out a laugh. "I don't know whether to be offended you thought I lived in squalor or proud that I've met your standards," he says.

"The second one. Definitely the second one."

We beam at each other like a couple of idiots. I swear if the lights were turned off we'd glow in the dark. Mac is the first to break. I could have stared at him all night.

"So, what's for dinner?" I ask, joining him in the kitchen. On the stove are two pots, a simmering sauce in one and barely boiling water in the other.

"Spaghetti, and I've got a salad and some garlic bread."

Mac gestures to the counter where, sure enough, there's a large bowl holding Caesar salad with what looks like homemade croutons. Unbaked garlic bread waits on the counter next to the salad bowl, and my mouth starts to water.

"Garlic bread? I hope you didn't expect me to kiss you very much tonight," I tease.

"Kissing! Jessica Matthews, this is study time, not sexy study time." He grins at me, and every organ in my body rearranges itself.

"Are those homemade noodles?" I point to the bowl of uncooked noodles sitting near the stove.

"They are," he says, his back to me. When he turns around he's got a spoon with some sauce on it. "Here—taste." Mac offers me the spoon, holding it like he's going to feed me.

I stare at him for just a beat, asking with my eyes if he really intends to feed me. He just moves the spoon a little closer to my mouth. I accept, closing my eyes against an onslaught of flavor. It tastes exactly the way it smelled, like someone went out to the garden this morning and picked every ingredient right from the backyard.

"That is delicious. You've got to be the only college student who actually knows how to cook."

"My mom is a great cook, as you may remember from Thanksgiving. I learned a lot from her. Plus, you can only eat so much caf food."

"Oh my gosh, is this Frodo?" I reach past Mac to a shelf holding a jar filled with white, bubbly liquid.

He smiles, proud as any sourdough daddy. I take a tentative whiff, the sweet, fermented, yeasty dough a feast for my senses. I can't even pretend not to be impressed. He's a great cook, a talented baker, he's smart and funny, and he keeps his apartment clean. He's almost too good to be true. I can't believe it took me so long to notice.

"Yes. And the garlic bread tonight is courtesy of that guy." Mac points to the jar.

"How much time did you spend today prepping for this meal?" I ask, replacing his jar of starter.

"I'll never say."

There's a slight blush to his cheeks, and I find all of this so endearing—the fact that he's blushing, the time he spent prepping this meal for me. I could scream with how much I like this guy. Why did I ever hate him?

I lean against the counter and watch as he finishes the meal, putting the bread in the oven right before he dunks the noodles in the water. Somehow all of it finishes at exactly the right time, and then the smell of fresh bread and garlic just about brings me to my knees.

"Go sit. I'll bring your food over," Mac says.

"I don't mind," I say and reach for the plates, but Mac gently grabs my wrists, guiding my arms back down to my sides.

"Let me." His tone is firm but kind. It's not a suggestion, and when he gestures to a small dining table tucked against a wall between the living room and kitchen, I nod and take a seat without another word.

"I would offer you wine, but I figured we should maybe wait until after we've done some of the coding," Mac says as he sets down two plates of food and takes the seat across from me. He pulls out his phone and clicks around until the soft sounds of Black Phantom float through a Bluetooth speaker sitting on his kitchen counter.

Dinner is a quiet affair, with just the music and the sound of us eating. But it's a comfortable quiet, like this is how Mac and I spend all of our Sunday evenings. I wonder if this is how we'll really spend all of our Sunday evenings. Flirting in the kitchen, me letting him cook for us, working on homework. I mull the idea over, trying to resist the smile I feel tugging at my lips. How is it that two months ago I could barely stand the guy, and now I'm at his house having dinner, picturing a life as his girlfriend?

"What's got you smiling?" Mac asks.

I thought I was hiding my smile okay, but apparently I'm easier to read than I thought I was.

"I was just thinking what it might be like if we did this more often," I say. It's all I'm brave enough to say.

"I'd like that," he says with no hesitation. "And I'll take that as a compliment to my cooking."

"It's a compliment to the cooking, to the company, to the vibes."

"The vibes are what I was most concerned with."

"I know. You can be a bit of a try-hard about it," I say, smirking when he gives me a faux shocked face.

"How dare you suggest I try hard at things. Everything comes naturally and easily to me, with minimal effort."

A few months ago I might have found this statement arrogant and overlooked his sarcasm as a reason to dig in on disliking him, but I see it for what it is now. I actually love his humor. I love so many things about Mac.

And I want to discover more things to love.

The conversation keeps us at the table for too long after we've finished eating, but by the time we relocate to the living room to work on the assignment, I'm still not quite ready to sit and focus. I explore the living space instead, starting with the giant entertainment center, shelves tastefully accentuated with framed photos and thoughtful knickknacks. Upon closer inspection, the small knickknacks look like travel memorabilia.

The first thing I notice is a small, carved wooden elephant. I reach up and stroke the elephant's trunk. The wood is smooth, and the elephant tips over at my touch.

"Shit," I whisper and put it back in place. "Where's the elephant from?" I ask.

Mac stands nearby, not hovering but also not giving me too much space. He's just out of my peripheral. "South Africa."

"Did you go there?" I ask, turning to him.

He nods with a humble smile.

"I've never even left the East Coast," I say, turning back to the shelves.

"Where would you like to go?" Mac asks.

"I'm not sure," I say quietly, running my finger delicately over a tiny ivory statue.

"That's from Rome."

"Rome," I whisper, a little in awe.

"Nowhere you dreamed of traveling even as a kid?" he asks.

"I've never really had the luxury to dream of traveling. I've spent most of my life in survival mode, just trying to help my parents pay the bills or take care of the house or my dad while my mom worked."

I pick up a photo of Mac and his parents and three brothers at the top of a mountain surrounded by a 360-degree view of snow-capped peaks. It could be the Swiss Alps, but after all the other places he's named, it could be literally anywhere in the world with tons of mountains. I set the frame down.

"You said that so matter-of-fact," Mac says.

"How should I have sounded?"

"I didn't really mean anything by it. You're right, of course. I just never considered dreaming like that was a luxury."

"I've started to let myself," I say, moving away from the knickknacks and scanning the next shelf, crammed full with books. "Dream, that is."

"What are you dreaming about, Jessie?" Mac's voice is soft and curious. It makes my stomach feel pinchy.

"Graduating. Going to grad school. I'd like to be a child psychologist eventually. I won't have any debt after college, hopefully, so once I'm established somewhere I can save up and travel. Which I think I would like to do. I just...never thought about it."

Mac's response is a humming noise in the back of his throat, but he comes up behind me, resting his chin on my shoulder. He wraps his arms around my middle and holds me to him. It's the kind of affection between couples, and it feels entirely natural for me and Mac to be entwined like this. I rest my arms over his, scanning his bookshelf. My eyes land on a *Complete Works of William Shakespeare* and I huff a small laugh. For a moment I wonder at the possibility of Jade's suggestion, that Mac was Sexy Shakespeare, but I dismiss it for all the reasons I already told Jade.

"Why'd you laugh?" Mac asks.

"Just thinking about...Shakespeare."

He turns me, digging his fingers into my hips so my lower body presses against his. He leans in for a kiss and my body arches backward with the pressure of his lips as he cups the back of my head. Our kiss is heat and fire, and I already know that when he stops I'm going to want more. I'm going to *need* more.

I grip his arms, trying to ground myself. I never feel fully anchored when we kiss. I'm unmoored on choppy waters, an unseasoned captain at the helm. I don't know how to navigate the storm inside of me that rages with every kiss, so I hold on for dear life.

He pulls back but plants a second quick and gentle kiss on my lips. "We should be working on our project," he says.

"Or...we could start that in, like...twenty minutes..." I say and push against his chest, nudging him toward the couch.

His hold on me tightens. Mac gets the hint and walks with me, a devilish grin on his face. When the back of his legs hit the couch, he sits. I climb onto his lap, one leg on either side of his hips, and run my fingers through his hair. He closes his eyes, pure pleasure etched into his features. I do it again, running my nails against his scalp. This time the motion elicits a groan, encouraging me. His fingers flex against my thighs and then clamp down. It's almost too much pressure, but it also feels good. It feels like desire, and knowing he's feeling everything I am eggs me on.

One last time, I run my fingers through his hair, but I curl my fingers and clench them, grabbing a fistful of hair at the base of his neck. Mac responds with another groan, his hands sliding up to my ribs and around to my back. He shifts my body so it collides with his, our mouths meeting with all the inevitability of a flood in springtime.

There's something so familiar about Mac, like maybe we've kissed before. Maybe we've kissed a hundred times in another life and in each new one we find our way back to each other. But it isn't just the kissing or his hands; it's the chemistry. Familiarity pricks at the back of my eyes, in the back of my throat. It crawls through me, growing and expanding until I can't ignore it.

I break our kiss and shake my head from side to side.

"Sorry, I got deja vu. Just...wanted to get rid of it," I say.

Mac acknowledges me with a hint of a smile and then leans in, tilting his head to my exposed neck, his breath brushing a spot just below my jaw. With the lightest touch he grazes my neck and a heat rises from my hips, spreading a familiar sense of longing and power through me.

"I'm sorry, it's just...this is so weird. This is so familiar. I feel like we've done this before."

"We have, silly. In the truck, when we listened to the album," he murmurs against my neck. I can hear a half-smile on his face.

"No, no, you didn't kiss my neck then," I say, leaning back a little.

Mac's neck stretches toward me like he isn't done yet, but I know he's only half-listening. His eyes are glazed with desire, his lips red and a little puffed from the kissing. He shrugs, giving me an "I'm not sure what to tell you" look.

I shrug too, shaking my head, and we kiss again, but not for long as I pull back once more.

"I'm sorry, it's just that you remind me so much of that guy. The guy I made out with at the Halloween party. The Sexy Shakespeare guy. I know that's so dumb. I'm not trying to compare you. It's just, sort of...I don't know, it's so familiar. Sorry I keep harping on this. It's just so...uncanny. So weird," I say, my sentences punctuated with awkward laughter.

Mac's face is rosy, his grin wide, his eyebrows raised, but there's something off in his eyes. His look has shifted as before. Now he has the look of someone who's laughing along with you but not fully connected to your words. "That's, uh...actually...because it was me," he says, choking out a chuckle. His grin turns to a grimace and his grip loosens on me a little.

A strangled, weird laugh escapes me. "You're hilarious," I say and lean back in to kiss him, but he turns his head just slightly. A rejection that hits harder than any words he just said. A punch to the stomach that kills any vestiges of the lingering mood.

"It was me, Jessie," Mac says with all the seriousness of a doctor delivering bad news.

I blink a few times, trying to let his words sink in. I slide off his lap and onto the couch, pulling my legs up to my chest. Every thought in my mind is frozen. All the cogs in the machine have stopped working.

"No. You would have told me."

"I should have told you. I tried to tell you."

"I don't understand," I say. I glance around the room, looking for someone to confirm or deny what he's telling me, but there's no one.

Mac bites his bottom lip. He looks pale, and his hands are twisted together in his lap. This is not the posture of a person who's joking. Or lying. He looks like he wants to say something, but his mouth moves without a sound.

"Oh my god," I say, covering my mouth. A curtain lifts inside of me and all the confusion is gone. The moment is crystal-clear. "You knew it was me," I say. "At the Halloween party when it happened."

"A cat costume is not a grand disguise. I swear, I thought you knew it was me. And the next day I thought you knew it was me. I didn't—" He reaches out, but I scramble up off the couch as if his touch might sting me.

"Do not...do not touch me right now," I hiss through gritted teeth.

Adrenaline pumps through my bloodstream, my heart racing. Blood thrums in my ears, anger pounding at my walls. Mac has been lying to me. Mac kept this from me. Intentionally. I carve my hands through my hair, clenching them just to feel the pull of that pain instead of the slow glide of the knife down my back.

"Why didn't you tell me? Immediately. Or the next day. You could have said something in class or after class," I say, my voice sharp.

"I swear I thought you knew it was me," he pleads.

"What!? It was pitch-black. I'd been drinking. You were wearing a mask and a wig. You had an accent!" My voice shakes with the effort of not yelling. My lips still tingle from our kiss, but the memory is tinged with pain.

"It wasn't that dark," Mac says, but not with a lot of confidence.

"You told me your name was Will, for fuck's sake."

"As in Will Shakespeare. I thought you..." He trails off.

"Yes, we already cleared that one up." The embarrassment of that moment still chafes, but it's overpowered by the red-hot rage boiling just under my skin. "Why didn't you say anything, Mac?"

"I tried. I really did. A few times."

"A few times! How hard could it have been?"

Mac's mouth works like a fish out of water, and the temptation to be cruel is so strong I have to bite my tongue to hold it back.

"Jessie." He reaches for me again, standing, but I jerk back, taking a few steps away.

"Why did you think I never brought up what happened? Or that we hadn't kissed again until now? Like, how did you justify this to yourself?" I ask.

"I don't know. I guess I thought we were doing a bit. And, like..."

"Involved in some elaborate roleplay? You thought this was a game! That we were doing a bit. Do you hear how stupid you sound? Did you not once think that maybe I just didn't know it was you?"

"Eventually, yes! I thought you'd talk about it when you wanted to."

"No. No, no. You're way too smart for this, Mac."

I can barely make sense of what he's saying. It sounds so illogical. I have sirens in my brain screaming, "BETRAYAL!" My eyes fill with tears and my chest gets so tight I wonder for a second if I'm having a heart attack. And over it all a bright red blanket making it impossible to see anything clearly.

Mac is cringing to the point of near cowering. He looks right on the edge of tears, but I can't dredge up an ounce of empathy right now.

"I didn't want to lose you," he says.

My rage bursts through the surface, a failed dam erupting with too much pressure. "So you lied to me?"

"I didn't lie. I never lied."

"Oh, I'm sorry, you 'withheld information,'" I mock him, but I also catch myself. I have to get out of here before I say something I'll regret, which I am absolutely about to do. I snatch up my bag from the couch and walk out, Mac calling my name after me.

I bolt from the apartment, not stopping to let myself cry or scream or fall apart, because I need to get as far away as possible as quickly as possible.

Get home first. Then fall apart.

But I'm halfway across the parking lot when I realize I've forgotten my jacket. It's too cold to walk back. With slowly numbing fingers, I find Jade's contact in my phone and call her, walking toward the road.

"I'm at the apartments. Come get me," I say.

"Be there in five. Are you safe?"

"I'm safe, just cold."

"Be there in four."

I hear her grabbing her keys and slamming the door behind her just before she hangs up.

Headlights come from behind me. I keep my head down and rub my arms, moving to a grassy area. The headlights come nearer, the car stopping. A door opens and shuts.

Mac approaches, holding my jacket. "Here." He holds it out, and I snatch it out of his hands. "Let me drive you home. It's too cold."

"Jade is coming to get me."

"Jessie, please let me explain."

"What's there to explain, Mac?"

"Okay, then let me apologize."

"Why? Why should I hear out your apology? This was just a game to you."

"That isn't true at all."

"Okay," I say with a nasty tone, rolling my eyes.

"I thought—"

"Mac, I don't care what you thought. You need to stop talking." My voice cracks and wavers. Tears have sprung loose from my eyes and streak my face. "Just...leave me alone."

He doesn't try to defend himself again. He concedes, nodding and getting back into his car. He stays there until Jade pulls up and jumps out of the driver's seat. She drapes my jacket around my shoulders and wraps me into a hug. Mac's headlights still beat down on us. Jade tucks me into the passenger's side and gives Mac the finger as she pops back into the car. She throws it in reverse and takes me back to our dorm.

Mac's headlights stay on for as long as I can see them in the rearview mirror.

CHAPTER EIGHTEEN

MAC

I don't care that it's only been four days since I blew up my relationship with Jessie. I miss her. I missed her within a day of the fight.

Before Saturday we'd been texting every day—memes, telling each other how we did on a quiz, asking schoolwork-related questions. I found reasons to text her, just excuses to start a conversation. Every morning since the fight I've reached for my phone, eager to type out a message to her, only to remember the way she looked at me when she realized I'd known, that I'd been an absolute asshat. The things she said rush back at me, and all over again I get a thick lump in my throat.

I still cringe at the way I tried to defend myself during our fight. Even Brody told me I was a dumbass at racquetball last night after I recounted the whole thing.

I should have tried harder to tell her before. I should have just blurted it out. I should not have been so fucking stupid. Should've, should've, should've. This is the refrain on repeat in my head every day. All day. I'm not normally a brooder, and I keep trying to find the silver lining, but I can't find a trace of silver in this, only ways I could have done better. *Should* have done better.

Today is the first day I'm almost guaranteed to run into Jessie. We share two classes in our schedules, and one of those classes is today. It will be the first time seeing her since Sunday, and I'm really considering skipping this class, but it's too close to the end of the year for that, and we're probably getting exam info today, so I need to be there. But I'm going to need coffee to do this. Preferably with some whiskey in it.

I stop by the campus cafe to get a latte the size of my face, but of course, when I walk in the only other person in there is Jessie's best friend. Jade.

Shit.

"Well, well, well, look what the cat chewed up, spit out, clawed up, and dragged across a gravel driveway and into the coffee shop," Jade says, turning to face me. She leans a hip against the counter and crosses her arms.

The barista making her drink snorts. This might be worse than seeing Jessie right now. Hell hath no fury like a best friend scorned.

I can't decide if I should try to explain myself, apologize, or just leave. I know girl code, and I have no doubt Jade already knows everything.

"Did you know it was me?" I ask, taking the offensive. Maybe I can steer our conversation.

"Are you fucking kidding me? If I did *I* would have told her," Jade says.

Ouch... But it's a fair point.

"I tried, I really did."

"Not hard enough," she says, turning back to the counter where the barista has finished making her drink. Jade removes the lid immediately to sip the whipped cream off the top.

"You're right," I say, but Jade makes no indication she wants to continue this conversation, so I move away from her to the register to order my drink.

Order placed, I return to the end of the counter to wait for my drink. I fidget, straightening up the cup of straws, organizing the sugars, and trying to make myself as small as possible.

I sense Jade's eyes still on me, and when I look over she's still there staring. Her eyes bore into me in a way that makes me want to curl up into a very small ball and hide until it feels safe to come out. Which it may never be so long as Jade lives and breathes.

"I have to know," she says, "are you just very inexperienced with women, or are you actually stupid?"

I swallow hard. I deserved that.

"Can it be option C, I'm actually just a coward?" I ask, averting my gaze. I have never wanted a barista to make a drink as fast as I do right now. The sooner I can leave, the better.

"Coward works."

The hiss of the milk frother fills our silence, and although the cafe always smells like coffee, the fresh espresso intensifies the smell as if someone lit an espresso-scented candle.

"You should know that I'm mad at you," Jade says as if her greeting and the dagger stares weren't communicating that. As I grab my latte and turn to leave, she gestures with a toss of her head to a table, inviting me to sit.

I hesitate. She just said she's mad at me—why would I sit? I know I fucked up, but I don't want to be lectured. I have no interest in being berated by someone else. I'm doing a decent enough job of berating myself.

"You have every right to be mad, I know I—"

"But," Jade interrupts, "I also think that in the grand scheme of your relationship with Jessie, this will just be something that brings you closer."

Grand scheme of my relationship with Jessie. Her words bounce around in my brain, slingshotting from one corner to the other. They disorient me like I've been spun around ten times and asked to walk in a straight line.

"Wait—what?" I ask, but Jade holds up a finger.

"Jessie is really hurt and really pissed, and rightfully so."

"Yes, obviously, that's—"

"But," Jade interrupts again, continuing her thought, "I think she'll forgive you because she really fucking likes you. That's why it hurts, but I think she has more grace in her than she realizes, and she may eventually come around."

Hope sneaks into my heart like a bandit.

"Is there anything I can do?" I ask with a sudden burst of energy. "Can I write her a letter? Or, like, send her flowers?"

Jade shakes her head violently. She does a hand-slicing motion in front of her neck. The energy leaves me as fast as it came.

"Listen, if I'm right and she does forgive you, you'll have years to make up for it. For now, just give her space."

I press my lips into a line and nod. I don't want to take space from Jessie, but I know she's right. I just hate it.

Jade and I both take a sip of our drinks. Our conversation feels like it's at its natural end, but she hasn't made any indication of movement. I dart my gaze around the room.

"I heard you might be taking a theater class next...semester? Next year?" Jade removes the lid of her drink, setting it on the table and cradling her cup in her hands. I swear she stares at me like she can see through my soul, and internally I squirm, but I won't give her the satisfaction of seeing it. Even if I should grovel a little. I can't help but think Jade is actually rooting for me and Jessie. For me.

"I guess Jessie told you?"

"Mm-hmm." Jade nods, eyebrows high, asking for more information.

"I'm just thinking about it for next year. I've got room in my schedule and I've always wanted to take a class, but I don't know. It's dumb." I pick at the plastic lid of my cup.

"Wrong crowd if you're looking for someone to agree. Theater isn't dumb. People who think theater is dumb are dumb."

"My dad."

"You said it, not me." She shrugs and takes a sip of her drink.

I want to agree with her, but it's ingrained into my brain. Rewiring my brain is a Herculean task, but how can I start if not by taking small steps?

"What's the deal with the improv night?" I ask. I stare at the photo I took of the flyer at least once a day, convincing myself to go, convincing myself not to go.

"You should come," Jade says. "It's open to the campus. People can come watch but also participate. It'd be a fun way for you to dip your toes in before getting fully wet."

Her words spark something inside me—the flicker of a match that's been struck but hasn't quite lit.

"Yeah, I was thinking about it. I don't know."

Picking at the plastic of the cup again, I refuse to lift my eyes to Jade's. The intensity of her gaze is almost too much. *How does Jessie deal with this all the time?*

"Ugh. It is exhausting when people don't just do whatever the fuck they want. Who gives a shit what your dad thinks? Is that all that's holding you back?"

It's hard to articulate exactly what's holding me back. I want to go, but what's the point? Participating in this doesn't earn me any respect from my father. It doesn't earn me any respect with my brothers, and it certainly won't be how I live up to the Baldwin name.

But what has that ever gotten me? What has the pursuit of my father's respect earned me except the silent treatment when I inevitably mess up again and don't meet his expectations?

Maybe it's time to actually do something I want for once.

"Tomorrow?" I ask.

"Seven o'clock in the theater."

"Is Jessie going?"

If she is I probably shouldn't go, and I think Jade knows that too. She shakes her head.

"I'll be there," I say.

I'M TOO EARLY for the improv event, but I've been swinging between anxiety and feeling like a kid on Christmas Eve eagerly awaiting Santa's arrival since yesterday when Jade and I parted ways.

It's the first time since my fight with Jessie that I've looked forward to waking up; that I've had something to look forward to instead of dread. I might be clinging too tightly to this thing, but if I don't, who knows when I'll get out of this dark place?

I barely slept last night, but this time it was event-related, not "I'm a jerk who ruined my relationship"-related. I had two classes today, and in between them I just paced campus, waiting for time to move faster. I probably looked crazy, walking past the theater building three or four times before walking away. I finally ended up in the library but had trouble focusing on studying. I was on high alert for Jessie but never saw her, and I couldn't stop wondering what the event tonight would be like.

What if I got the chance to go on stage? Would I be any good? I dream up about three hundred scenarios, ones where I get on stage and absolutely kill it, and some where I go up there and freeze. I'm a pendulum swinging uncontrollably between extremes.

By the time 6:30 p.m. rolls around, I'm staring at the doors of the theater, unable to wait any longer despite the fact I'll be way too early. I take a deep breath and pull open the door, trying to ignore my dad's voice in my head.

Some people are milling about in the lobby, but I don't see Jade, so I follow the signs posted for the improv event. They take me down a set of stairs into a much darker part of the building where Jessie and I watched the one-act plays. This basement-type area holds a stage too, and it's much smaller. There are probably less than two hundred seats down here and nearly everything is black—the ceiling, the walls, the stands holding the chairs. It feels simultaneously cozy and empty. Although, once the seats are filled, it will probably feel very intimate.

I didn't think much of the size of this space when I was watching a show, but picturing myself on the stage and being able to see people's faces in the audience makes my mouth dry. Maybe I shouldn't have come.

I know I shouldn't have arrived as early as I did. No one is in the audience, but students rush about the room setting things up. Still no sign of Jade. I'll wait in the lobby. She's sure to find me there.

On my way back up, a side room with a small loft area catches my eye. There's a booth at the bottom of the loft with a small countertop housing a board, maybe for sound. A pair of headphones sits on the chair, waiting for their human counterpart. Above the small booth is the loft, cramped stairs leading up to a space that looks so small no one could stand up there. There's another counter up there in front of a small window where two people are chatting, but they don't notice me, so I sneak back out before I get accused of being somewhere I shouldn't be.

I'm just leaving the room when I hear my name off to the side.

"Mac, hey! You're super early," Jade says. She's coming from a hallway that leads to who knows where. She greets me with a casual slap on the arm.

"Yeah, sorry. I—"

"Let me introduce you to some people," she says.

She introduces me to so many people, all their names kind of blur together. There's a Seth, a Jay, and an Anastasia, Kylie, Kristie, Sheila, Carter, Nate, Josh, and at least ten more people, none of whom I could identify in a crowd. And these are just the people in the stage and backstage area.

I glance up at the small window that peeks into the loft, where the two people I saw earlier are still sitting. There's a thin blond guy who looks like he's sitting in a clown car he's so tall and a shorter redheaded girl.

"Who are they?"

"I don't know their names," Jade says with a brief glance up at the booth. "Tech majors."

I mingle with Jade and her theater friends until students finally start to trickle in and take seats. I take one in the first row, just in case I feel brave enough.

The audience is nearly packed. I don't know what I expected as far as turnout, but it wasn't this. The pendulum swings to the nervous side, and I drum my fingers against my legs in no particular rhythm. Just something to get the nerves out.

One of the students Jade introduced me to hops up onstage and gets the evening started. He introduces himself and explains how the evening will go, how audience participation will work, and that this is not a regular show and laughing, clapping, hooting, hollering, and throwing money at the stage are all accepted forms of participation. The whole room cackles at this guy, and I do too, but I also feel a twinge of something I recognize from soccer.

When I was in middle school, I went to a soccer camp for a week in the summer. Some college-aged guys led the camp, and I remember being so impressed by their skills. I also remember this certainty I got in my head that I could do what they did at their level. There was one particular trick, elastico, that I knew was way above my skill level, and I also knew I was capable of getting it. So I worked my ass off, and sure enough, by the end of the week I'd mastered it.

I get that same feeling here. I know on an instinctual level that I could do what he's doing. I could make these people laugh. I know I could be just as entertaining. Given the chance, I could be really good at this stuff.

And tonight I'm going to take my chance.

The pendulum stills. Whatever doubt I had going into tonight disappears.

The first time they ask for an audience member, I shoot my hand up. I'm chosen quickly and join the other theater students on stage for a scene. We play a game called Taxi Cab that requires each player to have a distinct personality and be able—or at least attempt—to mimic each of the other players' chosen personalities. It's a riot, and I do as well as I thought I would. When my turn is over I go back to my seat, but I'm buzzing. For the first time all week, I'm smiling and I can't stop. For the first time maybe in my whole life, I feel the thing I've been searching for: belonging.

Even when I was in soccer, no goal scored felt quite this right. No grade earned, no scholastic honor, no pat on the back from my dad has brought me to life quite like being on stage for those few minutes.

I volunteer again and again, especially when it becomes clear not many of the audience members are interested. I go up as often as they let me, and I let them tease me for how often I go up. I don't care. All I care about is the crystal-clear certainty that whatever I've been looking for with my dad, approval or pride, I feel it for myself tonight.

I approve of this. I am proud of me for doing this. Like the shedding of an old skin, whatever I thought I may have needed from him, I don't need it anymore.

CHAPTER NINETEEN

JESSIE

The problem with not wanting to forgive Mac is that the desire only lives in the logical part of my brain. My body keeps cycling me through the Halloween party and all the moments that came after it. I relive every encounter we've had over the past six weeks. The small touches, the passing glances, the way his hand would brush against my thigh, against my hand...the night we listened to the album together. None of it blurs together for me. Every moment is distinct and precious and painful.

Every time I think about our fight, my blood boils. It's been nine days and I can't stop thinking about the look on Mac's face when he fessed up. When I replay that exact moment I feel the same stabbing pain in my chest. And now I've had the space to reflect on the fight, it's clear I wasn't exactly a saint. So I'm also at war with my shame and my anger. I haven't had a moment's peace in nine days. I've never been more distracted by my inner world, so I shouldn't be surprised when I run headlong into Ava Gold in the science building as I'm leaving class one afternoon, the papers she was holding falling to the floor.

"Shit, I'm sorry," I say as I help pick up the papers scattered everywhere.

"No worries. Are you okay?" she asks.

"Yeah, I was just...thinking. It's— I'm sorry. I should have been paying attention."

"It's not a problem," she says as I stack papers in her arms. "Actually, Jessica—"

"Jessie."

"You're just the person I wanted to see. I emailed you about an hour ago to set up a meeting with you. Any chance you're free now?"

"Uh, sure." My stomach flutters. I've never liked being summoned to teachers' offices even though I'm twenty-one now and there's no reason this meeting couldn't be good news. But my brain doesn't seem to think anything good can come of being summoned by a teacher.

I follow her down the hallway, taking deep breaths in through my nose and out through my pursed lips. She lets me into her office and gestures for me to sit as she sets down her disorganized stack of papers. I cringe.

"Sorry again about your papers." I point to the stack.

"Not a problem. I've had my head in the clouds a number of times," she says with a reassuring smile.

I smile back at her despite not having a thing to smile about, just eager for her to get on with it.

"So I wanted to bring you in and congratulate you because you have won the Walden Senior Scholarship." The smile on her face grows, and she holds her hands out in a celebratory jazz hands kind of way.

A thousand pounds lift from my chest and shoulders. I grip the handles of the chair because I might actually float away, the relief is so instant. Tears well in my eyes. I won't have to take out loans. I won't have to think one more minute about how I'm going to afford to finish college.

I think of the younger version of me, the little girl who cried in Miss Julie's office, and how grateful she was to have an adult who didn't tell her to dry her tears and get on with her day. I think of the slightly older version of me who found a safe space to speak her dreams out loud to another school counselor, how both of those versions of myself are celebrating this win with me today because they know I'm about to be one step closer to realizing my dreams of being a safe place for someone else who needs it.

"Thank you so much for letting me know," I say.

"It's my pleasure. You should be getting an email soon with more details, and of course the financial aid office will be in touch to work out details. Congratulations, Jessie. This was well-deserved."

I thank her again and leave, happier than I've been all week. I find a bench down the hall and text Jade immediately. She texts back within seconds.

AMAZING JOB BB!!! I KNEW YOU'D GET IT.

I'm radiating, little rays of sunshine bursting through my skin. I haven't had enough caffeine for this the jittery, wide-awake feeling to be anything but pure, undistilled joy.

A little breathless, I call my mom.

"Hey, chicken, how are ya?" She sounds tired, but I know she'll want to hear this.

"Mom, I won the scholarship." My cheeks actually hurt from smiling.

"Which scholarship?" I hear the water running in the background and dishes clanging. There's a TV on somewhere. I know she isn't trying to minimize this moment, but I'm ready to scream from the rooftops and buy a cake and tell everyone I see that I won this scholarship, and her lack of enthusiasm is bringing me down.

"It's the Walden Senior Scholarship. It covers everything my partial won't cover next year. I'm going to finish college, Mom. I'm going to grad school, and I'm going to—" I choke, my throat thick with emotion.

I'm going to do it. I'm going to make my dreams real.

"Jessie, that is amazing." I know she's mustering as much excitement as she can, and maybe another day she would have been jumping up and down with joy, but not today. At four o'clock on a Monday she's finished one work shift and will be getting ready for her next any minute.

"Thanks, Mom. I'll let you go. Tell Daddy I said hi."

She promises she will and we hang up. Pinches of disappointment snip away at my excitement, but I'm not going to let it ruin this moment.

For once I bask in my win with no shoulds, no guilt, no list of things I could have done better. I'm still so jazzed up, and I want to tell people. I want to celebrate.

I compose a text to Mac but stop myself before I can hit send. My eyes heat with the threat of tears as I remember we're not talking right now. My chest aches, the longing to text him nearly overwhelming. He would celebrate with me. He'd make me feel like a million dollars even though he didn't get it.

Oh my god. It dawns on me—if I won, it means Mac didn't win. I deflate, shrinking about two inches.

He deserved it just as much as I did. A flash of his brothers' faces enters my head, his dad's angry voice at Thanksgiving. *Is he okay?*

I hover my finger over his number, chewing on the inside of my lip. Maybe I should just check in and see how he's doing, how it went with his dad.

But our fight comes back to me. The guilt on his face, his admission, the feeling when I realized I'd been played.

I click my phone off. I will not be calling Mac.

My stomach grumbles. It's early, but I didn't have a big lunch, so I text Jade and ask if she's free to meet for dinner. When I look up, one of my psych professors is passing by.

"Hi, Professor Harris." I give him a polite smile and look back down at my phone, but he stops.

"Jessie! I just wanted to say that I heard about the Walden Senior Scholarship."

I smile, waiting for the inevitable praise.

"A second place for that scholarship is really quite an accomplishment."

Second place?

I cock my head to the side, brow furrowed. He doesn't pick up on my body language and plows ahead.

"You and Mackenzie have always been neck and neck for these things. I hope you aren't too disappointed he won it. You are both such deserving students."

But Mac didn't win.

He opens his mouth to say more, but I interrupt.

"Sorry, Professor, I don't mean to be rude, but I think there's been some mistake. Professor Gold just told me I won the scholarship..."

"Ah! Well, she is the faculty who knows the most about that. Perhaps we should clear the air about that. Have you got a moment?"

I nod because words are useless right now. Did Mac actually win? And if so, why did Professor Gold tell me I'd won? My stomach is in my throat and my throat is in my knees, and I start to shake a little.

I should not have gotten my hopes up. I should not have just taken Professor Gold at her word. I should have asked for proof. Like an email confirmation. Why didn't I get an email?

Oh god, am I going to have to call my mom back and tell her I didn't actually win?

Deep breaths, Jessie. In through the nose and out through the mouth. Do not throw up right now.

Ava Gold's office door is still open, and Professor Harris knocks and says, "Knock, knock."

Professor Gold gestures us both in, and Professor Harris launches into his explanation before she can even ask us what we need. Her face stays mostly neutral as Professor Harris talks. I keep looking for the confusion, but it never comes. Professor Gold looks a little pale and shifts in her chair.

"Ah. Yes." She clears her throat, tugging at the collar of her sweater. "Mackenzie did actually win the scholarship, but when I informed him, he declined it. And since Jessica was our second-place winner, she became the default winner. I didn't have a chance to send a correcting email to the faculty yet, nor did I find it entirely relevant to inform Jessica of such events. What matters now is that she is our scholarship recipient."

"Quite right," Professor Harris says, satisfied with this explanation, completely oblivious to Ava Gold staring daggers at him. He leaves the room with a pat on my shoulder, and I stand there for just a few minutes, feet rooted to the floor.

"Did he say why he did that?" I ask. My voice is raspy like I haven't spoken in years. "Mac. Did he say why he gave up the scholarship?"

"He just said he didn't need it and he hoped it would go to someone who needed it more than he did."

The room spins a little. I use the back of the chair to hold me steady.

"Did he know I was the second-place winner? When he said that, did he know?"

Ava Gold shakes her head.

Holy shit.

"Are you okay, Jessica?"

"Jessie," I say on autopilot.

"Jessie. Are you all right?" she repeats.

I nod despite the fact I'm not all right at all. My heartbeat thuds in my ears. It sounds like someone turned up the volume on my breathing and turned down the volume on the rest of the world. My mouth is dry, and suddenly nothing seems as important as getting a drink of water right now.

"Yes, I'm sorry. I can go..." I mumble as I walk out of her office. My feet weigh ten pounds each. I stumble to a water fountain, the ice-cold water a welcome relief. I stand over the water fountain, clutching the sides.

He didn't lose. He gave it up willingly. Despite his dad, despite the honor, he sacrificed the scholarship because he didn't need it.

It's the thing I wanted all along, so why doesn't it feel as satisfying as I thought it would?

IF HALLMARK CHRISTMAS movies could heal the pain of a broken heart, I would be completely cured. As it turns out, they don't, and in fact most of them have such poorly written plotlines and dialogue it's hard to completely ignore my sadness. I've stopped trying to ignore it at this point, and now I just let sadness sit with me. It's heavy and not a great companion, but I have no choice. It weighs as much as a whale, and I can't move it.

I spend my days doing the bare minimum. I got through my exams and I go home for the break tomorrow, but today, my last day on campus for a couple of weeks, I hide in my room until I have to leave for a shift at the cafe. I picked up work all week for different work-studies around campus, and tonight it's at the cafe as a barista. I don't know if Mac is still on campus, and I'm desperate not to run into him. I didn't have anything to do for Professor Campbell for the research project, but I did have to see him in class, which was hard enough.

I'm hoping that by next semester I'll be able to face him. Maybe not. And if not, I'll ask to be taken off the project. But right now I can't even bring myself to compose a text to him.

At least once an hour every day my thumbs hover over the keypad, a thousand things to say crossing my mind. Sometimes I even type up the message, but I always delete it. I wonder if Mac ever sees the little typing bubble appear and disappear. I chew on my lip, staring at our old conversation. Our last text exchange was right before I went to his apartment the night of our fight. I wish I could go back to being that girl who was blissfully unaware of what was about to happen.

I stuff my phone under my pillow, pull the covers a little higher up, and press play on my laptop. I've got a cheesy Christmas movie on, and I plan to watch as many as I can until I have to leave for work. Maybe eventually my brain will be full of mediocre movie romances instead of wondering what Mac is up to, and if I should forgive him, and am I being silly for being this sad? A million thoughts circle like birds of prey.

"Oh, Jessie."

Jade appears, standing in my doorway, taking me in. I'm a sight, I have no doubt. My eyes are swollen from all the on-and-off crying I've done all week, puffy from the lack of sleep. My hair has been in a knot on my head since I washed it a few days ago. There are empty cookie wrappers and some half-empty chip bags on my bed, at least three beverages at varying stages of empty.

Jade sets her bag on the floor and crawls into my twin bed with me after removing the trash scattered at the foot of it. I scoot to make room for her, and Jade spoons me.

"I like being the little spoon," I say, my voice a little shaky.

"I know, sweetie. How ya feeling?"

"Sad. Confused."

"He's such a shithead," she says, planting a kiss on the top of my head.

"He really isn't."

Before finding out about the scholarship earlier this week, I probably would have agreed with Jade, but I can't now.

"He isn't. I'm just trying to make you feel better," she says.

"He did a really, really shitty thing. But he also did a really, really kind thing. That's the worst part. I don't even think he's a bad person. He just hurt me."

"I am so sorry, Jessie."

"No, wait, that's not the worst part. The worst part is that I want to forgive him and call him and pretend it never happened. But this other part of me is like...I'm not sure I could trust him. Except that he just did this extraordinarily selfless thing, and I can't stop thinking about one or the other, and it's just a freaking seesaw in my brain."

"Then let's not do any thinking. Just Christmas movies." She snuggles me a little closer. A choir on the movie fills the silence—a Christmas hymn, of course.

"I don't want to go to work tonight," I say.

"Can someone cover for you?"

"No, I already asked around."

"I'd cover for you if I could."

Jade would be so lost behind the coffee counter. I won't be much better, but I did get a little training last year when I covered this shift. I know she'd really cover my shift if she could, and that's one of five billion reasons she's so amazing. For the past week, Jade and I have cuddled in my bed; she's bought us takeout and kept the freezer stocked with ice cream. Her schedule has essentially revolved around me since the Saturday she picked me up in the parking lot of Mac's apartment, and I don't know if I've ever felt so loved or cared for.

"What if he comes by and tries to apologize or talk to me? I can't..."

"Call me immediately if he does, and I will take care of it."

I take reassurance in this, because if I can trust anyone in this world, it's Jade.

"What about you?" I ask, tired of talking and thinking about Mac. "What's the update with George Greg and Threesome Anna?"

"I'm still balancing both non-relationships but starting to feel more and more guilty."

"Guilty, huh?"

I turn to face her, and Jade releases me from her hold. She lies on her back and throws her arms over her eyes.

"Ugh, don't."

"So you are catching feels?" I ask.

"Too many of them," she says, and I practically hear her roll her eyes.

"I knew it," I say, giving her arm a playful pinch.

She slaps my hand away. "Shut up."

"Which one of them do you have feelings for?"

"Both of them?"

"Uh-oh. Is this The Most Dramatic Finale of *The Bachelorette* Ever?" I say, imitating the commercial voice.

"I wish. I'd be willing to profess my love and choose between these two in Paris or Greece in a beautifully sparkly dress."

"You know, I can't make Greece happen, but we could set up a rose ceremony. I think both of them would respect you for that. Also, I'm going to skip over the fact you used the L word, mostly because I don't have the energy to unpack that with you."

"Yes, well, I didn't mean it. I don't love either of them. I just like them."

"You like-like them." I smile at her, egging her on.

She blushes, and even in the fog of my own sadness there's a pinprick of light, of excitement, for Jade. She doesn't catch feelings, always claiming she's "bad at love," so this is all a big deal.

"Yes, I like-like them." She sighs heavily, dropping her arms to her sides. She props herself up on one side, facing me now.

"You have to say something," I say.

"Why? I'm not exclusive with either of them. They could be seeing and sleeping with other people and that would be fine." She shrugs, trying to be casual, but it's the most forced-casual shrug I've ever seen.

I raise my eyebrows at her. "Except your tone tells me that maybe it wouldn't be so fine with you."

"Fuck off." She points at me and then pokes me in the shoulder.

"You can't tell me to fuck off when I say something true that you don't like to hear," I say.

"I can, and I will."

"Your response has been noted." I stare at her until she rolls her eyes, dropping face-down on the bed this time, face squished into my pillow.

"Fine. But do I have to tell them I've been seeing the other person and I like them too?"

"Probably."

"Boo," Jade says. "Being an adult is stupid."

"I agree."

"Can't I just break hearts and take names?"

"You could. But you're not that person."

"I actually am that person." She picks herself back up again to lie on her side, propping her head up on a hand. "But the fact that you choose to believe otherwise is what I love the most about you." She reaches out and pinches my cheek in a half-affectionate, half-teasing way.

I scrunch my face in response and turn back around to my laptop, which is propped on the nightstand, still playing my role.

Talking with Jade about her problems made mine disappear for a minute, but it only takes half a second for them to come back and haunt me. My heartbreak, momentarily forgotten, crashes back over me. A wave I tried to hold back with a paper wall. Salty tears paint my face for the hundredth time today.

We ignore the world for the Christmas movie, both of us avoiding feelings and situations that hurt too much to hold. For a short time we release them from our hands, cuddling until an alarm on my phone reminds me I need to get ready for the work shift.

I rummage through my drawers for an outfit while Jade sits cross-legged on my bed.

For the length of the movie, I didn't think about Mac once, but now I'm up and getting ready and my thoughts start to tornado again, picking up the debris of my feelings, causing utter chaos inside me.

"Jade, please just tell me what to do about Mac."

She presses her lips together in a thin line. "Well...what is your top option at the moment?"

I shake my head, tossing a shirt that's obviously dirty into my laundry basket. "I don't know. Try to forget he ever existed?"

"That's—" A long pause. "Yep, okay. Obviously, I fully support that."

I glare at her. "Out with it," I say.

"You don't need Opinion Jade right now, and I'm doing a really good job withholding that opinion. So maybe don't push it."

"I want Opinion Jade. I wouldn't push if I didn't want it."

"Are you sure?"

"Since when do you ask if I'm sure about hearing your opinions before you spout them at me?"

"You're delicate right now, and I'm trying to be delicate with you."

"I'm not that delicate," I murmur.

"You cried at a Rice Krispies commercial."

"Those are sad, okay?"

I am delicate, she's right, but I hate when people have something to say and don't say it. I don't want to be tiptoed around, not even now.

Jade pats the bed, and I finish changing quickly and lean against it. She takes my hands in hers and looks me dead in the eye.

"I think the fact Mac is Sexy Shakespeare is incredible. You know you have chemistry. You looked for him for a month, which is, like, sooo not you, and he was right there all along! Did he do something shitty? Yes. But we are human. And humans make mistakes. And I think this mistake is worth forgiving. And I think it's stupid for you to never speak to him again. Especially since I know for a fact that you love him."

"I don't love him," I say, grumpy that Jade has so clearly read my mail.

She just scoffs. "Fine, then at the very least you have insanely deep and intense feelings for him, and you're allowed to be hurt and sad for as long as you need. What he did was shitty, okay? I'm not saying what he did was okay. But I also think it's worth forgiving. Especially considering the chemistry between you two. It's palpable. I've never seen anyone so smitten with you. So obsessed with you. It's kind of gross, actually."

A smile cracks my face open. But just a little. "Damn it, Jade. No jokes. I'm trying to be sad."

"Oops. Sorry. Sad Jessie. Sad Jade. We can do that."

I gather my hair to one side and braid it slowly, chewing on everything Jade said.

"That wasn't so bad," I say.

"There's more."

"Uh-oh."

"Should I finish?"

I gesture for her to continue.

She cracks her knuckles but holds eye contact. Confrontation has always been a strong suit of Jade's.

"I think the reason you can't forgive Mac is because you haven't forgiven yourself."

I blink, but it's the only movement I can conjure. I don't even think my blood is moving through my body. My heart definitely stops beating for half a second. I've never understood deer more than I do right now. Jade's words resound so profoundly inside me my bones absorb the echo.

"You messed up freshman year. You had a really hard year and you partied a little too much that your grades slipped, and since then you've been unreasonably hard on yourself. You stopped having fun at all, to the point that when you did go out and try to let loose a little you couldn't enjoy it. I swear to god, you barely smiled for two years. But look what happened at the Halloween party this year. You let yourself have fun for the first time in a long time. Mac brought out my favorite side of you. Look what it led to! You found love."

"I found heartbreak."

"Your heart would not be hurting if you felt nothing for him." She pronounces every syllable so I don't miss a thing.

I shift from one foot to the other, avoiding eye contact. I twist a stray thread on the bedsheet around my finger.

"You do not have to forgive Mac right away. You can take all the time you need to heal from your hurt, but once you've healed, you don't have to be as hard on him as you've been on yourself. And while we're at it, stop being so hard on yourself."

"Being hard on myself is the only way I got my grades back up. If I stop then I'll slip again."

Even as I'm saying the words, I don't believe them. I've taken enough psychology classes and done enough therapy to know negative self-talk doesn't actually help anyone.

"That's just not true, Jessie." She reaches out and puts her hand over mine.

I meet her gaze, but I'm overwhelmed by the love in her eyes.

"Plenty of people do well in school without being an absolute ass to themselves."

The temptation to tell her she's wrong, to insist I have to do things my way and that she doesn't understand, is so strong, but I catch myself before any words come out. Jade is right. Her words and the truth of the matter settle on me like rain, pelting and pooling until there isn't a part of me that doesn't believe her.

"The way I see it, you just need to do a little work on yourself, and I wish I meant that in the dirty way, but I just mean you should forgive yourself and then forgive that poor, sweet man who just wants to bone you."

"What did I say about being Sad Jessie? No laughing." I fight a smile through the tears forming in my eyes.

"Sorry, you know I'm so bad at this."

"You're not though. You're actually stupidly good at it," I mumble.

"Oh, good. As long as you still want me to be your friend."

"You're stuck with me," I say.

"Thank god."

"Thank you." I reach out to hug her, and we hold each other until I remember I have to leave for work.

Jade's words ring in my head, clanging around during my whole shift. *Forgive myself, forgive Mac. Forgive him, forgive myself.*

Mac never stood a chance against my expectations. I barely stand a chance against my expectations. I'm always swimming with my head barely above water, paddling for my life under the surface, and even when I meet my goals I don't celebrate. I tell myself all the ways it could have been better and move on to the next thing. I am never enough for myself, so how could Mac have been enough?

Even if he'd told me within the week it was him at the party, I probably would have found a way to be mad at him about it. I would have found a reason to decide he didn't measure up.

My own mother is held captive by her mistakes. She admitted to me that she went to college, that she has loans she never told me about. Have I forgiven her? Of course not. Because Jade is right. I can't forgive others because I can't forgive myself.

The shame of this settles heavily on me. I don't recognize this version of me that I've become. The kind that holds onto resentments and expectations as if I acquire them for sport.

Should I continue to keep my mistakes in pretty cages? Feeding them, making them fat, never setting them free. If I keep other people's mistakes too, by the end of my life I'll have become a true collector, surrounded by a menagerie of resentments. A regular Mrs. Havisham, locked away in my home hoarding unforgiveness as I rot from the inside out.

My stomach turns, sour at this image of myself. I don't even know if I'm capable of letting go, but the cost of holding onto it all feels too high. I don't want to lose myself to my bitterness, but I don't want to get lost in unfamiliar territory.

What is the cost of unlocking all the cages, opening the windows, and setting my mother, Mac, and myself free?

The only answer is this: I won't know until I try.

CHAPTER TWENTY

MAC

I've never had a problem with being the extra wheel in the family. When my brothers started dating and getting married and our Christmas festivities grew from our original six to seven, and then eight, and now nine, it was never an issue for me.

Except this year.

Jessie's presence—or lack thereof—haunts me. She and I still haven't spoken since she left my apartment three weeks ago. We've somehow avoided seeing each other on campus for two weeks, except for the classes we shared, and even then we both acted like the other didn't exist. Or rather, she acted like I didn't exist. I fought every instinct and urge to sit by her, to talk to her, to stare at her from across the room, to text her, to brush past her—to do anything for a second of connection with her. Anything had to be better than silence. I did nothing, of course. I played my part and kept my distance, and I hated every second of it.

The only company I have in the silence is my guilt. And that is pretty shit company. I deserve it, I know I do. I just thought—I hoped—

maybe by now we could have had a conversation. I know it's too much to hope she might forgive me, and I've all but given up on reconciliation. At this point, all I want is a few minutes of her time so I can apologize properly, but I'm losing hope for that too.

Knowing I've lost her for good has pretty much ruined my Christmas. I'd hoped we'd be spending it together. I had her present all picked out but hadn't bought it yet: a Pilot Custom 823 fountain pen. I don't know anything about them, but I found a Reddit forum, made a post, got some advice, and learned enough to make a semi-informed decision. The pen is still sitting in my cart online. Just another reminder of what I lost.

I've been home a week now for the holiday break, and even though I'm not acting any different, everyone at home can sense my foul mood. I'm still the court jester, smiling and cracking jokes, but I'm the ninth wheel on the wagon that's making it all wobbly, and I'm guessing everyone is having more fun when I leave the room, which never happens. They probably sense the heartbreak under my laughter like the current under the waves. They're just hoping I don't pull them down with me.

I spend more time in my room than I might normally do over a holiday break. The worst part is, everything in my house reminds me of her because just a month ago she was here. Just a month ago I got to hold her and share a bed with her and watch her laugh and share meals with her in my home. Now I spend most of my days listening to Black Phantom, working out, trying not to text her, and wondering what she's doing nearly every second of the day.

I can't do this forever, and I won't do this forever. I know eventually I'll move on, but I can't yet. I'm not ready to let go yet.

Some days are harder than others, and I woke up this morning hoping it would be a good day. It's Christmas Eve, so we've already had brunch together as a family, and we have a whole day of activities planned. After cookie decorating, we have a church service, and then we'll have dinner and open stockings. Then it's a hot chocolate bar and pajama-party game night.

It's a lot of together time that is both the perfect distraction and the perfect torture. I snuck to my room for a few minutes to myself after brunch this morning, but the longer I sit here, the less I want to go back downstairs. Everyone is getting ready to decorate cookies, and I told them I'd be back in a few. The growing ache in my chest is almost too much. For the third time today, I hover my finger over her name in my phone, but a knock at my door keeps me from following through.

"Yeah?" I say, and the door opens, revealing my dad. He leans against the doorframe, a mug of coffee in hand. The steam rises out of the cup and I smell the caramelized, nutty, smoky aroma of it from here. Mom must have just put on a fresh pot.

"Hey, Dad."

"What do you say we play a little Christmas hooky and go for a round of golf?"

"Mom is okay with that?"

He gives me a reassuring nod, and I tell him I'll be down in five. I don't even like golf that much, but a little fresh air and movement and some time away from all the couples sounds really good to me right now.

It's a surprisingly warm day for December, in the upper fifties, and with the sun shining it still feels like fall. The country club my dad is a member of is just a five-minute drive from the house, and when we arrive they get us set up with a cart. We sling our golf bags on the back and we're on the green not twenty minutes after Dad appeared in my doorway.

I tee off first. The rule is always youngest to oldest when we golf. One of those unspoken family rules everyone's followed for so long no one remembers its exact origins. I haven't played in ages, so I'm rusty, but it's like riding a bike; all my old golf lessons come back to me, and even if I'm not playing my best game today, I'm happier than I've been in a while. With the sun on my face and the quiet of the greens it's hard to care about much else but what is right in front of me. I almost turn and thank my dad for bringing me out here, but I know he'll just grunt and wave me off. Even gratitude is too big of an emotional display for him.

We play in comfortable silence, as it usually goes if it's just us. My brothers are the chatty ones and always find a topic to interest my dad: sports, work projects, more sports. But I didn't come out here to chat with my dad; I came out to escape, and for some serotonin. It's working.

But a few holes in, Dad finally breaks the silence.

"You ever find out about that scholarship?"

I swallow hard. I'd hoped he'd start with a softer ball, something like, "How's school?" But leave it to my dad to throw a trick pitch first.

"I did," I say, shifting my weight as I watch my dad line up his next shot.

"You win it?"

"I did."

Did he hear the way my voice cracked when I said that? Can he sense I'm holding back? I know I need to be upfront about the scholarship, but my heart is racing, and despite the chill in the air I feel sweaty, clammy even. I pull my shirt away from my body. The material feels too heavy and sticky, as if all the places I'm sweating are actually glue holding the shirt against my body.

"Good. Four valedictorians in the house is something to be proud of. Expected nothing less from a Baldwin boy." My dad takes his swing and the ball soars through the air, landing probably just where he wanted it to. He pats me on the back as he heads to the cart, not even looking me in the eye.

All of this annoys me. His declaration about what a good Baldwin boy is, the fact he won't tell me even now that he's proud of me. I search for the familiar ache in me, the longing for my dad's approval, but it's not there. What lives there instead is the confidence that I don't have to just lie down and take his bullshit anymore.

"I declined it."

My dad freezes, his back to me. He stands stock-still. I imagine he isn't blinking or breathing. "Say that again," he says. It's not a question or a request. It's an order. His low near-growl sends a chill down my spine, but I straighten, channeling all the energy from my improv night.

"I said, I declined the scholarship."

He spins around, stalking toward me. He gets almost nose-to-nose with me. "Why the hell did you do such a damn stupid thing?"

My dad almost never loses it. He's a silent treatment kind of guy, so I know I've really hit a nerve.

"Because I don't need it. We have enough money, and that scholarship should go to someone who actually needs it."

"This is not about the money, Mackenzie Aaron Baldwin."

"Yeah, I know. It's about being a Baldwin. And pride. And whatever other macho thing it means to be a Baldwin boy. But I'm a Baldwin whether I earned it or not."

He looks like he's going to interrupt me, but I don't let him. I stand a little straighter, and the few inches I have on him feel like two feet of height. I puff my chest a bit, squaring my shoulders.

"I don't need a scholarship to earn my name, and if that's what I needed to earn your respect then that's a damn shame. I couldn't live with myself if I took that scholarship opportunity away from someone." *From Jessie.* "But I can live without your respect."

My dad stands there red-faced and speechless. I thought it would be terrifying to say these things to him, but it's actually incredibly freeing. I chuckle and walk back toward the cart, stuffing my golf club back in my bag and slinging it over my shoulder.

"Where the hell do you think you're going?"

"I'm done here," I say. "Oh. And I'm taking a theater class next year."

I retrace our path back up to the clubhouse. My dad doesn't follow me. He doesn't bring the cart around and yell at me or apologize. My heart is racing, and it isn't the pace at which I'm walking or the weight of the bag on my shoulder. I could run a marathon right now—I don't feel like I weigh anything. I watch my feet like an out-of-body experience, trying to stay tethered to the earth, but I'm on cloud nine, ten, and eleven. I can't believe I stood up to my dad like that. I can't believe how little I care about what he thinks of me. What took me so damn long to do that?

I call my brother Noah to come get me. He shows up less than ten minutes later with Charlotte in the back seat. I stuff my clubs in the trunk and join him in the front.

"Dad being...Dad?"

"Yep," I say. "I told him I declined the Walden Senior Scholarship, and he—"

Noah barks out a laugh.

"Exactly," I say.

I recount the whole conversation to Noah, who doesn't assure me Dad will come around because we both know he probably won't. He'll stay mad until it fizzles out and then he'll pretend like it never happened. It's the way he is, and none of us expect him to change.

"That seems healthy," Charlotte says as we park.

"Gotta get used to it, love," Noah says to her, helping her out of the car and planting a kiss on her knuckles.

"Is your family non-dysfunctional?" I ask Charlotte as I haul my bag from the trunk.

"Absolutely not. I wouldn't be nearly as interesting if I came from a well-adjusted household."

"Tell us about your dysfunction, my dear," Noah says.

We walk into the house and Charlotte does exactly that. The three of us spike some hot chocolate and find a spot in the living room to finish our conversation.

We barely get halfway through our hot chocolates before Mom comes in and reminds us to get ready for church and that we need to leave in an hour. Naturally, we spend forty-five minutes finishing our drinks and chatting and then get ready at the last minute. We hear Dad come in at some point, slam the door, and stalk through the house. I don't see him again until church. He doesn't speak to me, and for once I don't care.

During the service, I sit at the end of the pew, next to Charlotte. I liked her before she told us all about her childhood, but now I think she might be my favorite sister-in-law. Well, future sister-in-law. Maybe. I'll be harassing Noah later about when he's proposing.

I'm trying not to fall asleep during the sermon when I feel a tap on my leg. I look down and see Charlotte has typed out a note on her phone and is showing it to me.

How are things with the girl? Jessie?

Just seeing her name on the screen is like being punched. I successfully went a few hours without thinking about her, and now Charlotte's brought her up.

Thanks, Charlotte.

I open the notes app on my phone and type out a response.

Not great. I fucked everything up.

Charlotte types back on her phone.

What happened?

I type out the story and pass my phone to her. After she reads it she gives me a painful look. I type out another message.

Is this where you say "I told you so"?

Charlotte shakes her head.

What do I do? I ask in the notes.

Give her time and space. She'll come around. I promise. If she likes you as much as you like her...she'll come around.

I press my lips into a tight smile and mouth the words "thank you" to her. She nods and tucks her phone back into her purse. I want to believe Charlotte, but maybe I fucked up so royally there's no coming back from this.

I watched as the realization about the Halloween party played out on her face. I watched the light in her eyes dim. I watched her body language shift from open longing to "fuck off." The sting of that rejection still stabs at my ribs. I planned to take the truth to the grave, but the moment felt right. It was so casual, and she seemed so tickled by the idea I expected us to laugh about it. I thought it might become an inside joke. But it was more like a worst-case scenario, and the thing that I was trying to avoid all along happened: I lost Jessie.

Jade and Charlotte seem to think she'll come around, but hope is a slippery thing, and I'm losing my grip on it with every passing day.

HOURS after the service has ended and stockings have been exchanged and family games have been won and lost, I'm finally in bed, grateful for the silence and the time to myself. I'm just about to turn off my light and roll over when there's a knock on the door.

"Door's open," I say, certain it's one of my brothers. But my mom appears in my doorway. She looks tired, but in the satisfied "I just spent all day with my entire family" kind of way. Her eyes sparkle, but her smile shakes at the edges.

Her body slumps a little and she leans her head on the doorframe. She should be in bed asleep by now, but I know she's going room by room to check on everyone, and I also know she'll stay up a little longer just to get some time to herself.

"Merry Christmas Eve," she says with a smile.

"Merry Christmas Eve."

"You okay?" she asks, her forehead crinkled in concern.

"Yeah, why?"

"I heard about the scholarship from your father."

"Ah. Maybe you should ask if he's okay."

"He'll come around."

I nod. He will come around, but not in the way all of us hope he might. I don't know how my mom has put up with him for this long, but they seem happy enough. She's nothing like my father—she's proud of us for everything we've ever done, loving us endlessly and openly, and filling in the gaps he creates with his silence and disapproval.

"You know he's proud of you?" she says.

"He's not, but it's okay."

She presses her lips into a thin line. "It's not okay," she says, her voice a whisper. I can see tears in her eyes. I know she wishes he were different with us.

"It is, though, because I don't need his approval. I know who I am and I like who I am, and if that's not good enough for the Baldwin name, he's the only one who cares."

She walks into the room and pushes my hair back, planting a kiss on my forehead. She wraps her arms around my shoulders and holds me to her. I lean in, her floral laundry detergent scent enveloping me.

"I'm proud of you," she says.

"I know," I say. And it's enough. All of it is exactly enough.

CHAPTER TWENTY-ONE

JESSIE

"You have to talk to him."

"I don't though. I don't have to do anything, Jade," I say as I watch her do her makeup for a date with George Greg. She's not wearing nearly enough clothes for January, but I know if I point this out she'll change into something skimpier and insist that's what her jacket is for.

She's finally having The Talk with him tonight, and I know she's nervous, but she won't talk to me about it. So we're talking about me. Again.

"Don't be a child." She scolds me by pointing a finger at me like a mom.

"Don't be a mom."

"Did you develop an attitude over the holiday break?"

"Years of living with you have finally rubbed off on me."

"I'll rub off on you," Jade says with a wink, and I raise my eyebrows at her. She shrugs. "But seriously, Jessie, it's been more than a month."

While Jade and I talked on the phone nearly every day of the break, I still haven't exchanged a single word with Mac. It feels like it's been much longer than a month and also like no time has passed at all. I attempted to sort out all my feelings over the break. I sorted and unsorted, I cried and almost called him. I spent so much time journaling and processing and trying to figure out what to do that most nights I went to sleep with a little bit of a headache. We've been back at school for five days, and every day I wake up with butterflies. *Am I going to see him today?* It's been a few days of classes already, and he isn't in any of them so far. I still have a couple days left, and I can't help but think he's going to be in one of them. If I run into him without seeking him out, will we talk? Will we reconcile? Do I keep ignoring him?

A headache at the base of my skull thumps to life.

"My feelings are still hurt," I say with little to no conviction. This is my excuse for not talking to him, for not having called or texted.

"Maybe what you need is an apology."

"Maybe," I mumble.

"Which you can't get from him unless you *let him* apologize."

I sigh heavily and throw myself back on Jade's bed. The cloud of her down comforter *poofs* around me. She's right, and I've admitted as much to her. But my pride is a goddamn brick wall that isn't easy to topple.

"Listen, my little cabbage," Jade says.

"You spent too much time in France."

"It was just a week," she says, dabbing at her cheeks with a bright-pink makeup sponge. "But you're not going to like this, so brace yourself." She turns, setting her makeup down, so I prop myself up on my elbows, giving Jade my full attention.

A loose knot in my stomach tries to prepare me for whatever is coming next.

"There's no such thing as avoiding hurt feelings. And ultimately, the point is not 'Oh, he hurt my feelings.' The point is, did he own up to his actions? But if you don't open up a conversation and open yourself up to him, you might—"

"He could have reached out and apologized anytime," I say, sitting all the way up. It's a fight I'll probably lose, but I stick my flag in the ground anyway.

"No. No, no, no. You don't get to do that. You know as well as I do that yes, a text apology is an apology, but if he had done that you would have bitched about how he didn't say it to your face, that he took the easy way out. If he'd called, you wouldn't have picked up. And you sure as hell weren't meeting up with him to give him a chance to say it to your face."

"Why are you taking his side?" I cross my arms in front of my chest.

"I'm taking your side. You deserve an apology, and you deserve happiness. You deserve to be with someone who sends you into another universe when he kisses you. Throwing away what you and Mac have because you're too stubborn to have one conversation with him is dumb. I can't be more on your side than I am."

"But he hurt me," I murmur. It's the only defense I have, and it's weak and crumbling with every word Jade says.

She huffs, rolling her eyes. "Jessica Mae Matthews, listen very closely to me. Even if he didn't hurt you with this, and you two went on to be exclusive and you started bumping uglies, he would have eventually hurt you somehow. Because this is what we do to each other. We hold each other's hearts and sometimes we squeeze too hard. And sometimes we accidentally drop them. No one is one hundred percent safe, Jessie. Someone will always hurt you. But the good ones are the ones who apologize."

The knot in my stomach tightens and unravels and then tightens again. My wall of excuses crumbles to debris. I don't want to hold these truths, but they force themselves into my hands. But that is the funny thing about the truth: it demands to be seen. And now there's nothing left between me and Mac. No excuses, no really good reasons to stay away. Just me and my pride.

"You know, it's actually really annoying when you're right," I say.

"I'll try not to make a habit of it."

Jade makes the final touches to her makeup, and when she walks out of the room into the living room to gather her purse and jacket, I follow her.

"And by the way, he deserves an apology too," Jade says.

"What!"

"Didn't you call him stupid?"

I snort. "Fuck. Yes, I did." I hide my face in my hands.

"M'kay, bitch."

I throw a decorative pillow at her and she dodges, slipping out the door after blowing me a kiss. I sink onto the couch, pulling my knees up to my chest and resting my chin on them.

Am I brave enough for this? Everything I know I need to do sounds so vulnerable and scary, but Jade is right. I've been hurt by my parents and I still love them. Jade has hurt my feelings a time or two and we're okay. How is this thing with Mac any different?

It's not. And the sooner I let go of my need to be right, of my need to cling to my grudges, the sooner I could have Mac.

If he still wants me.

I need to get to him, and I need to do this now. The impulse is so strong it propels me off the couch and into the shower, and twenty minutes later I'm leaving my dorm on a mission to fix everything I've fucked up.

But where would I even find Mac on a Friday night?

I GREET DAISY, the librarian at the desk tonight. She looks bored, and rightfully so: the library is nearly empty. Who the hell would be at the library a week after the holiday break ended?

Hopefully Mac.

I weave through the tables on the first floor but don't see him at any of them. Nor is he in any of the private study booths. I don't see anyone, for that matter, and my pulse quickens despite my slow pace. I head upstairs to the stacks, starting at the front and weaving my way through.

I should have called first. Or texted.

What if he doesn't want to see me?

The stacks are woefully empty on this floor too, so I head to the third floor, but it's also empty. By the time I've climbed to the fourth and topmost floor, I'm a little out of breath and almost out of faith he's here at all. But I'll check this floor, and if he's not here I'll try the gym. If he's not there I'll do the cafe before I do his apartment.

Now that I'm thinking about it, the library seems like the dumbest place for me to have started. I should have started in a bigger space where he was more likely to be.

Why would Mac be at the library on a Friday night this early in the year?

For the same reason I would. Because school matters. It matters to me, and it matters to Mac, and that's reason one of one thousand that I would be an idiot to let him get away.

I just hope I'm not too late.

I'm nearly at the end of the rows and the end of my hope when I spot someone at the farthest end of the aisle. I freeze, ducking behind one of the shelves, and observe the person as well as I can from this far away. The lighting isn't great up here. Somehow it's dimmer, as if the maintenance person couldn't be bothered to get to the lights on the top floor.

The person in the aisle is a man, as far as I can tell based off body build and hair, although I don't want to be too presumptuous. They're hunched over a book, concentrating. Their phone dings, and when they pull it out of their pocket to check the notification, the screen lights up their face and I can see very clearly that yes, it's a man.

And yes, it's Mac.

My stomach dips and shoots up into my throat, and I get a little lightheaded. I press my back against the wood of the endcap. My heart pounds in my chest. I don't know if I can do this.

There's nothing to do, Jessie, except turn and walk toward him.

But my feet weigh a hundred pounds each, and I think my legs might have forgotten how to move.

Unlock the cage, Jessie. Set everyone free.

Somehow I find the courage to move, to walk down the library aisle toward Mac. He doesn't move a muscle until I'm almost six feet away, when he glances up briefly then returns to his book. Faster than I can blink he looks up again.

"Jessie?"

I try to smile, but it ends up being this pained half-smile thing. "Hi."

"What are you doing here?" he asks. His voice is eager and cautiously optimistic. It's like a punch in the stomach; all the air leaves my lungs.

He's happy to see me. He doesn't hate me.

He takes a few steps toward me, almost charging, but slows down. I have the instinct to lean away, but I force myself to stay rooted.

"What else would I be doing on a Friday night?"

The attempt at a joke falls flat, my lack of conviction and confidence too obvious.

"Are you here to talk?"

"Yes," I say, holding eye contact with him despite my desire to look away. I'm suddenly grateful the custodial service hasn't changed the light bulbs. I appreciate the dim lighting.

Mac snaps his book shut and sets it on a shelf, most definitely in the wrong place. "I'm sorry," he says quickly, like he's afraid I'll run. His shoulders sag after he's said it as if he's been storing up the words, waiting to use them. "I'm sorry I didn't tell you right away, and then I'm sorry I didn't tell you as soon as I realized you didn't know. And I'm sorry I was such an idiot and thought that the way to not lose you was to hide things from you."

He takes a step toward me, and then another. I take one toward him until we're within arm's reach of each other but not touching. Although the desire for him to reach out and touch me is strong enough to make me dig my fingernails into my palm. I thought this would be harder, but being around Mac feels as right as a dress tailored to fit my exact body shape.

"I am so sorry that I hurt you," he continues. "I never meant to, Jessie. Living with myself the past month, knowing how hurt you were —" He shakes his head, closing his eyes, unable to finish the sentence. He swallows hard, his face contorting like he might cry.

The familiar pressure of tears bears down on the backs of my eyes, and I take a deep, slow inhale, looking up at the ceiling to keep myself from tearing up.

"Jessie."

The way he says my name draws my gaze back to his.

"I missed you," he says, his voice a whisper. His words are an arrow straight to my heart, and it takes every ounce of self-control I have not to just throw myself into his arms.

I clasp my hands in front of me, squeezing them together so I don't do just that. His gaze is so intense I avert my eyes, scratching a pattern into the carpet with the toe of my shoe.

The very big, strong wall I built around my heart was so sturdy before this moment, but here in the dim, dusty library, with Mac spilling his heart at my feet this way, the wall, originally made of stone, turns to dust. His apology is more healing than I expected it to be. Jade was right: I did need to hear this. And just the fact that Mac believes I deserve an apology is proof he is exactly the kind of guy who's safe for me to be vulnerable with.

And is there anything more vulnerable than an apology?

I take one more steadying breath and meet his eye again. "I'm sorry too." I'm surprised by how easy it is to say the words.

He furrows his brow and tilts his head to the side. "But you didn't—"

"Yes, I did. I called you stupid and I was just...mean. You didn't deserve that, and I'm sorry."

When Mac reaches for me, I let him take one of my hands into his own.

"Thank you," he says.

And then neither of us says a word. It doesn't feel necessary. The way he looks more relaxed than he did a few minutes ago, the way his smile reflects my own, the way he grips my fingers—all of it says more than either of us could with words.

A song pops into my head, but I feel too shy to sing while looking into Mac's eyes. I look down and start to sing quietly.

"You light me on fire, from inside I burn..." I tentatively lift my eyes to meet his as I start the next lyrics. *"When you're near I desire..."*

And then he joins me.

"To be lit on fire... When you're far it's too cold, it's too cold."

Our voices are shaky and quiet, but as we sing together, the massive library shrinks to just us. There could be a hundred people here and I wouldn't notice a single one but Mac right now. I squeeze his hands, my muscles aching for more contact with him.

So when he gently pulls me toward him, I let myself be pulled.

And when he dips his head, his eyes darting between my eyes and my lips, I let my body melt against his. He wraps both arms around me, one hand snaking up into my hair. I indulge the overwhelming need to touch him and let my hands splay out on his back. His body is both new and familiar to me. I remember so much of him, and I want to discover every inch.

He pauses just before his lips touch mine. His proximity is dizzying, the press of his body against mine intoxicating. The air between us is charged as if everywhere we stand, lightning strikes, and Mac and I are live wires absorbing the current.

Deja vu sweeps through me, but this time I know why. I've been here before. I've been in these arms, and I've been kissed by these lips, and the urge to have them on mine again is overwhelming, but Mac waits.

"Mac," I say, his name a whisper, and it must have been what he needed to hear because he closes the space between us.

When his lips find mine, that same insatiable hunger flows through my blood and my bones. He kisses me like I'm the exact thing he's been craving all his life. It's a kiss to end all kisses, and I know if I said the word I could have this whenever I wanted.

And I will. I'll say whatever it takes to make Mac mine. If it takes a thousand apologies, I'll say them all.

He moves, but I have no sense of where I am until my back is pressed against the shelves. I had no idea I wanted to be pressed against books and kissed like this until Mac did it, but now I'm not sure I want to have it any other way.

He pulls away for a moment, both of us breathing like we've run up the stairs. My lips are tingling. I can't tell if we kissed for one second or an entire lifetime, but I want more. I dig my fingers into his back and pull, but instead of his lips landing on mine, they land on my jaw. They just brush against my skin, and when his mouth travels down my neck I groan in his ear, little fires blooming all over my body.

His hand travels down my side, over my hip, and along my thigh. He hitches my leg up around his hip, and when he grips my ass to pull me against him I forget how to breathe for a second.

"God, Mac, we're in a library."

I do nothing to discourage him, though. I explore him with my hands, eventually winding my fingers through his hair, holding his mouth against my skin.

"Agree to be my girlfriend and I'll stop," he says against my neck. His breath tickles my neck where his lips just kissed.

I go still.

Girlfriend.

Do I want that?

Yes. More than anything.

"And if I don't want you to stop?"

Mac pulls back enough to meet my gaze. "Is that a yes?"

The corners of my lips lift into a smile. "Yes."

And then he kisses me again. Library be damned.

EPILOGUE

JESSIE

Four months later...

I clear my throat and glance around, hoping I haven't disturbed anyone in the library. It's a Friday night, so there aren't a ton of people here, but it seems like everyone who is here has headphones in and my noise doesn't seem to have bothered anyone.

I shift in my seat and lean on my hand, staring at the textbook in front of me. I need a break soon as the words are all starting to blur together.

Fingers brush against my neck, moving my hair back, startling me, but when I smell citrus and that clean detergent scent I relax. Lips brush my neck where his fingers just danced across my skin, and I shiver.

"Mac, we're in a library," I whisper as the tension in my shoulders eases. I tilt my head to the side as he places slow, firm kisses along my neck.

"Then don't make any noise," he mumbles, his lips hovering just over my jaw.

I bite my lip and close my eyes, savoring the moment. His tongue slides over the skin of my neck and I grip my textbook. I should definitely make him stop, but I can't seem to bring myself to say the words.

Someone clears their throat. My eyes snap open, and both Mac and I turn toward the sound.

Daisy gives us a look from behind the main library desk. "Get a room," she says in an exaggerated whisper, and my cheeks burn.

"Should we?" Mac smirks, taking a seat across the table from me.

"Definitely," I say, my smile full of mischief.

He reaches for my book and starts to close it, but I slap my hand down on it, forcing it to stay open. "After we finish studying."

Mac's expression changes rapid-fire between excited, shocked, and disappointed, but it lands on a grin. The very same one that used to annoy the hell out of me.

"I would complain, but this is one of my top three favorite things to do with you," he says.

Mac slings his backpack off his back and sets it on the chair next to him. He's still sweaty from the gym, and it takes all my self-control not to crawl across this table and climb onto his lap. Four months of dating and I still cannot get enough of this guy. It doesn't matter if he's sweaty or wearing a suit or jeans—I can't seem to keep my hands off him.

"What are your other two favorite things to do with me?" I ask.

He smirks, raising his eyebrows. "I'll show you later." And then, adorably, he opens his textbook and starts to actually study.

I take a moment and drink him in, remembering the time I spent resenting him, taking all his academic success as a personal attack on me. It was so easy for me to take his compliments as criticism when that was all I gave to myself. And our dynamic is way more fun now knowing it's coming from a place of support and friendly competition rather than rivalry. Last I heard, we're tied for a chance at valedictorian next year. But even if Mac got it and I didn't, I think I'd still feel like I won.

Mac peeks up from his book as if he can sense my eyes on him. He smiles at me, and the desire to reach out and touch him is too much to resist. I open my hand, leaning forward a little. His warm hand envelops mine, and he gives my fingers a squeeze.

"Whatcha thinking about?" he asks.

"How ridiculous I was for so long about seeing you as my competition."

He squeezes my hand again. We've talked about this as much as a couple can talk about anything. It's always accompanied by an apology from me for my atrocious behavior.

"I'm still your competition," he says, raising his eyebrows again.

"Barely," I scoff.

"I'm sorry, who got the better grade on our sociology exam last week?"

"One of those questions was a trick question and it wasn't fair at all," I say, pointing a finger at him.

He smirks, and all my insides turn to mush. The way he looks at me makes me feel like I'm living in a goddamn Taylor Swift song.

"Hey," he says, glancing sideways and then back to me. "Come here." He lowers his voice into a soft whisper. He pulls on my hand, and I get out of my seat and walk over to him, checking to see if Daisy is still at her desk. She's not, so I sit on his lap.

He coils an arm around me, and I lean into him as he holds me up. I wrap my arms around his neck and he rests his free hand on my upper thigh. It sends warmth through my whole leg.

"I was thinking..." he starts.

"Dangerous."

"Move in with me next semester. For our senior year."

My stomach climbs up to my throat. "Really?"

"Really. What's the point of having two apartments? You'll be at mine or I'll be at yours all the time anyway."

I glare at him, skeptical. "This isn't your way of, say, paying for my housing, is it? Trying to 'take care of me' financially?"

"Absolutely not. But financially speaking the logic is there."

I chew on the inside of my lip. Jade has offered multiple times to pay for an apartment for both of us, but I've always refused. I would refuse Mac outright too if I didn't think he was right. I've practically been living at his apartment this past semester. Jade complains all the time that she never sees me anymore. Mac has slept more than a few nights on my twin bed with me because I've felt bad leaving Jade.

I'd feel bad leaving Jade next year for Mac. We've lived together for three years; I don't want to abandon her now.

"Not your strongest argument, but not your weakest. What about Jade?"

"We'll get a two-bedroom apartment."

"You want Jade to live with us too?" I chuckle.

"I feel like you two are a package deal, and if that's how I get you, then that's how I'll take you."

"And if you and I break up?"

He smiles at this, the weirdo. "I'll move out," he says.

I know what he wanted to say. He wanted to say, "Won't happen," which he does say occasionally when I mention the possibility of a breakup. So this answer both surprises me and puts me at ease. He's taking my concern seriously and answering in a way he knows I appreciate. He's not pretending like this is forever, which he sometimes likes to do, because maybe it's not, as I like to point out. But it's for now, and I want to soak in every minute I get with him.

I lean in and kiss him, and even though we've kissed a million times in the past four months, it feels like the first time. I'm no longer in the library; I'm outside of space and time. His arms tighten around me, and

I can sense he wants more, that he wants to deepen this kiss and kiss me until I'm dizzy. But he ends the fun, pulling back just a little.

"Is that a yes?" he asks.

"Yes, if Jade says yes too."

"She already did," he whispers against my lips.

I feel rather than see his lips form a smile. "You sneaky—"

But he interrupts me, his lips against mine. He tilts his head, parting his lips, and when his tongue slips past mine my whole body wakes up. Desire pools in my lower belly, and I don't know how much longer I can stay in the library if he's going to keep kissing me like this.

There's a tap on my shoulder. I sheepishly turn and make eye contact with Daisy.

"Seriously, you two. I don't know how many times I have to say this, but you cannot do that in here. Get a room."

Mac and I give Daisy our most apologetic faces, and when she walks away we both start to giggle. I have to hide my face in his neck to keep from laughing out loud.

"Should we? Get a room, that is..." Mac asks, his voice low and seductive in my ear.

"Yes, please," I say.

And we do.

Did you enjoy Deja Vu?

Love it to pieces?
Mildly tolerate it?
Finish reading it out of spite?

....

LEAVE A REVIEW!

Reviews help other readers find my book! And they help other readers decide if this book is for them or not. Please take a minute and tell the world your thoughts. It's not every day you get to post your opinions on the internet!

....

READ ON FOR A SNEAK PEAK AT JADE'S STORY...

CHAPTER ONE
JADE

Jade

"Aw fuck. She's listening to Sondheim."

Jessie's voice follows the slam of the front door of our shared apartment. Even over the sound of my music, I can hear her and her boyfriend Mac, both my roommates, shuffling in from their evening at the library. I click the volume buttons on my phone to turn the music down to a more respectful level. Just because I want to drown in show tunes doesn't mean everyone in the apartment has to.

"Is that what that weird music is?" Mac asks.

Weird music!? I scramble up from the floor where I've been laying for the last two hours to give Mac a piece of my mind. Merrily We Roll Along by Stephen Sondheim is not only my favorite musical of all time, Stephen Sondheim is a legend in the musical theater world. Hand on the knob, a fight already brewing in my gut, Jessie starts talking again, so I wait.

"Oh stop, it's just a musical. I don't remember the name of it, but I do know it's some guy named Sondheim."

"Sond-who?" Mac asks, his voice louder, probably passing my room to put his things down in his and Jessie's shared room.

"Of course you don't know who that is you uncultured numpty," I say, whispering from my side of the door. I don't mean it. Mac is probably more cultured than both Jessie and I combined, but I'd never admit that to him.

"SondhEIm," Jessie explains, her voice also getting louder then quieter as she disappears into their room. "He's a musical theater composer or something. I only know him because it's Jade's Code Red music"

My Code Red music? What the... I tighten my grip on the handle, but hold back, my arm practically shaking with the effort of not opening the door. My curiosity wins out over my temptation to join in on the conversation, and I lower the volume of my music a couple more steps to hear them better.

"What does that even mean? Do I have Code Red music? Do you?" Mac asks.

"It's not really about the music. It's about levels of sadness."

"Levels of sadness?" Mac asks

"Yeah, like, different behaviors that indicate how upset she really is and how worried I should be. Code red is the highest, obviously."

Their voices grow louder and then quiet again as they both go back out into the kitchen. What the hell is she talking about? Level of sadness? Why has she never mentioned it to me? I shift my weight, crossing my arms across my chest with a tight squeeze. I'm tempted to pop out of the room and confront her for an explanation, but I've never been able to eavesdrop on my best friend talking about me and I'm not about to miss that opportunity.

"You've piqued my curiosity," Mac says. "What are Jade's levels of sadness?"

"Well, level one sadness is, like, she gets rip-roaring drunk, wakes up with a hangover and she's back to herself."

I scrunch my nose. That barely counts. Everyone in college is getting rip-roaring drunk when they're a little sad. They're also doing it when they're celebrating or when it's a day that ends in Y.

"But Jade parties, like, every week." Mac says. I clench my fist around the doorknob.

"Yes, but she can hold her liquor. When was the last time you saw Jade get absolutely hammered?" Jessie asks. There's a silence while Mac thinks. He doesn't respond, and Jessie continues.

"Exactly. She actually doesn't get drunk very often. It's rare. She can really keep her shit together when it comes to alcohol. "

"Thank you," I whisper to no one with an eye roll, relaxing my clenched fists.

"Okay so level one sadness, drunk. Check. How many levels are there total?" Mac asks.

"Four. Levels one, two, and three, and code red. Level two is a food binge."

Four?! Now I know she's made up these levels and I'm going to make her say them to my face. I reach for my phone sitting on my night-stand, ready to storm out of my room, but when I have to move a chip bag stuffed with the trash of a few candy wrappers to get to my phone, I stand down. Instead, I lean against the door again, ear pressed against the wood, lowering the volume of my music again.

The coffee machine crackles sending the smell of fresh-brewing beans my way. Jessie and Mac are probably going to be studying for a while if they're brewing coffee at ten o'clock in the evening. Studying this late on Friday night? I would judge them but I'm crying to show tunes alone in my room on a Friday night, so for now I'll withhold that judgment.

"What's level three?" Mac asks.

"Hallmark Channel."

The scrape of a mug across the counter sets my teeth on edge. Or maybe it's the fact that Jessie sees right through me and that's a level of vulnerability I didn't fully sign up for.

"Hallmark Channel?"

"Yeah, if she's on the couch just watching Hallmark Channel movies, we're on level three sadness."

"You do that too," Mac says. "Is that one of your levels of sadness?"

"Yes, but that's like level five for me."

That's true. She watched cheesy Christmas movies for three days when shit hit the fan with her and Mac last year. I take great comfort in fake stories, whereas it takes only the greatest levels of emotion and distress to knock Jessie off her feet. If she's binging movies or TV of any kind, it's warning bells for me.

My armpits are sweaty and I'm practically shaking with the effort of staying put. I'm desperate to join the conversation, to put in my two cents. But it's not often you get to hear what people really say about you when they think you're not there, and I want to know where the rest of this conversation is going.

"And level four is—" Mac says at the same time that Jessie says, "Code red is—"

"Sondham," Mac says.

"SondhEIm," she corrects.

WANT UPDATES AND NEWS ABOUT WHEN JADE'S BOOK WILL BE RELEASED?

SIGN UP FOR MY NEWSLETTER!

Go to my website to sign up at
www.lizleiby.com

ACKNOWLEDGMENTS

This book would not exist if not for the people who carried me through the writing and revising of it. Revising a book during a divorce is as brutal as it sounds, and there's no way I could have done it without these people.

Sheila, there isn't enough gratitude for the way you showed up for me both as a friend and a writing wife. Our weekly Wednesday writing night was an anchor in the chaos. Thank you for brainstorming with me, for alpha and beta reading, and for weathering the storm of my self doubt, stepping in to captain when I couldn't.

Julie, if I could thank you in every language I would. Thank you for being one of the handful of people I trust with my early drafts, your beta reading feedback is a north star as I navigate my drafts. Thank you for the near daily check ins, for all the encouragement, and for loving my characters as much as I do.

Kayla, thank you for being one of my newest beta readers, and for checking in with me, for being excited when I was excited and sharing in all my joy.

Ashley Lewis, the original cheerleader. Thank you for brainstorming with me and helping me elevate my story. For beta reading, for listening, and for believing in me since I started this journey nearly a decade ago.

Josh, for reading an early draft of Deja Vu and helping me get my brain around turning the first draft into the second one. I am so grateful to have you as my arch nemesis.

To the rest of the Stark Exchange: thank you for your critiques and encouragement, it means the world to me. You guys are... (this time it's intentional)

Destinee, thank you for beta reading and for loving my characters!

Shea and Gabe thank you for your check ins and for cheering me on. It meant so much to me, I put you in my book!

Seth, thank you for the soccer trick and for being part of the chorus of voices to check in on me.

Bryony, as always, a privilege and honor to work with you. Your encouragement and kind words mean so much to me, you are a true professional when it comes to working with authors and the vulnerability of sharing our works. Your edits have once again taken my writing to the next level. Thank you is such a measly few batch of syllables for the depth of gratitude I have for you!

Erin, your light touch and thoughtful proofreading have made me eternally grateful to have had the chance to work with you. This final version is as great as it is in part because of you. My deepest thanks for your work.

Mallory, it is a huge joy to get to collaborate with you. Thank you for using your gifts and talents in creating stunning book covers.

And to my parents, your unending love and support in the making of this book has been vital.

ALSO BY LIZ LEIBY

<u>Love Again</u>

BUY ON AMAZON!

After a devastating breakup six months ago, Mara, a famous but anonymous painter, lost her ability to paint, and with it her sense of self. Low on funds and desperate to find herself again, she moves into her grandparents' old cabin in Copper Springs, Colorado.

As Mara settles into her new life, a phone call from her agent puts her career on the line: deliver a new collection of paintings in fIve months or watch her career tank. Mara strives to reconnect to her old magic, but every time she lays brush to canvas, she fails to create anything worthwhile.

Despite her attempts to stick to herself and focus on keeping her career alive, small-town life proves to be more helpful than she anticipated when the handsome local cheesemonger catches her eye and the quirky art store owner insists on friendship.

Faced with crippling self-doubt, the ghosts of her past, and a sudden shift in her deadline, Mara must decide if it's safer to hide herself from her new friends for the sake of protecting her art and identity, or if it's worth the risk to learn to love again.

ABOUT THE AUTHOR

Liz Leiby is an emerging romance author. She holds a bachelor's degree in theater from Birmingham-Southern College and lives outside of Atlanta, Georgia with her sweet cat, Opal.

When she's not writing, Liz likes to bake, solve puzzles, practice yoga, and read. She hates ketchup and season 8 of Game of Thrones. Her dream is to travel to New Zealand one day.

Follow me on Instagram! @lizleibyauthor
Website: http://lizleiby.com
Newsletter: Sign up